To Love Again

CHRISTINE ANDERSON

CAPSTONE
FICTION

WATERFORD, VIRGINIA

To Love Again

Published in the U.S. by:
Capstone Publishing Group LLC
P.O. Box 8
Waterford, VA 20197

Visit Capstone Fiction at
www.capstonefiction.com

Cover design by David LaPlaca/debest design co.
Cover image © iStockphoto.com/Elena Elisseeva
Author photo © 2007 Countryside Studios, Madison, New Jersey

Scripture verses are taken from the *Holy Bible*, New International Version®. NIV®. Copyright © 1973, 1978, 1984 by International Bible Society. Used by permission of Zondervan. All rights reserved.

ISBN: 978-1-60290-011-0

"For nothing is impossible with God."
Luke 1:37

To Meredith, Kelly, and Michael:
Hold onto your dreams,
persevere and pray,
knowing always that you are
the treasures of my heart.

Acknowledgments

I have loved to write stories since I was a teenager, and this book is the culmination of a lifelong dream. Some would say that writing is a solitary process, and while it is true that I've spent a lot of hours in front of a computer alone, weaving words in my head, it would have been impossible to finish the race without a lot of support and encouragement from some very important people in my life. To them all I owe a debt of thanks.

To the wonderful women of Creative Living Bible Study—some who have encouraged and mentored me, and some of whom I have been privileged to encourage and mentor as a result—thank you for your constant support and your prayers.

To my friends and colleagues on the New Vernon Volunteer First Aid Squad: Some of what I have learned at your side found its way into this story. You perform a vital service for no money and few accolades—all for the chance to help those in need. It is an honor to have served beside you in caring for our community.

To Mary Ellen Sullivan, friend and soul sister who wouldn't take no for an answer and kept inviting me to join her at Creative Living Bible Study. It was a life-changing introduction, and I will always be grateful. Thank you also for all the time you have taken over the years to read and edit my work. Your words of encouragement have helped me to persevere.

To Heather-Jo Taferner, my little sister and a fabulous editor: You helped me to be honest in my story-telling, pushed me to show the emotions behind the actions and never to take the easy way out. Thanks for never letting me get away with anything but my best effort.

To Meredith, for her wise edits and unerring ear for real dialogue.

To Kelly, for her smiles and her joy in sharing the successes.

To Michael, for doing all those little things I asked and giving me the time to write. And for Wednesday nights together enjoying our favorite TV show.

And to Rodd, my husband and best friend, for all the years of hard work in supporting our family and taking such good care of us. You gave me the time to pursue my dream and the family to share it with. God has truly blessed us!

One

"She lied to us, Scott." Maddie Alexander skewered the massive sirloin and placed it on a platter. She handed the meat across the granite counter to her husband, then glanced at the clock. The Baldwins would be here any minute.

Plate in one hand, Scott grabbed the barbeque fork and headed out to the grill overlooking the lake. "Kylie wouldn't do that. She's never given us a reason not to trust her."

"She's sixteen. Remember what you were doing at that age?"

Scott turned at the screen door, his broad shoulders backlit by the June sunset. "Yeah, I do, but Kylie's a good kid . . ."

"Yes, she is, but lately she's made some bad choices. Like sneaking out last week. And lying to us about going away this weekend with Larkin and her parents."

"Where was she really going?"

"To the beach, but without a parent in sight."

Scott's eyes narrowed. "I take it Kevin was going too?"

Maddie nodded, her blond curls falling into her face.

"I never liked that kid. Kylie never lied to us before she started dating him." Scott kicked the door open and stepped out onto the cedar deck. "And speaking of Kevin, you'll have to stay on top of that relationship this summer. Make sure things don't go too far."

Maddie hated when Scott continued a convearsation as if he'd never left the room. She grabbed the spinach salad and followed him outside. "I intend to, but what will you be doing?"

"Working six days a week if we get the Hingeman project. I'm presenting my designs for the new wing later this week."

"What about our vacation?"

Scott laid the platter aside and fired up the grill. "You'll have to take the kids without me."

"Just like last summer," Maddie fumed.

"I can't take time off at the start of a new job."

"You never take any time off. I feel like I'm raising our kids by myself."

Scott spun around and braced both hands on the back of a deck chair, his muscles tense. At just over six feet, he loomed over Maddie. Behind him, the lake lay still, the evening calm contrasting with his stormy expression. "Hey, I'm here now. I even canceled a dinner meeting. And it wasn't my idea to have Annie and Phil over tonight."

"They're about the only friends we have. You never make the time to see anyone else."

"Since when is my job bothering you so much? I thought you were used to it by now."

"Oh, I'm used to it," Maddie shot back at him. "What choice did I have? It was either get used to it or fight about it all the time. Besides, it's easier to be a single parent in a marriage than out of one."

As soon as the words hit the air, Maddie knew she'd gone too far. The flash of anger in Scott's brown eyes couldn't mask the sag in his shoulders. Maddie bit the inside of her cheek, wishing she could take the words back as she spotted Annie and Phil coming around the side of the house.

Scott shot her a warning glance, and she knew this discussion was over. For now.

"I hope we're not late." Annie hurried up the stairs while her husband, Phil, followed at a more leisurely pace. She wore a yellow sundress, tinted sunglasses and flip-flops with butterflies, making Maddie feel a bit frumpy in linen pants and a blue man-tailored shirt.

"You're right on time." Maddie hugged her, taking the plate of brownies from Annie's hands. "Thanks for bringing dessert."

Phil stepped up behind Annie and planted his chin on her shoulder with a grin. His blond hair hugged his head in a crew cut reminiscent of his days as an all-American lineman.

"I'm not supposed to tell you, but the brownies are leftovers from the store."

Annie and Phil owned the Stoddard General Store, an old-fashioned lakefront market they'd taken over when Annie's parents retired a year ago.

"Well, I didn't want them to go to waste." Annie elbowed him in his ample midsection.

"No chance of that," Phil said, "but I guess tonight I'll have to share."

Scott stepped up and shook Phil's hand. "Want to give me a hand with the steak?"

Phil eyed the barbeque. "Lead the way." He dropped a quick kiss on Annie's cheek and then, rubbing his hands together, advanced on the grill.

Envy washed over Maddie as she led the way inside to get the drinks. She wasn't usually the jealous type, but Annie and Phil had such a great marriage. They really liked each other. Anyone with eyes could see that. Married for ten years, they'd managed to avoid the pitfalls of taking each other for granted. They didn't have any children, and children naturally changed any marriage, but their infertility could have driven them farther apart. Instead it had drawn them together.

"I brought you something else." Annie reached into her bag. She handed a folded sheet of paper across the kitchen counter. "It's the flyer you were staring at in the store. Auditions for the musical are tomorrow night."

Maddie unfolded the sheet, her stomach queasy.

"You should try out. You know you want to," Annie prompted.

"I will if you will."

"Not a chance. The last time I sang in public I embarrassed myself in a college coffee house."

Maddie's gaze lingered on the page before she set it aside. "Thanks for the thought."

Annie leaned on the counter. "So where are the kids?"

"Shaun's working on a class project at a friend's house, and Kylie's sulking upstairs." Maddie gave an abbreviated version of Kylie's latest escapade while she set out a tray and filled four plastic tumblers with ice.

"So, how'd you figure out she and Larkin were going away with the guys?"

"Because I did it myself a long time ago. Only we went to the Outer Banks."

Annie's eyes widened. "How did it turn out?"

Maddie retrieved a pitcher of ice tea from the refrigerator. "Not well, actually. I spent the whole weekend fighting to keep something I didn't think I wanted."

"What's that?"

"My virginity." Maddie tried to make a joke of it, but it wasn't funny.

"Did you tell Scott that?"

"Why would I?"

"So he wouldn't feel like a washout as a dad." Annie pushed her sunglasses up onto her head, making her red hair stick out at odd angles. "Admit it, when it comes to Kylie, you've got the inside track. You've been there. He hasn't."

"You always stand up for him."

"Maybe I'm just waiting for you to do it." Annie came around the counter and slipped an arm around Maddie's shoulders. "But Kylie's not really the problem, is she? When was the last time you and Scott talked about anything besides your kids?"

"I don't know."

"Then it's been too long."

"I don't know if talking is going to help. We may be too far gone." Maddie leaned her head against Annie's, trying to keep the mood light though a hint of truth colored her tone.

"Nobody's too far gone. You just need to start talking, and a little touching wouldn't hurt either." Annie grinned. "Didn't you tell me something about a double sleeping bag and a second-floor porch?"

"That was years ago, when we first moved in."

"Still have the porch?"

"Of course."

"Might be time to start using it again," Annie suggested, her tone light but her gaze serious.

Maddie squirmed under her friend's watchful stare, unwilling to admit to anyone, not even Annie, that she couldn't remember the last time she'd slept with her own husband. They still shared the same bed, but the king-size left acres of room between their turned backs. "Maybe we should start with a civil conversation."

"Great idea. How about a picnic? You could sail out to the island in the Sunfish." Annie pointed over her shoulder at the tree-covered island in the middle of the lake. "But you need to set a few ground rules. No talking about kids, sports teams, or home repairs."

"What else is there?"

"A whole world of things. Give it a try. Every journey, you know..."

"... starts with a single step." Maddie groaned. "You are relentlessly cheerful."

"Not always." Annie grabbed the tray, ice clinking against the plastic.

Maddie closed her eyes, suddenly filled with remorse. How had she forgotten? "Oh, Annie, I'm sorry. What happened when you and Phil went for the interview?"

Annie sighed, carrying the tray outside. "You would think the state

4

of New Hampshire had more foster parents than they know what to do with. Our application is going to take months."

"Why so long when you were all ready approved in Massachusetts?"

"Different state, different regulations. We have to start from scratch with the classes, the home inspection, and the fingerprinting."

"That's crazy."

"I know they don't want to place vulnerable kids with convicted felons, but we were just licensed before we moved and now . . ." Annie's voice faded to a whisper before she shook off the wistful mood. "Don't get me started. I'll talk your ear off."

Maddie felt like a louse for going on about her problems when Annie had enough of her own. Her struggles with the foster-care system were the latest in a decade of attempts to have a child. "I can't think of anyone who would be a better mother. How do you stand the waiting?"

"Not on my own, believe me."

"You mean you share it with Phil?" Maddie glanced at the two men bending over the steak like they were operating on it.

Annie shook her head. "Nope, someone bigger."

Maddie laughed, staring at Annie's linebacker-sized husband. "Bigger? Who's bigger than Phil?"

"God."

Maddie's smile wavered. She'd been singing in the church choir for years and never discussed religion with anyone. "So, what do you do?"

"I just talk to Him."

"And it helps?"

Annie nodded. "It does. I mean, my life's still the same, but I trust that He's got a plan for me about the foster care, about our family, about everything."

"That's a lot of trust."

"I used to think so too, but just because I can't see the plan doesn't mean it isn't there."

Annie smiled at the two men coming toward them, triumphant grins on both their faces. "You sure you two have got that just right now?"

"Rare on the inside . . . ," Scott offered.

"And seared on the outside," Phil concluded. "It's perfect."

Their glee was contagious. Maddie couldn't help but grin. "Then let's eat."

Easy conversation flowed throughout the meal, making Maddie feel like she and Scott were a normal married couple, despite their earlier harsh words. The couples laughed as they wrangled over politics. But on one issue they all agreed: the increased stress in their lives. Jobs. Financial pressures. Keeping fit and well informed. All added up to more stress.

"Everyone needs something they do just for them, apart from their job or their family," Annie continued, picking up the thread of their dinner conversation as she dug her fork into a brownie smothered in ice cream.

"So what do you do?" Maddie sipped her coffee, wishing she'd opted for dessert instead of taking a pass on the calories.

Annie glanced at Phil and smiled. "Do you think I know them well enough to tell them?"

Phil stole a forkful of Annie's dessert having already finished his own. "Go ahead, I think your secret's safe."

Annie pushed her plate closer to him. "I'm a painter. Not a very good one, but I'm learning."

"Where do you paint?" Scott asked.

"In the attic over the store. Phil put two skylights in the roof to improve the lighting. I can get lost for hours up there."

"Sounds soothing," Maddie said, loving the idea of having a creative outlet. "What about you, Phil? What do you do that no one knows about?"

Phil sipped his coffee. "Actually, I restore old boats."

"You're kidding." Scott set his cup aside, his voice eager. "Do you have one you're working on now?"

Maddie pictured the warped and dusty Blue Jay in their boathouse. The boat belonged to the previous homeowner who'd thrown it in along with the sale. Scott had intended to work on it ever since.

"No, I just finished one and sold it before we moved here."

"Ever work with anyone?"

Phil eyed him. "Not yet. What did you have in mind?"

Scott's eyes gleamed. "I'll show you sometime. Why don't you stop by after basketball next weekend?"

"It's a deal." Phil carved off a forkful of brownie but left the last bite for his wife. "Okay, Maddie, your turn. What do you do just for you?"

Caught off guard, Maddie didn't have an answer. "I don't know . . ."

"There must be something you'd like to do."

Maddie's gaze met Annie's across the table. "Well, I was thinking of trying out for the community theater's summer musical."

Scott leaned back in his seat, folding his arms behind his head.

"Why would you do that?"

Maddie flinched at his tone, so casual and yet so derisive. Once he'd loved to hear her sing and now he didn't even remember she could. "It's something I've wanted to do since college."

"Then you should do it," Phil said with an encouraging smile.

Scott's eyes narrowed. "You're not serious? You haven't done anything like that in years. You'll never get a part."

A hot flush spread up Maddie's neck and she dropped her gaze to the table. She closed her eyes as a wave of sweat broke out across her back and chest. An awkward silence fell over the table. Maddie's cheeks burned, her pride wounded as much by Scott's attitude as his words.

"I was thinking of trying out for the show, too," Annie said, breaking the silence.

Maddie looked up and caught the surprise on Scott's face, and the loving admiration on Phil's.

Annie popped the last of the brownie in her mouth. "Maddie and I are going to do it together, right?"

"Right. It'll be fun." Maddie shot her husband a scathing glance, daring him to contradict her.

Scott merely shrugged. "Well, good luck then. I hope you two get what you want."

"I'm sure we will," Maddie said, her humiliation replaced by a steely resolve. It would be a long time before she forgot Scott's cutting words or his cavalier dismissal of her dreams.

Two

Scott hit the button for the CD player. "Born in the USA" filled the BMW coupe. He drummed his fingers on the steering wheel, resigned to the lengthy commute from New Hampshire to Boston and the architectural firm of Sanders and Lowenstein. After seventeen years, the drive was monotonous. Fortunately, he didn't do it every day. Often he stayed in the city when dinner with a client left him too tired to drive home. He'd become a regular in the suite the corporation kept for executives and major clients.

The country road dipped and weaved along the lakeshore. Sunlight glinted off the water and fell in dappled patterns on the roadway. Pine groves scented the air before the road veered away from the water and through the tiny town.

Stoddard, New Hampshire, had seen better days. In the sixties many of the houses on the lake were summer rentals, making for an influx of tourists from Memorial Day to Labor Day. During the eighties many of the lake houses were bought by baby boomers who renovated the properties and then used them for just a few weeks each summer. Tourism waned and the town slipped into a state of disrepair. A gas station, general store, and volunteer fire department were all that remained of the commercial district.

Scott pulled up to the Stoddard General Store and cut the engine. He stepped onto a porch that stretched the length of the white clapboard store. The screen door yielded to his touch with the same loud squeak that had heralded a customer's arrival for decades.

Phil finished with the customer he was waiting on and turned to Scott with a lopsided grin. "What can I get for you? A little arsenic with your coffee?"

Scott reached for his wallet. "Coffee, black. Hold the arsenic. I'm sure Maddie will take care of that when I get home tonight."

Phil poured a steaming cup and secured the lid with a snap. "She was fuming last night. Why'd you say it?"

8

"I thought she was kidding about trying out for the show."

"You embarrassed her."

"I'll make it up to her," Scott said tossing a five-dollar bill on the counter.

"By the look on her face I'd say you better do it today."

"Can't. Not tonight. I've got a stack of work waiting for me when I get home."

"Forget it. Do something with your family," Phil suggested. "Take them to dinner or out for ice cream."

"I haven't got time for that. It'll blow over with Maddie. It always does." Doubt tinged his words as Scott recalled Maddie's remark about being a single parent.

"Are you really willing to take that chance?"

Scott laughed, scooping up his change. "It's not like Maddie's going to divorce me over this."

"I wasn't talking about divorce." Phil placed the coffee in a bag and handed it across the counter. "Have I ever mentioned my brother?"

Scott shook his head. "I didn't know you had a brother."

"Cameron worked seventy hours a week as a trial lawyer right up until his first heart attack. Afterwards all he wanted to do was play Candyland with his son and push his daughter on the swings."

"So what did he do? Retire?" Scott asked, his curiosity piqued.

"Never got the chance. He died."

Scott stared at his friend, hearing the resignation in Phil's tone.

"He survived the first attack but then had another two days later. That was ten years ago. Right after Annie and I got married."

"How old was he?"

"Thirty-eight. And he never saw it coming. No symptoms, no pain, and a clean check-up three months before." Phil glanced up as a family of four came through the door.

"How old are your niece and nephew now?"

"Rachael's fourteen and Danny is sixteen."

"What do they remember about your brother?"

A sad smile played across Phil's face. "A little here and there, mostly from pictures. But Cam worked some long hours so he wasn't home much." Phil started to unload a basket of groceries for an older couple. He looked up at Scott as he punched the first item into the register. "We still on for basketball this Saturday?"

Scott nodded and retrieved his keys from his pocket. "My turn to drive. I'll pick you up at 10:00 a.m."

In his car he sipped his coffee, unable to shake off the peculiar dread he felt after hearing about Phil's brother. *Thirty-eight.* The guy was so young. It made Scott wonder just what his kids would remember about him if he died.

Sailing on the lake or skiing in the mountains, maybe? No, Maddie had done most of that with the kids. The vacations on the Outer Banks, perhaps?

Every year since the kids were toddlers they'd spent two weeks vacationing along the North Carolina shore. It was the only vacation he took all year. Scott had taught Kylie and Shaun how to body surf and fish, and helped them create intricate sand sculptures. They fashioned whales and elephants, mermaids and seals, even the traditional sand castle.

Scott backed the car out and headed for the highway. The last two years he hadn't made the Outer Banks trip. The kids were older and able to make the trip without two parents to supervise them. And with the house quiet he'd completed a major project in half the time, pleasing the Sanders board and earning himself a substantial raise.

So, he'd missed a vacation or two? That didn't make him a bad dad, just a busy one. And hands down he was a better father than his own had been. Ray Alexander had run out on his wife and kids before Scott was in second grade, and never sent them a dime.

Scott cared about his kids, about who their friends were, and how they were doing in school. But sometimes he felt like a stranger in his own home, relegated to the role of bread winner while his children shared their lives and their hearts with Maddie. He loved Kylie and Shaun with a fierce love that sometimes surprised him. But beyond the subject of school and sports he found it difficult to talk to them. His attempts at conversation usually met with an uncommunicative shrug, especially from Kylie.

Scott's phone vibrated and he plucked it from his pocket.

"Scott, when will you be in?"

He stifled a groan and gripped the steering wheel harder. A call from his boss at this hour of the morning was never a good thing. "I should be there by 9:00. What's up, Rob?"

"I've arranged a dinner for tonight with the Hingemen board, and I want to go over those plans for the new wing as soon as you get here."

Scott tensed. "We weren't scheduled to meet until the end of the week. What's the rush?"

"Our competition is presenting their preliminary plans tomorrow. I want to beat them to it." The tension in Rob's voice grew more pronounced. "Our plans are ready?"

"I just have to put the finishing touches on them, but yes, they're ready."

"Good. I'll need you to get me up to speed before the dinner."

Scott punched the brakes to avoid hitting the car in front of him. The multimillion-dollar oncology center, to be named in honor of the Hingemen's daughter, had been a design challenge. "You're taking this meeting yourself?"

"I am."

"The plans are complex. I'm familiar with the details. You might want me to make the presentation."

"Oh, you'll be there, but I'll do the talking."

Scott had worked on the Hingemen design for the past two months, and now Rob Sanders was going to step in and sell the job to the client?

"And Scott, this meeting could go late. Plan on staying in town tonight so we can get an early start tomorrow on any revisions."

"Anything else?" Scott's clipped reply barely hid his sarcasm.

"Nothing that can't wait." Rob's tone was brisk before he added, "Have you ever considered moving closer to town? Do you know how much time you waste commuting from the sticks?"

Scott refused to comment on what was clearly a rhetorical question. "I'll see you when I get in." He punched the off button on his phone.

Why had he stayed with Sanders and Lowenstein for so many years? He should have left them long ago and started his own firm like he'd planned coming out of college. But the corporate life and the corporate money had lured him in. He'd been able to buy the house on Whitefish Lake and to renovate it a few years later. If he'd been out on his own he never could have afforded the seedy, but sprawling Colonial in its perfect lakefront setting.

They'd moved in when Maddie was seven months pregnant. As they'd sat cross-legged on the floor in the empty living room, eating sandwiches by candlelight, Scott had gathered Maddie in his arms. The sandwiches forgotten, he'd kissed her tenderly, unable to contain the swell of contentment that made his chest ache with joy. They were home.

Scott hadn't thought about that day in years—the sweetness of Maddie's kiss, the fullness of her pregnant body, and the intensity of his love for her. A smile lifted the corners of his mouth at the memory before quickly fading into a frown.

Maddie.

He supposed he owed her an apology for last night. He hadn't thought she was serious about auditioning for the show, but these days he knew so little about his wife.

Switching into the left lane, Scott found that thought strangely depressing. He had everything a man could want. A great job. A sizable bank account. A beautiful home he'd designed. But he could barely talk to his own kids, and his wife ran their home without even consulting him.

He'd fulfilled his boyhood dream of having a stable family with no financial worries. He should be proud—happy even—yet he spent three nights a week sleeping in a sterile hotel suite with no one to talk to but the waiter who delivered his room service.

"Kylie, you're going to miss the bus," Maddie called up the stairs, her irritation growing.

The sound of tires screeched behind her. Eleven-year-old Shaun lay sprawled on the family room floor, working the video game's control pad with furious skill. The noise grated on Maddie's nerves, her mood still edgy with embarrassment at Scott's callous words last night.

A disembodied plea floated down from the second floor. "Can't you drive me just this once?"

"Not today. I have to take Shaun in because his final history project is too big for the bus and the high school is in the opposite direction." Maddie looked up as her lanky daughter descended the stairs. At sixteen, Kylie was a taller version of her mother, only with dark hair. Her facial features were all Finnegan. Wide eyes. High cheekbones. Straight nose. So like Maddie and her brothers. But at five-foot-nine, Kylie had a good four inches on her mother, her thin athletic build and straight hair an offshoot of the Alexander family tree.

Kylie tossed her book bag on the counter and pulled open the refrigerator. Her tight jeans hugged her hips, her T-shirt riding up to reveal several inches of creamy white skin.

"And I suppose you're picking him up, too?" Kylie grabbed an apple before closing the door with her hip.

"No, he's taking the bus home, same as always." Maddie's icy tone seemed lost on her daughter. "And I want you home right after school. Your four-week grounding starts today."

Kylie spiked her bangs with one hand, her mouth fixed in a permanent pout. "I still can't believe you called Larkin's mother."

The last thing Maddie wanted to do was rehash yesterday's confrontation. "I made that call because that's my job: to keep you safe."

"I don't need you looking out for me," Kylie shot back.

"I think you do. You proved it when you lied."

"You just don't want me seeing Kevin."

"That's not the point." Maddie hadn't liked Kevin since the day he'd come to pick Kylie up and honked the horn from the driveway. "You can see him, but it has to be here, in this house."

Kylie eyes widened, her face a mask of misery. "You want to ruin my whole summer, don't you?"

"You did this to yourself."

"You never would have let me go if I told you the truth."

"You're right. I'm trying to keep you from making bad choices, and going away for the weekend with Kevin is a really bad idea," Maddie said.

Kylie grabbed her backpack. "I wouldn't be doing anything at the beach house I couldn't be doing here if I wanted to."

"That's true, and I can't make those choices for you. But we've talked about this. You know I don't want you having sex while you're still in high school."

"Face it, Mom. You want me to wait until I'm married."

"Yes, I do. It's hard enough being a teenager without adding pregnancy and STDs into the mix." Maddie checked her watch. This was hardly the time for a discussion about abstinence. "You better get going."

"Did Dad go ballistic when he found out?"

"Let's just say I'm sure he'll want to talk to you when he gets home tonight."

"I won't hold my breath," Kylie mumbled.

Maddie looked her daughter square in the eye. "Listen, you're getting off easy. Try it again, and you'll be home until your senior prom."

Kylie groaned and rolled her eyes before the bus honked and she hurried out the door.

"You let her off too easy." Shaun muted the volume on the Playstation. "Two months and no phone would be more like it."

"I'll remember that when you're in high school and try to pull the same stunt."

"Oh, but I won't get caught," Shaun said with a sly smile.

"You think so, huh?" Maddie crossed the room and tipped back the brim of his Red Sox cap. "But you know better because . . ."

"Yeah, yeah, I know, you've got spies everywhere." Shaun tugged the hat down again to shade the dusting of freckles that covered his face. "That's not really true, is it?"

"Wouldn't you like to know," Maddie said as she helped him carry his replica of the Boston Tea party to the car.

As they sped down Lake Shore Drive, Shaun stared out the window, kicking his backpack in time with the music pouring from the speakers.

"Shaun, stop that, please," Maddie said.

"What?" He turned in his seat, his tone confused. His straight blond hair stuck out from under his hat as he stared at her.

"Stop kicking your backpack."

Shaun glanced down at his foot as if it didn't belong to him. "Sure, Mom. What's the big deal?"

Maddie stifled a sharp reply. "No big deal. I just have a headache."

She reached for the radio, twisting the volume left until the speakers barely hummed with the rap message. Shaun shrugged and turned back to the window, making Maddie feel like her irritation was an everyday event. She hit the gas, her mind replaying as it had all morning Scott's cutting words. Last night she'd been angry, but this morning she found herself more depressed than irate. How had their marriage gotten to the point where a callous comment wouldn't even warrant an apology?

She'd tried so hard to raise her children in a house filled with love instead of the cool politeness of her Southern upbringing. Her parents rarely spoke to each other, and she and Scott were well on their way to repeating the family pattern. They never laughed together anymore, and even talking was a function of essentials. Somehow they'd lost the invisible connection that allowed them to finish each other's sentences or to start humming a tune only to find the other was humming the same one. All of that had been worn away until what was left was a thin veneer of a marriage, still beautiful to look at, but superficial and fragile.

All of which made Annie's suggestion about a romantic outing on the porch as frightening as it was absurd. She'd need to lose ten pounds first. When they'd married she was barely a size eight. Now she was every inch of a size fourteen. And while she certainly wasn't obese, she wasn't svelte either. Maddie shook her head, knowing that was just an excuse. She was self-conscious about her weight but what kept her from seriously considering Annie's plan had nothing to do with pounds and everything to do with pride. What if she tried to reconnect with Scott and he rejected her? Sweat prickled Maddie's skin and her heart raced. She couldn't take that.

Seventeen years ago they hadn't been able to walk by each other without reaching out a hand to touch, to caress. When the kids were little, that simple contact had been a promise of the evening to come when they'd slip out onto the porch, alone together at the end of the day. Maddie shivered, recalling the fall night's chill, the warmth of the flannel-lined sleeping bag, and the heat of limbs so closely entwined that nothing but a thin sheen of sweat lay between them.

"Mom!" Shaun's shout cut through Maddie's fog.

The car barreled toward a huge tree stump at a sharp bend in the road. Maddie jerked the wheel left, veering back into her lane with a screech of tires. She missed the tree by inches.

Maddie's pulse thundered, her palms slick against the steering wheel. She glanced at Shaun. "You okay?"

His hands gripped the door, his eyes wide with a mixture of terror and relief. "Yeah, I guess."

Behind them a siren yelped. Blue and red lights flashed in the rearview mirror. Her heart still racing, Maddie pulled over onto the shoulder.

Shaun turned as the squad car pulled in behind them.

"I'm sorry, Shaun. I should have been more careful."

"And you say I'm spacey," he joked, though Maddie heard the slight crack in his voice.

The officer approached the car. "License and registration, please."

Maddie flipped open the glove compartment. She'd scared her son and probably gotten herself a whopping ticket. But the memories lingered, unbidden and tantalizing.

Maybe Annie was right about the porch after all.

Three

Maddie was still mulling over Annie's suggestion as she entered the Kerry Community Theater later that night. Rows of seats upholstered in blue and divided into three sections sloped down to the stage. The familiar scent of old costumes, dusty curtains, and new paint made her smile.

Maddie cast a glance at Annie as they waited to sign in. She'd worried Annie might back out of the audition for *The Music Man*, but here she stood, shuffling sheet music and looking queasy.

"You don't have to do this," Maddie whispered.

Annie looked up. "Actually, I think it will be fun if I can get past the audition. Aren't you nervous?"

Maddie nodded. "I just hide it well." Her stomach had been doing flip-flops all afternoon, though her nerves had more to do with people staring at her onstage all alone. Scott's cutting remark to the contrary, Maddie knew she could sing, but she'd never been comfortable in the limelight. "Anyway, if we make it, they'll probably put us in the chorus."

"Fine by me, but why didn't you bring any sheet music?"

"I was in this musical in high school." Maddie smiled at the memory. "Some things you never forget."

A middle-aged woman with corkscrew curls sat at a table in front of the stage. She handed them each a numbered card. "I'm Emily Tuttle, the director. When we call your number tell the accompanist what you will be singing. We also have a short scene for you to read."

Annie scrawled her name on the sign-in sheet then glanced up at Maddie with a nervous laugh. "I've heard you sing. There's no way I'm going after you."

Emily Tuttle handed them each a page of dialog. "I'll be posting the results of tonight's audition on our Web site."

Maddie and Annie took a seat in the back row. Around them men and women chatted in small groups. Several brave individuals sat alone and a good number of children waited with their parents for their number to be called.

As Maddie watched the auditions, she realized the level of talent varied widely. Some of those auditioning were capable singers, others barely so. One young woman in her late teens clearly had some theatrical experience and would likely get the part of Marion the Librarian, the female lead. Maddie mentally picked out the most likely candidates for each of the main roles. Marion's little brother would likely go to the precocious seven-year-old who dropped in and out of the required stutter with ease. A short, rounded woman in her fifties with a very good Irish brogue would likely be cast as Marion's mother. What she had yet to see was a man who could pull off the part of Professor Harold Hill, the con man who comes to town to sell musical instruments for a boy's band. Hill's rapid-fire sales pitch and charming spiel would not be easy to master, and so far the only candidate was a man with great oratory skills but a good twenty years too old for the part.

Annie leaned toward Maddie, her voice a low whisper. "So, given any thought to my suggestion about taking Scott out to the island for a picnic?"

Maddie shot her a sidelong glance. "Maybe, but the island's too far."

"Sounds like you've got a plan."

"I might," Maddie hinted. "But I could use your help."

"Number twenty-two," Emily Tuttle called out.

Annie froze. She stared at the number in her hand, an expression of horror lighting her eyes. "I don't think I can do this."

Maddie hooked an elbow under Annie's and brought her to her feet. "You'll be fine. I'll even say a prayer for you."

"You will?" Annie flashed a grateful smile and made her way down the aisle.

True to her word, Maddie offered up a silent plea for her nervous friend. Annie's voice was soft and tremulous, and her reading rushed, but Maddie beamed with pride as her friend exited the stage a few minutes later. It took courage for Annie to face her fears. That she'd done it for Maddie made the feat a true act of friendship.

"Twenty-three."

Maddie gave Annie a thumbs-up as they passed in the aisle.

"My White Knight," she told the accompanist, trying to ignore her fluttering stomach. She quickly pulled her hair back into a bun and stepped onto the stage. As the music began and she took up the melody, memories assailed her at the familiar tune.

She'd been a freshman in high school and cast as a member of the chorus while Nancy Cooper sang the lead. Maddie had wanted to be her. And all the more so when Nancy got to kiss Byron Williams in the second act. The memory left her strangely sad, and tears stung her eyes as she sang about finding a man who would love her forever.

The reading passed in a blur and then she was back in the aisle, retrieving her purse from under the seat.

"You were great!" Annie whispered.

"Thanks," Maddie said softly. "Let's go. We can check the Web site to find out how we did."

A smile tugged at her lips. She'd actually gone through with it. Whatever the outcome, she was proud of herself.

Behind her a powerful baritone took up the rapid-fire verse of a song early in the first act. Maddie turned toward the stage. The man wasn't tall, maybe five foot ten. Dark curly hair, a wiry build, and a long angular face made him interesting rather than handsome. He had an impressive voice and a command of the lyrics that seemed effortless. As he cocked his hat back on his head and leaned against an imaginary pool table, Maddie knew he was the next Harold Hill.

"He's got that part locked up," Maddie said pushing open the lobby door with Annie right behind her.

Scott signed the credit card receipt as his dinner companions adjourned to the bar for one last drink. Rob Sanders had nearly blown the predinner presentation to the Hingemen board. Scott bailed him out, supplying the details his boss had forgotten, but Scott had no illusions about Rob's reaction to this rescue. He wouldn't be thankful but embarrassed and surly as evidenced by his abrupt exit right after dinner, leaving Scott to wrap up the evening with the client. Pocketing the receipt, Scott took a last sip of coffee and got to his feet.

In the bar, Jared Duffy, managing director of Hingemen Hospital Corporation, ordered a round of drinks for his associates as well as the other members of Scott's team.

"What'll you have, Scott?" Jared asked.

"Club soda," Scott replied, recalling Rob's parting instructions to

18

meet him at the office at 7:00 a.m. The hotel suite at the Meridian would be his home for another night.

Jared's assistant, a model thin blonde in a navy silk suit, joined them as the bartender handed Scott his drink. Mariel Kensington was in her early forties, her air of purpose and efficiency mellowed by all the chardonnay she'd had with dinner. "Scott, the designs for the atrium, can they still be changed?" Mariel asked with a slight slur.

"Nothing is set in stone. Just tell me what you're looking for and we can incorporate it into the final drawings."

"I have a few ideas . . ."

Jared gave a chuckle and sipped his drink. "Give it a rest, Mariel. We're finished with business for tonight. I'm sure Scott and his team are about ready to go home."

"Oh, we're not talking anything major. I spoke with Mrs. Hingemen and she would like a day-care center included in the ground-floor space."

"You know Mrs. Hingemen's imput is always welcome," Scott replied.

"Perhaps we could get together later. I have Mrs. Hingemen's ideas on the laptop in my suite."

"Why don't you fax them over to me in the morning and I'll take a look at them." Scott tried to avoid Jared's smirking stare. "If you'll excuse me for a moment."

Scott left the bar and found the restroom. Staring at his bloodshot eyes in the mirror, he splashed cold water on his face, determined to find a quick way to wrap up this evening. All he wanted was a good night's sleep. Reluctantly, he exited the restroom and made it as far as the bar before colliding with his junior associate, Michelle Collins.

"You do know she was hitting on you?" Michelle said with a smile.

"I figured it might be something like that." Scott glanced at the empty bar.

"Don't worry. They're gone. Jared hustled her out before she could make a fool of herself. He told me they really like your designs."

"Our designs. It takes a team to put together a project this big. Come on. I'll walk you out."

Michelle led the way as they left the restaurant. "Do the late nights ever bother your wife?" she asked over her shoulder. "My husband has been giving me grief about it lately."

"Maddie's used to it by now," Scott replied, glad the evening was finally over. "She knows after seventeen years it comes with the territory. The company dinners. The long hours. It's all part of the deal."

They stepped out into the warm evening and Scott waved down a cab.

"Doesn't make for much family time. Not that I'm complaining, mind you, but once you have kids it must be hard," Michelle said. A cab pulled up to the curb and she opened the door. "Can I drop you somewhere?"

"No thanks. I think I'll walk."

Scott watched the cab pull away, considering Michelle's earlier question. Time management seemed to be a problem for everyone in his business. But the mention of family time made him uneasy. The last time his family had done anything together was Kylie's graduation from eighth grade.

Scott walked the three blocks to the hotel. He'd just stepped into the lobby when his cell phone rang.

"Hi, it's me."

Maddie? Scott's jaw clenched, his stomach suddenly queasy. "Everything okay with the kids?"

"Fine. I just wanted to see if you were on your way home?"

Scott frowned, wondering why she wasn't still mad about last night. "It's too late to drive home. I'm staying in town tonight."

"Will you be home tomorrow?"

"Of course, I'm always home on Friday."

"So, I'll see you then?" She sounded tentative as if she'd started to say something else and then changed her mind.

"Sure."

"Good night, Scott," Maddie said softly.

Scott closed the phone, surprised at the call. What was that about? Usually Maddie assumed if he hadn't made it home by eleven that he was staying in town.

Scott hit the elevator button. Before the Hingemen project he'd intended to take a vacation, spend some time with his family and a few days looking into the prospects for a one-man firm in New Hampshire. But with Sanders and Lowenstein one major project inevitably led to another, and time away from the office took him off the fast track for the best projects. Besides why go on vacation when you lived on a lake?

Lived on a lake? Who was he kidding? These days he lived in downtown Boston in a hotel suite as sterile and lifeless as what remained of his dreams.

Four

Candles flickered on the porch Friday night. A light breeze slipped through the screens making the lights shimmer and sway. Maddie lit the last candle and carried it over to the wicker table.

Resting a hand over her nervous stomach, she surveyed the surprise she'd planned for her husband. A picnic basket filled with Scott's favorite foods rested atop a plaid blanket spread out on the floor. Two large floor pillows rested on opposite corners. A bottle of wine chilled in an ice bucket on the coffee table.

Maddie reached for the wine bucket. Ice clinked against glass as she studied the bottle's label with a smile. She and Scott had visited the vineyard on their honeymoon trip through Napa. They'd both agreed the full-bodied chardonnay was the best vintage of the day.

After three attempts, Maddie finally managed to hold the bottle steady and extract the cork. She brought it to her nose and sniffed. Though she wasn't much of a wine drinker these days, she thought it smelled fine. Pouring half a glass, she sipped. Not bad. Maybe not quite as good as she remembered but then that day long ago had been tinged with emotions that had nothing to do with fine wine.

Glancing around the porch, a wave of nervous energy drove her into motion. She plucked the pillows from the sofa and patted them until they were round and full. Turning, she straightened the white wicker chairs before lifting the lid of the picnic basket.

Fried chicken. Flaky biscuits. Homemade cole slaw. Chocolate cake smothered in fudge sauce.

A breeze off the lake made the candles dim to a mere flicker. Maddie glanced at her watch and again debated her choice of white capri pants and a pink top with spaghetti straps. Stepping into the bedroom, she cast a critical eye at the mirror on her closet door. She turned and glanced over her shoulder, wincing at the ample spread of white linen across her backside. Why had she chosen these pants? White made her look huge. She considered changing her clothes but realized she'd already tried on most of what fit. Besides it would be dark soon and, knowing Scott, he would be more concerned with the food than her figure. She grabbed a fleece throw from the blanket chest. The lid swung closed, leaving a hint of cedar in the air just as the phone rang.

"So are you nervous?" Annie asked with a lilt in her voice.

"Nervous and nauseous and wondering what ever possessed me to do this? Scott's going to think I'm crazy." Maddie rubbed her stomach at the reminder. Annie was enjoying this too much.

"Maddie, it's just dinner. Relax."

Cradling the phone between her shoulder and ear, Maddie stepped out onto the porch and sank onto the sofa. "Thank you for taking the kids into town. I appreciate it."

"Kylie was so glad to be out of the house I don't think she minded taking her brother to the movies."

Maddie reached for her wineglass and tried another sip. "Sometimes I wonder why parents are so fond of grounding as a punishment. It tortures the parents as much as the kids."

Annie laughed. "Phil's going to get them after the movie. They'll be home by 11:00. So enjoy yourself."

"I'll try."

Setting the phone down, Maddie curled up on the sofa with the fleece blanket. She sipped the wine, her stomach fluttering as she glanced at her watch. Scott should be home anytime and the kids would be in town for the next three hours.

The surface of the lake shimmered in hues of pink and orange, the colors muting as they fell away to the shallows of the lakeshore. This was the weekend she and Scott usually put the float in the water, Maddie recalled, then cut the thought short. No talking about the house or the kids. A light breeze breached the screens and Maddie shivered. She drew the blanket up to her chin, hoping it wouldn't be a silent evening.

Scott slung his portfolio case on the counter. He shrugged off his sports jacket and flipped on the kitchen lights. Where was everybody? Too early for bed. It was only 10:30. Maybe Maddie had taken the kids to a movie.

Scott unbuttoned his shirt and studied his briefcase. He had hours of work to do this weekend. He should get started, but instead he detoured upstairs to change clothes. Tomorrow was soon enough to start those projects. Right now all he wanted were his old sweatpants and the Red Sox' game on TV.

Taking the stairs two at a time, Scott bounded into the bedroom and tossed his shirt on the chair. He was halfway to the bathroom when he spotted a light coming from the screened-in porch off the bedroom.

Scott froze. On the porch, a picnic basket rested on a plaid blanket surrounded by dimly flickering candles. His gaze shifted to the sofa where Maddie slept beneath a blue blanket. A bottle of wine and an empty glass sat on the floor beside her. Scott stepped onto the porch and lifted the lid of the basket. The tangy aroma of fried chicken made his mouth water. Clearly, Maddie had gone to some trouble. So why hadn't she called him and told him what she was planning?

She had. Last night. On his cell phone. Scott grimaced. He sat on the coffee table facing her. Candlelight softened the straight line of her nose, while sleep made her lips puffy and full.

"Maddie?" Scott brushed her shoulder with one hand. The blanket fell away, leaving her bare skin soft and warm beneath his touch. "Maddie, I'm sorry."

She stirred, her voice a mere whisper. "Scott?"

"If I'd known about dinner . . ."

"Are the kids home yet?" Maddie groaned and pushed herself to a sitting position, letting her feet fall to the floor.

"Not yet. Where are they?"

"Movies." Maddie leaned forward, her hands pillowing her head. "Where were you?"

"At work. Rob called me into his office just as I was leaving and then I hit some traffic on the way home." Not exactly the truth, but close enough.

Maddie looked at him, her gaze weary and tone resigned. "I thought I'd learned this lesson long ago."

"What lesson?" Scott brushed the blond curls from her eyes but she leaned back, wrapping the blanket around her shoulders.

"Never to make dinner for you without checking first. My mistake."

The edge of sarcasm in her tone cut through his remorse. "Maddie, I was working."

"Well, that explains it. Work always comes first."

"Do you think I like working the kind of hours I do?"

Maddie got to her feet and stared down at him. "Frankly, yes."

"That's not fair. Sanders and Lowenstein is a job, not my life."

"But it conveniently gets you out of all those tiresome chores you'd rather not do." The blanket trailed behind her as she began blowing out the candles.

"I don't know what you're talking about."

"Like last month when Shaun had the flu and couldn't keep anything down. He spent the better part of three days in the bathroom and where were you?"

"At the office."

"My point exactly. Not exactly a hands-on parent when it comes to sick kids." Maddie grabbed the picnic basket and carried it into the bedroom.

Scott followed, her tone igniting his temper. "You have no idea what it takes to do what I do every day."

"How could I?" Maddie swung toward him. "You're never home to tell me."

A knock sounded at the door and Kylie flung it open, one hand on her hip and the other on the doorjamb. "Just thought you'd like to know we're home. Nice to know nothing ever changes around here. Keep it down, will you? Shaun's going to bed." She pulled the door closed with a bang.

Scott's features hardened. "We can't let her talk to us that way."

"I know. I'll take care of it . . . tomorrow." Maddie moved to the bed, pulled back the edge of the comforter, and slipped underneath.

Scott lifted the abandoned picnic basket. Maybe some of it could be salvaged. He'd take it downstairs and put it in the refrigerator. Thinking about his favorite foods, Scott stopped in the doorway. "Maddie, about dinner . . ."

She rolled toward the wall. "Forget it, Scott. I know I plan to."

Maddie pulled a chair up to the computer in the kitchen. She logged onto the Internet and typed in the web address for the Kerry Community Players. She'd told the kids about the audition, but after that fiasco with Scott Friday night, she hadn't mentioned it to him. Not that they talked much all weekend. Scott had spent most of the weekend in his office. After church on Sunday, she and the kids had hauled the float out of the boathouse and anchored it out on the lake. Then at Shaun's prompting they'd rented *The Music Man* on video and curled up with popcorn and chocolate sundaes to watch the movie.

Maddie tapped her teeth with one finger as she waited for the page to load. She wouldn't get a major part, especially since this was her first audition with the company, but some small speaking part would be nice. She hooked one foot over the edge of the chair. Hugging her knee to her chest, she scrolled down the theater menu and double-clicked the mouse on audition results. While the page came up, she thumbed through the pile of mail on her desk then glanced at the screen. Her name was first on the page.

Laughter tickled her throat and she bit back a giggle. After more than twenty years she was going to play Marion the Librarian. Leaning back, she stared up at the ceiling, a cry of triumph escaping her lips. And even after their silent weekend, Maddie wondered if Scott might be proud of her.

"Hey, Mom, what's up?" Shaun appeared in the kitchen.

"I got the part," Maddie said, exhaling her pleasure.

"Which one?"

"I got the lead."

"You mean, the librarian, the one Shirley Jones played in the movie." Shaun leaned on the seat back as he peered over her shoulder. "Did Annie get a part?"

Maddie turned back to the screen with a wince. She hadn't even looked. She scrolled down the cast list and found Annie Baldwin listed as one of the townspeople. She pointed to the screen.

"Can I tell Kylie when she gets back?"

"Tell me what, Brat?" Kylie jogged into the room, her hair damp from a run.

"Kylie, don't call him that." Maddie's automatic response was maternal but the grin never left her face.

"Mom, it's just a nickname. I've called him that ever since he tricked me into riding the chairlift with this really cute French guy who didn't speak a word of English."

Maddie shot a glance at Shaun, who suddenly seemed very interested in finding a snack.

"She got the lead in the summer show," Shaun said as he grabbed a box of cereal and started eating it by the handful.

"For real?" Kylie asked.

Maddie nodded, not sure what to expect from her daughter.

Kylie stepped over to the computer, her expression doubtful. She glanced at the screen and then threw her arms around Maddie. "That's pretty cool. Out of all those people they chose you."

The back door from the garage slammed closed. The jangle of keys preceded Scott's entrance into the kitchen. "Chose who for what?"

"I got the lead in the summer show," Maddie said, a touch of pride in her voice.

"You're kidding." Scott slid his briefcase onto the counter. "You tried out?"

"I told you I was going to."

"But I didn't think you'd actually do it."

Why had she dared hope he might be proud of her? Maddie bit her lower lip and shut down the Internet connection with a quick tap of the mouse. "Well, I did."

"So how much time is this show going to take?"

Kylie rolled her eyes at his words and made eye contact with her brother. She cocked a thumb over her shoulder, and they cleared the room like animals scurrying for cover from a storm.

Maddie watched them go, their communication so sure and speedy she knew they must have done this many times. She didn't think she and Scott fought that often, but her children's reaction said otherwise. Maddie glanced at her husband. Did Scott even see it? "We'll be in rehearsal for six weeks."

"Who's going to take care of things around here?" Scott strode down the hallway to his office.

Maddie clenched her fists and raised her voice. "I can manage. Rehearsals are only a few hours a day."

"Well, don't expect me to pick up the slack. I just got the Hingemen project and the timetable we're looking at is much tighter than I thought." His voice drifted out to her from his office.

"You got the project?" At any other time, Maddie would have congratulated him with a sincere smile. But tonight she couldn't see past her frustration. Why did everything always have to be about Scott? He hadn't said a word about her news. All he cared about was how it would affect him.

Scott's voice hummed with pride. "That work I did over the weekend must have clinched the deal. I submitted it by fax this morning and they gave us the job this afternoon."

"I'm glad for you, Scott," Maddie said quietly as she shut off the computer and followed her children upstairs.

When Scott returned to the kitchen she was gone. His shoulders sagged. He opened his briefcase and lifted out the bottle of champagne. Cold against his palm, it couldn't chill the fire building in his gut. He'd just landed the year's biggest project and his whole family had walked out on him.

Scott wrenched open the refrigerator and jammed the champagne in among the juice and milk. He'd been working his tail off for the last two months trying to please the Hingemens. Maddie knew the hours he'd put in. So where was she when it finally paid off?

After seventeen years of working for the financial stability of their family, he'd succeeded only to find that his wife and kids took his efforts for granted. His kids would have an education free from the massive student loans he'd taken out to pay his tuition. Maddie had new cars, a beautiful home, and the freedom to volunteer her time to any number of charity organizations, but did she see what this job took out of him? The drain on his energy? The shriveling of his imagination?

Sure, there were perks to his job, but on the whole it was just hard work. Scott braced his hands on the counter, his head bowed as disappointment replaced his anger.

Why was he working so hard? For what?

It was all for them, Maddie and the kids. Scott caught himself in the lie. No, he had to admit to a certain amount of ambition. He liked being a major player at the firm, and he liked pulling down the major jobs with his designs. So he wasn't as selfless as he made himself out to be.

Scott frowned. He knew he wasn't perfect, and certainly their marriage wasn't perfect, but in the last few years he and Maddie seemed to have more and more misunderstandings. He winced, thinking of the picnic basket on the porch. Well, now they were even. If she wanted him to know what it felt like to be ignored, he got the message.

Scott straightened as Maddie came downstairs and reached for her keys.

"Going out?" He kept his tone even, pushing aside his

disappointment.

"Choir practice," she said, not meeting his gaze as she turned back toward the stairs. "Kylie, are you coming?"

She appeared, carrying her violin. "You sure this is okay?"

"Absolutely. Vincent called and asked if you'd come."

"He did." Kylie beamed.

"Who's Vincent?" Scott cut in.

Maddie turned. "He's the choir director. He asked Kylie to play a piece on Sunday."

"That's great, honey. Maybe I'll come and listen."

They both stared at him as if he'd said something surprising.

"You'd come to church?" Kylie asked.

"Sure, to hear you."

Kylie smiled. "11:00 o'clock on Sunday then, okay?"

Scott nodded. The door closed behind his wife and daughter and he headed for his office.

So, his marriage wasn't perfect. It was still a far cry from his parent's' marriage. Scott loved his family and a real family stuck together. He would never leave his wife and kids the way his father had done. He would never make them suffer through the agony of doubt about what they'd done to drive him away. His kids would never lay awake at night and wonder if he ever really loved them.

He was a better father than that. A better husband. Scott stopped in his office doorway and listened to the silence all around him. Wasn't he?

Five

Saturday afternoon Maddie and Annie joined the cast members at the Kerry Community Theater. This first rehearsal would be a full read-through before vocal rehearsals began on Monday.

Maddie hadn't eaten anything, too anxious about the run-through to bother with food. Now she wished she'd driven through Dunkin Donuts on the way over. Her stomach rumbled loud enough for the whole room to hear. Maddie pressed a hand to her noisy stomach as she leaned over and whispered to Annie, "Last time we were here you were nervous. This time it's definitely me."

"If I had the lead I'd be nervous too, but since I'm just one of the peons I'll just sit back and watch," Annie teased.

Her red hair was pushed back from her face with a folded bandanna. Maddie marveled at how pretty she looked in khaki pants and a blue work shirt having come straight from the store. Maddie had chosen a long jean skirt and white linen top, hoping she wouldn't be overdressed. Though she fit right in with the cast's attire, the long, lithe bodies of some of the dancers made her sigh with longing.

Emily Tuttle crossed the stage, coming toward them with the man Maddie had seen as they left the audition.

The director's smile was wide. "Maddie, there's someone I'd like you to meet. Adam Slater, this is Maddie Alexander. She'll be playing Marion to your Harold Hill."

He held out a hand, a quizzical smile making his brows dip above blue eyes. "Nice to meet you, but I think we've met."

Maddie got to her feet and shook his hand. "I don't think so."

"Did you ever do an interview for the *Kerry Sentinel?* I'm the managing editor, and I'm usually pretty good with faces."

"Well, I've never been interviewed for the local paper or any other paper for that matter."

"It'll come to me." Adam accepted a script from Emily, who also handed one to Maddie. "Anyway, I'm looking forward to working with you. I heard your audition. You have a beautiful voice."

"Thank you. You did a great job yourself."

"And that would be why we're here. See you later."

Maddie sat back down next to Annie in the circle of chairs set up center stage. "He seems nice."

"Good thing because you've got a lot of scenes together," Annie replied, thumbing through her script.

The reading started and again Maddie was impressed with Adam Slater's command of the con man's spiel, his voice and demeanor perfect for his character. He was a good actor. In fact the whole cast was good. As Maddie had suspected, the woman with the Irish brogue, Rita Meyers, had gotten the part of Marion's mother. A young seven-year-old named Nate Higgins was playing her young brother, Winthrop. And the older man with impressive oratory skills had found the perfect part in the town's mayor.

Maddie tensed as her first scene began but soon fell into character as the reading progressed. She tried to appear professional but a warm flush heated her cheeks as she noted the kiss between Marion and Harold in the second act. She hadn't kissed anyone but Scott in seventeen years. This wasn't a real kiss though, and Maddie hoped she wouldn't break out in a cold sweat when it came time for the performance.

The reading ended and the group broke up with the director's call for everyone to be on time on Monday.

"This is going to be fun. I just hope I can remember all my lines." Annie laughed as she rolled her script up and tucked it under one arm. "Give me a minute? I want to say hello to Rita. She and my mom are friends."

Maddie gathered her script and her bag.

"I think I figured it out." Adam Slater appeared at her side. "Have you ever served on the local school board?"

Maddie winced. "No. I ran for the school board but missed being elected by three votes."

Adam snapped his fingers with a smile. "I covered the candidate's night for the paper. Must be what, ten years ago?"

"Nine, actually. I can't believe you were there?"

"Yes, and I wrote a brilliant piece about the young mother trying to unseat the elderly incumbent."

"Experience versus earnestness," Maddie said with a start. "That was you? My daughter was so proud she hung the article on the refrigerator."

"I'm flattered you remember. Actually, I'd just started working at the *Sentinel* so I got all the plum assignments. Quite a change from the *Globe*."

"The *Boston Globe*?"

He nodded. "I started with them right out of school and stayed for about six years."

"What made you decide to work for a local paper?" Maddie asked, enjoying his easygoing manner.

"The *Globe* had me doing major crimes, mostly homicides. All that violent death gets to you after a while, and I'd already seen enough death to last me a lifetime." His sneaker brushed the floor before he looked up at her. "Besides my dad lives not far from here so the move made sense."

"Ready to go?" Annie asked, her face flushed as she rejoined Maddie.

Maddie nodded and introduced Annie to Adam.

"Nice to meet you." Adam reached into his pocket for his keys as Annie hurried Maddie toward the door.

"Well, you're in a rush. What's up?"

Annie turned to face her, walking backwards. "Rita's daughter recently adopted a baby from Asia. She gave me the name of the agency she used."

Maddie smiled at her animated friend. "I didn't know you were considering foreign adoption."

"We've talked about it, but it always seemed so out of reach. We don't have the money to pay for the travel expenses, but Rita said the agency helped arrange financing to cover the costs."

"Sounds like it might be worth looking into," Maddie said cautiously.

Annie beamed. "I can't wait to tell Phil."

Sitting in the choir loft the next morning, Maddie scanned the aisles below, her stomach churning. She cast a sidelong glance at Kylie. Her violin rested in her lap as she watched the church fill, her face carefully neutral.

Maddie spotted Shaun sitting alone a few rows from the back. Where was Scott? He'd promised he'd be here. He couldn't do this to Kylie, not again. He'd missed field hockey games and band concerts in the past. But Kylie always gave him another chance, her tone eager with anticipation when he made yet another promise.

Maddie clenched her fists, her ire growing. The service began, and still no Scott. By the time the ushers took up the collection, Kylie's shoulders sagged and she no longer glanced over the balcony rail. And at that moment Maddie truly hated her husband. Her anger burned, mixed with a pure maternal longing to take her daughter in her arms, one parent trying to make up for the deficiencies of the other.

Vincent Morelli, the young choir director, leaned out from behind the organ. "Maddie, you're up."

Startled, she realized she'd forgotten all about her solo. She got to her feet.

Vincent paused, fingers poised over the keys. "You okay?"

Maddie managed a nod.

"Don't worry. It's a hymn of praise. God won't let you mess it up."

God? Here she was in church and she hadn't even thought about God.

"Sorry about that, Lord," Maddie said under her breath as she stepped to the side of the organ. Vincent nodded to Kylie with an encouraging smile and played the first notes. She rested her violin under her chin and glided her bow across the strings, the sound sweet and lilting in the silent church.

The bars of introduction faded and Maddie took up the melody. A slight quiver in the first few measures didn't last long. Heads in the congregation turned, but she barely noticed. The music had her in its flow. The choir joined in for the chorus, their voices raised in melodious sound.

Later outside the church, Maddie accepted the compliments of several parishioners.

"You were awesome." Shaun snuck up on Maddie. "And you weren't so bad either," he admitted to his sister.

"Gee, thanks, Squirt," Kylie said, but with none of her usual sarcasm.

Vincent Morelli bounded down the stairs, making his way toward them. At twenty-four, Vincent was fresh out of college with a degree in music and Maddie had never seen the usually serious young man look so animated. His long angular features looked almost handsome as he swept dark hair out of his eyes.

"Maddie, I'd like to try something more challenging next week. Are you game?" Vincent asked.

"I suppose so," Maddie agreed cautiously. "Vincent, I'd like you to meet my son. This is Shaun."

Vincent stuck out his hand. "Call me V.J."

"What's it short for?" Shaun shook the older man's hand.

"Vincent James. My mother's idea, but it works well on job applications. Makes me sound serious."

"You sure can play the organ."

"You should hear me on the keyboard. I really let it rip. I'm part of a band that plays at The Rafters."

Kylie's eyes widened at the mention of a band.

"Do you play?" Vincent asked Shaun.

Shaun shook his head, pointing at his sister. "Not me. Kylie got all the musical talent in the family."

"Well, I don't know about all the talent, but she plays an awesome violin."

Kylie blushed, staring at the pavement in awkward silence. "So you have a band?"

Vincent nodded. "We play at a little coffee house in Kerry. You should drop in some time."

"Maybe I will." Kylie smiled for the first time all morning.

Maddie shot her a cautionary glance. Clearly Vincent was being kind, and she didn't want Kylie taking his invitation the wrong way.

"Anyway, Maddie that was great." He waved a hand and headed for his beat-up silver Civic.

"You know, for a choir director he's kind of hot," Kylie said, staring after him.

Maddie could almost see her daughter's mind at work, but this morning she was glad of the distraction. Anything to get her mind off Scott. "But he's twenty-four. And you're still in high school."

"Not for much longer. So, where exactly is The Rafters?" Kylie asked as she climbed into the car.

"I don't know," Maddie said. "And you're still grounded, remember?"

"But this is music, not a date or anything."

"Three more weeks and then we'll talk about it." Maddie started the engine and pulled out of the parking lot.

Kylie turned her face toward the window in sullen resignation. By the time they pulled up to the house her self-imposed silence couldn't be contained any longer.

"I knew he wouldn't come." Kylie slammed the car door. "I should have known not to trust him."

"I'm sure he just got caught up with work and lost track of the time," Maddie said, making excuses for Scott not because he deserved it but because Kylie deserved a better explanation than her father would ever give.

"Like always," Kylie shot back at her.

"He's got that big project," Shaun chimed in and Kylie turned on him.

"Yeah, just like all the projects during baseball season when he didn't make it to any of your games."

"He did too," Shaun shouted defiantly, though his lower lip began to quiver.

"Enough you two. We can't change what's done." Maddie stepped between them throwing an arm around each one. "So what do you two want to do today? Go swimming? Take a sail?"

"How about fishing?" Shaun beamed, perking up.

Kylie glanced at her feet. "Sure, why don't you two go fishing and I'll just call a few people and invite them over to swim."

Her mother laughed and tipped her chin up. "Now you didn't really think you were going to get away with that, did you?"

"Hey, it was worth a try. You never know, you could be feeling sorry for me because Dad dumped me." She'd said it in jest but the words seemed to stick in her throat, her eyes suddenly moist.

Maddie's heart ached. "Kylie, honey, he didn't dump you, he just got—"

"Save it, Mom, I've heard it before, okay?"

Maddie reached out to hug her. Kylie stepped away, shoving her violin case in Shaun's direction before she fled down the path to the boathouse.

Six

tanding onstage Monday night, Maddie's nails bit into her palm as she recalled her daughter's pain. Kylie had trusted her father to keep his promise and Scott had let her down . . . again. It was one thing for Scott to pull this on her, Maddie reasoned. She was used to it. But Maddie was ready to throttle him for breaking his promise to Kylie. And worse, he hadn't even remembered making it at all.

When Maddie had confronted him, Scott was all apologies, but it was too little too late. Kylie barely looked at him the rest of the day.

Maddie tried to shake off her anger as she waited offstage for her cue. She thumbed through her script, noting the parts she'd highlighted. She had a lot of lines and lyrics to memorize and, though she was familiar with the show, she worried about her recall. Her nearly forty-year-old brain often left her standing in front of an open refrigerator with no clue as to what she'd opened the door to get. A whole script suddenly seemed daunting.

"Maddie, we're ready for you," Emily Tuttle called.

Maddie stepped from the wings. The scene was a short one. She simply had to walk across the stage looking annoyed at the stranger trying to get her attention.

"Now, here's the trick, Maddie," the director said. "You have to look like you're in a hurry, but you actually have to walk slow enough to let Adam get his lines in before you reach the other side of the stage."

Adam gave Maddie a lopsided grin. "Don't worry. I'll be such a pest you won't get very far."

"Thanks." Maddie smiled.

"Okay, let's try it."

Maddie set her script aside. She entered from the left and walked purposefully across the stage only to find her path cut off by Adam. She sidestepped around him as he delivered his line but found he was in front of her again. Maddie's annoyance grew. She'd be lucky to make it to the other side of the stage if he kept this up. Adam popped up in front of her again, grabbing her hand and bending to kiss it as she snatched it away. She delivered her one line and pretended to slam the door in his face.

"Excellent." Emily turned a page in her script. "Maddie, I loved that look. I thought you were really mad at him."

"I was," Maddie admitted with a chuckle, staring at Adam. "You make the motivation in this scene really easy."

"I aim to please." He tipped his hat.

"Let's try it one more time and then we're moving on," Emily called. "Just like before."

Maddie walked faster this time but Adam cut her off at every turn.

"You are far too good at that," she said to Adam as they finished the scene. "Being annoying, I mean."

"That's what my dad tells me too. Good thing I know he's joking."

"You and your dad are close?" Maddie asked as she crossed the stage to retrieve her script.

Adam nodded. "We talk almost every day and get together once a week for dinner." He rolled his script and used it to tip his hat back on his head. "How about your family? Are they around here?"

"Just my husband and kids. My parents still live in North Carolina where I grew up."

"Which would explain the accent. Do you get much chance to see them?"

"Only during the summer. I take the kids to see my parents for a week in late August and then go on to the Outer Banks." Maddie winced, recalling the strained farewells as her mother would try and persuade her to stay longer. "I'm the only girl in my family and my mother wishes I didn't live so far away."

"So you have brothers?" Adam reached down and picked up her script, handing it to her.

"Four, actually. Spread out all over the country. I don't see them much." Maddie flipped to the next scene in her script. "Do you have any siblings?"

"Nope, I'm an only. It's been just me and my dad for a long time."

Maddie looked up at him, noting his wistful tone.

Adam spied Emily waving him over. "Time to get back to work. See you later, Maid Marion." Adam bounded across the stage back in character again.

Maddie stared after him, wondering what it would be like to have such a small family. Maddie had to admit she took her parents and siblings for granted. They weren't close, a family of common heritage more than love, but Maddie recalled her boisterous escapades with her brothers with fondness. Her parents hadn't known half of what they'd done, anything to keep them out of the house and away from the stilted silence of her parents' loveless union.

Maddie had left for college and, like her brothers, had never looked back. She'd taken summer internships and spent most of her school vacations with friends, returning only briefly for the holidays. Even now Maddie dreaded the one week each year she dutifully spent with her parents and the last two years had been silent torture without Scott there to serve as a buffer.

Maddie glanced across the stage. Adam's wistful tone made her realize just how much she wanted her own family to be different. She wanted her children to feel comfortable in their home but now she feared the angry outbursts between she and Scott might make their children as eager to live elsewhere as she had been twenty years ago when she fled the South.

The rest of the rehearsal passed in a blur of blocking as Maddie covered her script with notes. Set in 1912 and written in the 1950s, *The Music Man* harkened back to a way of life that now seemed so antiquated it was quaint. Women wore full-length dresses and children were reprimanded for saying *darn*. The Wells Fargo wagon delivered long-anticipated purchases, decades away from Airborne Express and twenty-four hour satisfaction. Granted even then there had been a seamier side to life, but this musical's depiction of Iowa in the early 1900s was a watercolor view with soft edges and moral certainties, where good triumphed in the end and love could change a wayward con man.

"Remember principals only tomorrow for vocal rehearsal," Emily Tuttle called as they broke at ten and headed out to their cars.

Adam caught up with Rita and Maddie in the parking lot. He gave Rita a big hug.

"Working on another one together, Rita?"

"After *Brigadoon* you'd think I'd know better than to work with the likes of you," she laughed, practicing the Irish accent she would use in the show.

Adam turned to Maddie. "Don't believe a word she tells you."

Maddie feigned innocence. "About you?"

"Actually I hadn't gotten to that part yet," Rita joked. "But I will."

"Then please be kind." Adam pulled open the door of a black Volvo coupe.

Maddie and Rita watched him pull away in the sporty car. "So I take you it you've worked with Adam before?""

"The last two summers. His job at the newspaper may be his livelihood, but he's talented enough to pursue a professional acting career. Comes by it honestly, though. His mother did summer-stock productions for years when he was a kid."

"Not anymore?"

"She died when Adam was a boy. Twelve, I think. He's been doing the summer show ever since. Kind of a family tradition, I guess."

"No wonder he's so good."

Rita unlocked the door of an old station wagon. "You are too. This is going to be a great show. See you tomorrow."

Maddie arrived home from rehearsal to find Shaun sprawled in front of the PlayStation. His fingers danced over the keypad, controlling a gold Camero as it raced for the finish line.

Maddie tossed her keys on the counter and nudged his foot with her shoe. "Getting late, Bud."

Shaun peered over his shoulder. "Friday was my last day, so it's not like I have school tomorrow. Another ten minutes?"

Maddie nodded at his impish smile. "Where's your sister?"

Shaun resumed his game. The squeal of tires off the starting line almost drowned out his words. "She went for a walk with Kevin."

Maddie froze. "Kevin came over tonight?"

"Yeah, after you left. Kylie said you said it was okay even though she was grounded."

"I meant when I was here," Maddie said, her irritation growing. "Where'd they go?"

"Down by the lake."

"I'll be back in a minute. Stay put." Maddie grabbed a flashlight from the hall closet. She hadn't seen Kevin's car when she pulled in, which meant he'd parked farther down the lake road. Kylie hadn't misunderstood Maddie's instructions; she'd deliberately ignored them. Maddie jerked the door closed behind her and switched on the light. She strode down the grass to the water, sweeping the beam in large arcs.

The lakefront was quiet, the only sound the gentle lapping of water on the rocky shore. The flashlight's beam touched the float, the dock, and the Sunfish, tied up and bobbing in the black water.

Where was she? Maddie tried to fight the panic that threatened to override her anger. Kylie had deliberately disobeyed her. Sure, Kevin had probably talked her into it, but she'd gone along with him. Maddie couldn't believe Kylie had thrown away her last ounce of common sense and left her eleven-year-old brother alone in the house while she went out with Kevin.

Maddie shook her head. Maybe she was naive, but Kylie wouldn't have gone far, knowing Shaun was alone. So where was she?

The Sunfish bobbed against the dock's padding with a loud squeal. Maddie whirled to face it, suddenly sure she knew just where they'd gone.

Her stride deliberate, she took the path that paralleled the shore, growing more incensed with each step. The flashlight's beam shone on uneven ground before the path ended at a ramshackle boathouse. Just last week she and the kids had removed the canvas-covered float stored there. Scott's old Blue Jay and a few plastic lounge chairs were the only items left in the boathouse.

Her temper fully piqued, Maddie reached for the door handle and then stopped. Her hand wavered. What would she find in there? One part of her didn't want to know, but still she grasped the handle and pulled. The warped door squeaked on rusty hinges as Maddie shone the light inside.

A gasp. A grunt. The rustle of an old sail broke the silence before a creamy shoulder, almost white in the flashlight's beam, appeared around the corner of the Blue Jay. The straps of Kylie's bikini top dangled loosely as she scrambled for her shirt.

"Mom!"

Kevin lurched to his feet. He dove for his blue jeans, trying to avoid the light. And while Maddie allowed her daughter a moment of privacy to straighten her clothes, she took angry satisfaction in showing no such mercy to Kevin. His awkward struggles were highlighted in the stationary beam. He finally heaved the jeans past his hips and grabbed his shirt. Maddie barely controlled the impulse to kick him in the rear as he scurried by without apology. He disappeared into the darkness like the coward he was, leaving Kylie to take the heat.

Maddie closed her eyes, mustering every ounce of self-control she possessed as her daughter stepped into the light, looking scared but defiant. Maddie wanted to scream, to rant at Kylie about lying, about leaving her brother alone, about nearly having sex with a boy she barely knew in a smelly old boathouse. But Maddie knew she would gain nothing by yelling. Kylie was expecting that.

"I don't even know where to start," Maddie said, her shoulders so tense her muscles twitched. She drew in a deep breath and blew it out slowly. "Then again, yes, I do. You are not allowed to have anyone over when we're not home. And you went ahead and did it anyway." Maddie shone the light up the path.

Kylie got the hint, and started, shoulders hunched, toward the house. Her voice was barely audible. "Kevin's leaving on vacation with his family, and I wanted to say good-bye."

"Which doesn't give you the right to leave your brother alone while you do it. You deliberately chose your boyfriend's company over your brother's safety."

"He's not five; he's eleven. He can call 911 as well as I can."

"Don't even go there, Ky," Maddie said, her tone steely. "You can't talk your way out of this, and an apology would go a long way toward showing me you understand the bad choices you made tonight."

"I'm sorry." Kylie glanced back over her shoulder. "But I had to say good-bye."

"Looked like more than good-bye to me," Maddie said, trying not to let her anger overpower her good sense. This discussion was too important.

"This isn't going to be the birds and the bees lecture, is it, Mom?" Kylie groaned.

"No, I'm pretty sure you've got a handle on the facts, Ky. It's the feelings I'm worried about." Maddie pulled up short a few feet from the porch and turned off the flashlight.

"I know what I'm doing."

"Which is what?"

In the light from the front windows, Maddie saw her daughter blush.

"I'm still a virgin, if that's what you're asking."

Relief eased the tension in Maddie's neck. "I'm glad about that, and I want you to think before you take this relationship any further. You've only been seeing Kevin a short while. It takes a real commitment to enter into a sexual relationship."

"You do know everybody is doing it." Kylie crossed her arms over her chest. "I don't know anybody who's still a virgin."

"Not even Kevin?"

Kylie squirmed under Maddie's pointed gaze.

"How does that make you feel, Ky?"

"It's no big deal. It was just some girl he was dating last year."

"I just don't want that to be you next year." Maddie took her daughter by the shoulders. "You only get one first time, Kylie. Do you really want it to be in a dirty old boathouse?"

Kylie's silence was more chilling than her earlier protests.

Had she and Kevin really been that close? Maddie wondered. Why hadn't she realized the two of them were getting so involved? Because she didn't want to see it? "We'll talk about this some more tomorrow."

Kylie's eyes widened. She'd been prepared for a longer lecture but now saw the end in sight.

Maddie burst her bubble. "And there will be consequences for leaving your brother alone as well as having Kevin over."

"What kind of consequences? I'm already grounded," Kylie said, her tone suspicious.

"Like I said, we'll talk tomorrow."

"Mom, you don't have to tell Dad about this, do you?" Kylie's eyes were pleading.

"I don't keep things from your father."

"I won't do it again. Just please don't tell Dad."

"Ky—"

Kylie threw her arms around Maddie in a desperate hug. "I can't talk to him about this. I can't even mention sex in front of him."

"I'm not making any promises."

Kylie kissed her cheek and then disappeared through the front door, smart enough to know sometimes saying less was more.

Maddie sank onto the porch step. Did she really have to tell Scott? Of course, she did. He deserved to know what was going on in his daughter's life. But when Maddie pictured the inevitable uproar, she tended to shy away from what was morally right.

Wrapping her arms around her knees, Maddie stared into the night as she considered what amounted to a lie of omission. Certainly, she and Scott didn't always see eye to eye on parenting, but Maddie had never lied to him. So, she would tell him. It was the right thing to do.

A cool breeze blew in off the lake. Goose bumps rose on Maddie's arms and back.

Of course, she would tell him, when he came home.

Scott pushed open the door to his hotel room. He tossed the keys atop the suite's minibar. He'd been in charge of the Hingemen project less than a week, and Mariel Kensington was driving him crazy. The woman wanted to change parts of the project already approved by the Hingemens. He'd have to speak to Michelle tomorrow and ask her to run interference.

Scott laid his laptop on the coffee table and reached for the phone. He glanced at his watch and dialed home.

"Hey, Bud, what are you still doing up?" Scott asked when Shaun answered on the sixth ring.

"Just playing video games."

"Where's your mom?"

"Out on the porch. Want me to get her?"

"No, it's okay, just tell her I got held up in the city and I'm staying in town tonight. Got it?"

"Sure. Will you be home tomorrow, Dad?"

"I hope so, Shaun."

"Me too. See you."

"Night, Bud."

Scott held the phone to his ear and listened to the silence, suddenly longing for home. Sometimes he felt so removed from his family, not just in miles but in everyday experiences.

Since when did Maddie sit outside in the dark at this time of night? In June, she often stayed indoors especially after dusk, claiming the bugs would eat her alive.

And where was Kylie? Usually she grabbed the phone on the first ring and tonight Shaun had answered. Which meant he wasn't in bed, and it was almost 11:00 p.m.

Ever since Maddie started rehearsals for that show, things at home had been chaotic. Scott frowned.

Maybe the show would have to go.

Seven

Annie poured fresh coffee beans into the grinder and turned it on with a smile. She loved this time of the morning. The first rush of customers was over, and she could finally pour herself a cup of coffee. Morning sun angled through the front window, its warm light giving the wooden countertop a golden sheen. The scent of freshly baked muffins wafted from the box delivered earlier by the Kerry Bakery.

Annie had loved the idea of moving back to Whitefish Lake and the little town she'd grown up in. When her parents decided to retire and offered to sell them the business, it seemed like a perfect opportunity. After years of living in big cities, she savored the slower pace of the little New England town. Her only qualm had been the timing. Their approval as foster-care parents had just come through. They'd had only one emergency placement, a baby who stayed with them only a few days before the court granted temporary custody to a relative from another state. They moved soon after.

The old screen door squealed.

"Is Phil ever going to fix that door?" Maddie crossed to the register and leaned a hip into the counter.

"He's working on scraping and painting; then we'll see about the door." Annie waved a hand at the coffee bar behind the counter. "What can I get for you?"

"Coffee black, and four of those muffins. Blueberry, if you have them. I promised Shaun."

Annie put the muffins in a bag. "Anything for you?"

Maddie hesitated, then shrugged. "I shouldn't, not with costume fittings in a few weeks, but do you have any cinnamon rolls?"

"Always." Annie added one to the bag.

"Just the sugar rush I need. I didn't sleep much last night."

Annie peered at her friend with a sly smile. "Was Scott home last night?"

Maddie held up one hand, palm out. "It's not what you think. Or it is, but it has nothing to do with me."

"We are talking sex here, right?"

"Right, but it's not *my* sex life I'm worried about; it's my daughter's." Maddie paid for the muffins but left the bag on the counter. "Have you got a few minutes to talk?"

Annie poured two cups of coffee, covered them with lids, then turned to the back room. "Phil, got a few minutes to watch the register?"

Dressed in paint-spattered jeans and a navy sweatshirt, Phil leaned out of the storage room. "Sure, no problem."

Annie led the way through the storage area, stopping just long enough to drop a kiss on her husband's cheek before Maddie followed her out the back door. They threaded their way down a narrow path through the trees. Russet-colored pine needles carpeted the path, the needles dry and slippery underfoot.

Minutes later, they stepped onto a weathered boat dock jutting out into the lake. A covered motor boat bobbed at its moorings. Annie unsnapped the canvas boat cover and whipped it off. With an agile leap she climbed aboard, collapsing onto a beige vinyl seat. Maddie followed suit.

"Now this is what I missed. The lake, the sun, the quiet." Annie sipped her coffee. "I thought when I went to college that I would never come back. I was sick of small-town America. Now I can't imagine why I ever left."

"You wouldn't have met Phil if you hadn't."

A soft smile quirked the corners of her lips. "All a part of the plan." She pulled her knees up onto the seat and balanced her coffee cup atop them. "So what's going on with your daughter's sex life?"

Maddie sighed. "I found Kylie and Kevin nearly naked in the boathouse last night."

Annie's sneakers hit the deck as she leaned forward. "I can see how that might keep you up nights."

"I didn't know what to say. I was so mad I was tripping over my own tongue." Maddie jumped to her feet. The boat tilted from the sudden movement and she leaned against the stern. "I mean, what are we supposed to tell our kids about sex when all the messages they're getting from the media and from friends tell them to go ahead and try it?"

"You could tell her what my dad told me." Annie slipped across the deck and sat next to Maddie.

"Which was?"

She smiled at the memory. "When I was about thirteen my dad caught me making out with Tommy Rollins in the rowboat down by the dock. Now he could have told my mother, made a big stink about the whole thing, but he didn't. Instead he sent Tommy home and then took me out for a row around the lake. I was prepared for a lecture but what I got was the best explanation of sex I'd ever heard."

"Well, I can use all the help I can get. What did he say?"

Glistening prisms of light tipped the lake's surface as Annie continued. "He told me to think of sexuality as a gift and I'm the one who gets to decide who is worthy of something so rare and wonderful. Now the catch, of course, is that you only get to give the perfect gift one time so you have to weigh carefully who will get it. It should be someone you trust, who has proved himself capable of appreciating the true value of it. So what is the gift?"

Maddie smiled, squinting in the bright sunlight. "Your virginity, of course."

Annie shook her head. "That's what I thought, too. No, the gift is more than your sexuality. It's your whole being, because to enter into that kind of relationship you must be willing to give your whole self and you have to trust that the person you give it to will handle it with the utmost care."

"We don't always make the right choices, though," Maddie said softly.

"All the more reason why we have to take the time to choose wisely. You can't get to know someone in a week, or a month, even a year. But the gift can't be damaged if you wait until the prefect moment to give it."

Annie turned to the island just off the eastern shore, recalling how her dad had let the boat drift as they talked. "Before that afternoon I'd thought of myself as an awkward teenager. But that day my father told me I was a gift from God to my future husband, and I deserved to be treated that way. Gave my self-esteem a real shot in the arm, let me tell you."

Maddie nodded in agreement, though a quizzical frown wrinkled her brow. "I agree with the sentiment, but do you think it's realistic today, when kids can go to the movies and see couples having sex or go to parties and watch their friends hooking up?"

"Do I think it's easy?" Annie shook her head. "Not a chance. Especially these days. But God told us to wait and that's the best reason I can think of to do it."

"Does it actually say that in the Bible?"

"As a matter of fact, it does. The Bible says, 'It is God's will that you should be sanctified: that you should avoid sexual immorality, that each of you should learn to control his own body in a way that is holy and honorable.' "

Maddie still looked a bit skeptical. "Isn't sexual immorality kind of a broad term?"

"Not really. It means having sex outside of marriage. God wants us to use His gift of sexuality within the context of a blessed relationship—in other words, marriage." Annie gathered the coffee cups and jumped up onto the dock. Then she turned and offered Maddie a hand.

"Whatever happened to Tommy Rollins?" Maddie grabbed the proffered hand and bounded up next to her.

"Senior year he got his high school girlfriend pregnant and their parents pressured them into getting married. He never went to college, and after the baby was born he spent a lot of time hanging out in the local bars. He got arrested for DUI a few times and last I heard was serving ten years in prison for vehicular manslaughter."

"Good thing you didn't marry him."

"Don't I know it," Annie said, walking backwards up the path to the store. "So are you going to tell Kylie about the gift?"

"Hopefully after rehearsal tonight," Maddie said, lifting her hand to shade her eyes. "Annie, thank you. How did you get so wise?"

Annie smiled. "I've got a great teacher."

Angry shouting brought Maddie up short as she came through the door after rehearsal. Shaun sat on the staircase. Tears streaked his face as he cast a fearful glance upstairs.

Maddie raced to her son and crouched down beside him. "Hey, Bud, what happened?"

He looked at her, his brown eyes shiny with tears. "I didn't mean to tell him."

Above her Scott shouted, his words muffled by a closed door. Much as she wanted to rush up there, Maddie needed to know what was going on first.

"Shaun, what did you tell Dad?"

46

"It just slipped out, about Kylie having Kevin over last night and about them going for a walk. Then Dad started shouting, and Kylie ran upstairs. He followed her, but I didn't know what to do so I stayed down here to wait for you."

"Okay, slow down. None of this is your fault." Maddie slipped an arm around Shaun's shoulder and pulled him to her.

His face nestled in her shoulder. "Feels like it is."

"Dad and I needed to talk to Kylie about this and you just got it started." She hugged him and then wiped his cheeks with her thumbs. "Now why don't you play a video game and I'll play referee. And if they keep it up I'll send them both to their rooms."

Shaun managed a tiny smile. "Can you do that?"

"Sure I can."

Shaun sobered as another bellow erupted from upstairs. "Just make them stop yelling, please."

"I will, Bud." Maddie kissed the top of his head and then hurried upstairs to Kylie's room. At the door, she drew in a deep breath, catching part of Scott's tirade as she pushed it open.

". . . and if you think I'm going to let that punk set foot in this house again . . ."

"Mom!" Kylie screamed. She flew across the room to hug Maddie in a fierce embrace.

Scott glared at them. "We aren't finished here, young lady."

"How about we take a break and you and I talk first, Scott. Then we can both talk to Kylie about her punishment."

Scott scowled, his face flushed. "I don't need you running interference every time I want to have a conversation with my own daughter."

But Kylie had already slipped out of the room.

Scott stared at the empty doorway before turning on Maddie. "I had it under control."

"Didn't sound like it. I could hear you from downstairs." Shadings of guilt tempered Maddie's righteousness. If she'd called Scott and told him about Kylie and Kevin, this whole scene might have been avoided.

"Okay, maybe I raised my voice but . . ."

"You scared Shaun," Maddie said softly.

Scott's anger ebbed. "I didn't mean to, but when I think of Kylie and that little punk in the boathouse . . ." His fists clenched in impotent rage.

"Kylie told you about the boathouse?"

"She thought I already knew." Scott's tone hardened. "So why is this the first I'm hearing about it and where were you last night anyway?"

"At play rehearsal."

"Our kids need you home. You can't be running out every night."

"This isn't my fault."

"I know that." Scott ran a hand over his face, clearly more frustrated than angry. "But you need to be here to supervise the situation."

"What are you suggesting?" Maddie closed the door, afraid the next explosion would be hers.

"Maybe you should quit the show."

"And maybe you should spend more nights at home."

"Last time I looked all those late evenings helped pay the bills around here," Scott shot back.

"And if I'd known our finances were such a burden to you, I'd have gotten a full-time job long ago."

"That's not what I meant," Scott said, his shoulders tense.

"I know that." A tinge of regret made Maddie's tone more reasonable, if not quite an apology.

It was always like this. A blow-up, followed by a few digging remarks, then silence with nothing resolved. Didn't they care enough to have it out? Or were they both so afraid of confronting their dismal marriage they opted for peace at any price?

Scott broke the silence. "About Kylie . . ."

Maddie sighed. They'd played this same scene for years. Always dealing with the kids' problems and ignoring their own. "Well, we won't have to worry about Kevin for a while. He's on vacation with his family until early August."

"And Kylie is still grounded so she won't be going anywhere. Let's give her an extra two weeks on the grounding and take away her phone and computer for a month, which should give her time to think about what she's done. Agreed?"

"Fine."

Scott strode to the door.

"Scott, about the play . . ."

He didn't even turn. "I'm not going to give you an excuse to hate me. Do what you want, Maddie; you always do."

"I could never hate you . . ."

The door closed behind him. Maddie's words hung in the silence even as she wondered if they were true.

Eight

Scott stared at the design for the day-care center, unable to keep his mind on his work. He'd come into the office early to finish the preliminary drawings, but he wasn't making much progress. Last night's angry exchange with Maddie kept playing over and over in his head. Just once he'd like to get through a discussion with Kylie without Maddie's interference. She always assumed she was right. The woman was a control freak. Granted, he should have kept a hold on his temper, but he had every right to discipline their daughter. And did Maddie understand his words were driven by fear and not anger?

The thought of Kylie having sex with some guy who wouldn't know her name next year scared Scott to death.

A knock sounded on the door frame and Rob Sanders stepped into the office. "Scott, got a minute?"

"What can I do for you, Rob?"

"I just got a call from Mariel Kensington. It seems she's having a problem getting through to you."

Scott's jaw clenched. "Michelle gave me her messages, but I've been dealing directly with Sarah Hingemen."

Rob looked surprised. "You've spoken with Mrs. Hingemen?"

"Several times, yes."

Somewhat mollified, Rob adopted a less challenging tone. "You know, of course, how important this project is to the firm. We don't want any problems with the Hingemen people. Just meet with Mariel."

"It's a waste of time. Her suggestions almost always contradict Sarah Hingeman's."

"Just have lunch with her and put out any fires before they start."

Scott's fist closed atop the unfinished design. If he blew two hours on lunch, he'd have to finish the work tonight. "Fine."

"Who knows, Scott, you might enjoy it. She's not bad-looking." Rob smirked.

Scott bit back an angry retort. This day was going downhill fast.

Maddie and Annie hurried down the aisle to join the cast onstage. Emily Tuttle clasped her script in one hand as she pointed a finger at the dancers and counted out loud.

"We're one short." Turning, the director advanced on Annie as she came up the stage steps. "Can you dance?"

"I took tap back in high school," Annie said.

"Perfect. I need one more for the library scene. Pull that hair back, and you'll pass for a teenager."

"I think I'm flattered," Annie said in an aside to Maddie. "Except she's desperate."

The choreographer, a lithe older woman who looked like she'd taught a lifetime of ballet classes, began to position the dancers onstage. She motioned Annie to a seat on the library set. Maddie suppressed a smile, noting that her slender friend fit right in with the other dancers. But Maddie's smile quickly faded. She was dancing in this scene too. And all she wanted was to get through it without looking like a klutz.

Adam Slater stepped next to Maddie, noting her frown. "Don't worry. In a few weeks this will all be second nature."

"I hope so. Playing Marion is a lot harder than I thought."

"How so?" Adam withdrew a leather pouch from his jacket pocket, smacking it against his palm. The clink of marbles made the choreographer turn and glare at him. Adam smiled at her and held the bag steady.

"Well, besides the dancing, which I haven't done in years, there's a fine line between making Marion a prissy prude and making her a believable character. It's hard to hit the right note and give her a softer side."

"So just let my charm whittle it out of you. At first you'll be stoic and I'll be charming." Adam came around in front of her and executed a courtly bow. "Then you'll be interested but reserved, and I'll be charming, and then you'll be won over."

"And you'll still be charming." Maddie laughed.

"That's the idea." Adam straightened up. "There's a part of Marion that wants to take a chance on love. She's ready to fall, and Harold is there to catch her. The part he never sees coming is the change she'll bring about in him. That's the beauty of this story."

"Nice analysis of the motivations. Maybe you're ready for the big job." Maddie pointed at a frazzled-looking Emily Tuttle consulting with the set designer on paint colors.

"No, I'm too much of a ham." Adam grinned. "I've got a day job where people read my words, but never see my face. I'll take a little recognition where I can get it."

Maddie laughed, finding his honesty refreshing. "Well, then this is the right show. You're in almost every scene."

The choreographer waved them over to center stage. "Mr. Hill, you will enter from stage right, and Ms. Purue, you'll be here behind the librarian's desk."

When Adam stepped onstage moments later, the leather pouch was nowhere in sight. He leaned on the librarian's desk and oozed charm as he asked Marion the Librarian to go out with him. When she refused, he reached into his coat pocket and held aloft the bag filled with marbles. With a mischievous smile he threatened to upend the bag in the silent library unless Marion changed her mind.

The choreographer then walked the dancers through a simple routine that eliminated any difficult dance steps for everyone except Adam. Having worked with him before, she'd mapped out several measures of more intricate footwork to showcase his talents.

Maddie blushed at her own clumsiness as Adam led her in a waltz step around the librarian's desk. As the number came to a close, Adam held the bag aloft and tossed it in the air. Maddie lunged over the desk and just managed to catch it.

The director clapped her hands. "That looks great. Let's take a ten-minute break. I'll need principals only for the rest of the night. Everyone else can go on home."

Winded and thirsty, Maddie hurried out to the lobby, bypassing the fountain in favor of the vending machine and a bottle of water. Grabbing a second one, she spotted Annie across the lobby talking on her cell phone.

Maddie offered her the drink and Annie took it with a distracted nod.

"Anything I can do?" Maddie asked, when Annie joined her moments later.

Annie's eyes brimmed with tears. "That was Phil. The bank turned us down flat for the loan. So that means no foreign adoption."

"Oh, Annie, I'm sorry." Maddie hugged her, her heart aching. How many times had Annie gotten her hopes up only to have them shattered again?

"They said we haven't got enough collateral because the store is still owned by my parents."

"What if someone cosigned the note?"

Annie sighed. "I can't ask Mom and Dad."

"I wasn't talking about your parents. Scott and I could cosign the loan for you."

"We couldn't ask you to do that."

"Why not? We know you're good for it. Besides, I can't think of two people who would be better parents."

Annie dried her face with the heel of her hand, her voice tentative but hopeful. "Maddie, thank you. I can't tell you how much I appreciate your offer, but I need to talk to Phil first and then we need to pray about it together."

"Do you think God will give you an answer?" Maddie asked, not quite able to keep the incredulity from her tone.

"I do." Annie nodded. "It's just this time I'm afraid the answer may be no. It may be part of God's plan for us to serve Him in some other way than being parents."

Maddie was amazed by Annie's continued faith. "Do you think God would keep you from something you want so badly?"

Annie stepped back, her eyes still shiny but her demeanor certain. "I have to believe that God knows more than I do, that He can see the whole picture while I can see only a tiny corner. A few years ago I trusted Him with my life, and whatever the outcome, someday I'll understand why it had to be this way."

"That's a whole lot of faith."

"It's what gets me through."

Maddie glanced over her shoulder. "Well, I think you should go right home and talk to Phil about my offer."

"But we came together. How will you get home?"

"I'll call Scott." Maddie patted her on the shoulder and turned her toward the door. "Don't worry about me. Just drive carefully."

"You sure you'll be okay?"

"I'm fine. Just go." Maddie gave Annie a light push to send her on her way.

Maddie watched her go, awed by her friend's quiet peace. Annie wanted a child so badly, but despite her pain, she radiated an acceptance Maddie had never seen before. Annie was truly committed to living her life God's way. Maddie didn't think she'd ever asked God's advice before making a decision. She always went ahead and did whatever she thought was best. She couldn't imagine trusting anyone that much. Not even God.

"Do you need a ride home?" Adam's question interrupted her musing. He took a drink from the water fountain before dipping his face into the stream. "I couldn't help overhearing."

"No, thanks. I'll just call my husband," Maddie said.

Adam shook his head, sending droplets flying. "That's hot work in there."

"Especially when you have to push me around the stage."

"I thought you caught on faster than most."

They started back toward the theater before Adam waylaid her with a hand on her arm. "I was serious before. If you can't get your husband, I'll give you a lift home."

"I appreciate the offer, but I'll be fine." Maddie smiled. "Thanks anyway."

"So how'd it go with Phil?" Maddie asked the next morning as she tucked the portable phone into her shoulder and poured herself a cup of coffee. She grabbed her script and headed out to the deck.

"He was floored by your offer, Maddie. But he'd like to think about it, if that's okay?" A box cutter zipped through cardboard in the background. "So, how'd you get home last night?"

"I called Scott. He drove in and got me. Couldn't very well leave me stranded now, could he?"

"It's lucky he was home."

"Otherwise I would have had to take Adam up on his offer."

Annie paused, the box cutter silent. "Adam offered to drive you home?"

"He did. Nice of him too, since he barely knows me."

"You two seem to be hitting it off."

"He's a nice guy and easy to work with."

"And he makes you laugh."

Maddie sipped her coffee and settled into a lounge chair, curling her feet under her. "Good thing, since we've got weeks of rehearsal before opening night."

"You two could be pretty friendly by then."

"What do you mean?" Maddie picked up the script, thumbing through the pages.

"Only that Adam could be a pretty tempting distraction."

"Distraction?" The script fell open in Maddie's lap as she started to laugh. "You're not serious."

"Don't tell me you haven't thought about it."

"Well, now that you mention it—" Maddie broke off with a suggestive pause—"that kiss in the second act could be fun . . ."

"I'm sorry I brought it up."

"Annie, listen, I know you're trying to look out for me and I appreciate it. I haven't had anyone do that since my brothers hand-picked my boyfriends."

"It's just when you spend a lot of time with someone it's natural you could get close . . . oh forget it. I was just giving you a heads-up in my own inane way."

"You're a good friend."

"With a big mouth . . ."

"And a heart in the right place."

Maddie pulled her knees up to her chest. Her script slipped off the lounge and landed on the deck. "I mean, we both know that Scott and I don't have the best marriage, but I'm not about to throw it away on a fling. Our family is too important."

"I'm sorry if I overstepped. Listen, I've got a customer. I have to go. See you tonight."

"My turn to drive. I'll pick you up at 6:30 p.m."

Smiling, Maddie retrieved her script. She was lucky to have a friend like Annie, even if she was completely off base on this one.

Maddie gazed out over the choppy white-crested lake. Sure, she'd thought about the kiss, wondered what it would be like to kiss someone besides Scott. But when she thought about it, her first emotion wasn't desire but embarrassment. Was a stage kiss the same as a regular kiss without the passion? She blushed, hoping her inexperience wouldn't cause them to bump noses like two teenagers on their first date. Goose bumps rose on Maddie's arms as a cool breeze cut through the pine trees. The script fell open to the scene where Marion meets Harold at the footbridge. Her eyes drifted down to the stage directions.

THEY KISS.

And despite her earlier denials, Maddie shivered and her heart beat faster at the words.

Annie poked her head in the back room where Phil was doing inventory on the computer.

"I think I just did a really stupid thing." Annie leaned against the doorjamb, keeping one eye on the store.

Phil spun his chair around, giving her his full attention. "What'd you do?"

"I warned Maddie about getting too close to Adam during rehearsals."

"You've got good instincts, Annie. Something made you think you needed to say that; what was it?" Phil pushed himself out of his chair and came to stand beside her.

"Adam is flirting with her. Nothing serious, but I'm afraid I may have put an idea in her head that wasn't there before."

"You aren't the one putting the idea in her head. You just saw the inevitable result of them spending time together."

"I planted a seed, though."

"A seed of warning, and later Maddie may need to remember that." Phil draped an arm around her shoulders.

Annie leaned her head against his muscular shoulder. "It's just that Maddie has no defenses against this temptation. She and Scott have a miserable marriage that neither one of them seems to want to fix. They love their kids, but they're not invested in each other anymore."

"And neither one of them knows the Lord, right?"

Annie nodded. "Scott I can understand, but Maddie is in church every Sunday with the kids. She hears the words, sings the songs, but it's all just head knowledge. It's never touched her heart."

"That's why she has you." Phil squeezed her shoulder. "You're here in this place for a reason. We both are. And maybe one of those reasons is Maddie."

"She's a good friend." Annie looked into his eyes. "Can you believe she offered to cosign our loan?"

Phil turned her to face him and his hands settled on her waist. "I've been thinking and praying about that, and I don't know if we should do it."

Annie flinched, trying to keep the pleading from her tone. "We would never default on the loan so they'd never have to pay it off."

"I know, but there's a bigger question here. Should we be spending money we don't have for something that may not be God's will for our lives?"

"I've prayed about it, but I think God's answer is all mixed up in my head with what I want for us. I can't tell the difference anymore."

"And even if we got the loan I don't know as foreign adoption is the way to go. Maybe we should help a child who lives here in the USA." Phil tilted her chin up, forcing her to look at him. "I know this may not be what you want to hear. It sounds like starting from scratch . . ."

"I just want a baby so badly," Annie whispered. "It hurts."

Phil hugged her. "I know, Annie."

He didn't say any more. This was a problem he couldn't solve and words, no matter how eloquent, would not make it better. Long ago he'd learned to offer comfort in silence. He drew Annie close and held on tight.

Nine

S cott sipped his beer, sinking lower into the deck chair. He stretched
his legs out and closed his eyes with a sigh. Even if he did have
work to do, he was going to enjoy this holiday weekend. Maybe
take Shaun fishing or go sailing with Kylie—anything to get his mind off
work. The Hingemen project was prestigious, but more work than he'd
anticipated due in large part to Mariel Kensington. His lunch with her
earlier in the week had been long and tedious with little accomplished.

Late afternoon sun warmed his face as Scott savored his temporary
freedom. Even driving into Kerry the other night to pick Maddie up
from rehearsal had been a welcome break. The summer night had been
perfect for a drive. Windows down, he'd pulled into the theater lot and
watched Maddie wave good-bye to a young boy with white hair and a
dark-haired man. Sweat glistened on her brow as she climbed into the
car. And even with the few extra pounds she'd put on since they married,
she still looked like the girl Scott first met in college.

"Thanks for coming to get me," she said.

"No problem."

"Were you working?"

"Yes, but it's nothing that can't wait until tomorrow."

"Sorry to make you drive all the way in here," Maddie said.

"What was I going to do—leave you here?" He intended the words as
a joke but instead heard their gruff edge....

Sitting on the deck now, Scott winced. He never seemed to hit the
right note with Maddie anymore.

Behind him the screen door slid open with a metallic hum. "You're
home early." Maddie sounded surprised as she stepped outside.

"I wanted to beat the traffic so I left after lunch." Scott turned from
the lake. "Kids around?"

"I just brought Kylie home from work. She's upstairs, and Shaun's
spending the night at Jack's house."

Scott nodded, closing his eyes as the roar of a motorboat signaled the start of the weekend. "Do you have rehearsal tonight?"

"Yes, but not for a few hours. Then we're off until Tuesday."

Scott nodded. "Uh-huh." He folded his arms across his chest, content just to listen to the rhythmic slap of waves against the dock.

"I wanted to talk to you about something."

"Okay," he murmured.

"You know about the problems Phil and Annie are having with the foster-care system, right?"

"Not really. Phil and I don't talk about that stuff."

"Well, they want a child so badly," Maddie said, elaborating on the details. "And they were accepted as foster-care parents before they moved up here, and now that's not working out because they live in a different state."

Scott inwardly groaned. Much as he liked Phil and Annie this was more than he needed to know.

"So they're considering adopting a baby from overseas."

Scott pushed himself up in the chair and opened his eyes just a slit. "Is there a reason I need to know all this?"

"Yes, I'm getting there. Since foreign adoption is so expensive Annie and Phil applied for a loan but the bank turned them down."

"Because Phil is working freelance restoring boats and has no steady income except the store."

"And they have no collateral because Annie's parents still own the store." Maddie paused, smoothing the fabric of the chaise lounge. "I offered to cosign the note for them."

Scott's jaw tightened. "You mean, you said we'd cosign the loan."

"Yes."

His anger mounting, Scott got to his feet. "So you went ahead and made a decision for both of us without even talking to me first."

Maddie squared her shoulders, though her tone sounded nervous. "It was just an offer, and I'm pretty sure they won't take us up on it . . ."

"But if they do . . . how much is it for?"

"Twenty-five thousand dollars."

Scott stuffed his hands in his pockets. "You've backed me into a corner, Maddie. I can't very well say we won't cosign the loan without looking like a lousy friend."

"So we'll do it?"

"Is that all you care about?" Scott snapped. "You're so intent on looking like the Good Samaritan you don't care who you have to step over to do it."

"That's not fair . . ."

"It's just like all the other unilateral decisions you make around here—about the kids, about the house, about this show you're doing." Scott leveled her with an accusing stare. "I find out after the fact when no one can stop you from getting what you want."

Maddie surged to her feet. "If this is about the money . . ."

Heat rose in Scott's face. "It's not about the money. It's about you making all the decisions around here without even consulting me." Scott turned his back on her and sat down with a weary sigh. Leaning his elbows on his knees, he stared out at the water, the evening's earlier promise tainted by the tenor of their words.

"Don't do this to me again, Maddie."

He didn't turn to look at her as the screen door closed behind him.

Maddie collapsed on the edge of the stage and tried to catch her breath. Glancing around, she wasn't the only one breathing hard. Dancing the Shipoopee had proved the ill state of her aerobic health. She should use this holiday weekend to start getting in shape.

"No rest for the weary, I'm afraid." Adam stood above her and held out his hand. "Emily wants us to block out the footbridge scene while the others take a break."

Maddie took his hand and let him pull her to her feet. "Right now?" She dusted off the back of her shorts.

"I think Emily is starting to panic."

Maddie noted Adam's grin. His face was flushed and gleamed with sweat, but he didn't seem winded. Evidently he was used to this. "Does she do this every year?"

He nodded. "Like clockwork. Don't worry. She'll calm down once all the blocking is done."

Emily waved them over to down stage right. "Adam, you'll be here at the bottom of the footbridge," Emily began as Maddie used the sleeve of her T-shirt to wipe her dripping brow. "Maddie, you'll enter from stage left and hurry over to him. Okay, you two face each other, and Adam you take her hand. Next week we'll have the footbridge along with the railing; the footing will be different because it's sloped . . ."

Adam tipped back on his heels imitating the slope. He fell backwards and pulled Maddie with him. She laughed at his antics but then grew quiet under Emily's stern gaze. They ran through the lines and then the song "'Til There Was You."'

"Very nice," Emily said matter-of-factly. "At the end of the song, Adam, you'll kiss her."

Maddie blushed, heat flooding her face. She kept her chin tilted upward when all she wanted to do was look at her feet. Adam leaned forward. He brushed by her cheek without touching, his face just inches from hers as Emily bustled away calling for Harold Hill's sidekick to make his entrance.

Adam straightened and looked into Maddie's eyes. "When I was little I used to watch my mother from out there in the theater." He cocked his head towards the seats with a smile. "She was the most beautiful woman in the world, no matter what part she played. But I was always a little jealous for my dad that some other guy was going to kiss her."

"Did you ever tell her that?" Maddie asked, liking the note of fond remembrance in his tone.

Adam nodded. "She told me it was just a stage kiss, and my dad would never have anything to worry about because she saved all her real kisses for him . . . and for me." His mouth curved in a sad smile. "Then she kissed me on the forehead and hugged me so hard I had to wiggle to get free."

Maddie laughed, thinking of Shaun. "How old were you?"

"Nine."

"Thanks for telling me," Maddie said, stepping back.

"Got us through the awkward kissing moment, didn't it?" Adam squeezed her hand, then released it.

"Yes, it did."

The rest of the scene was straightforward, thanks to Adam's story and his professionalism.

"That's great, better than great for a first run-through. You two are fabulous together. What chemistry," Emily crooned. She flipped through her script and made a few notes. "The scene ends with another kiss, but we'll save all that for the performance. Nice work."

"Thanks," Maddie said, as the cast assembled on stage again to run through the earlier number. "You made that easy."

"Because I remember my first stage kiss." Adam took his place behind her and placed a hand on her waist. "Actually it was my first kiss ever."

Maddie glanced back at him. "Really."

"I was sixteen and scared out of my wits."

But before Maddie could ask another question, the music began and they were off and running with no time to do anything but dance and breathe.

Hours later, Maddie slipped into bed exhausted but happy. Her muscles were sore and her throat scratchy from all the singing, but with several more weeks of rehearsal she'd be ready for opening night.

Beside her, across the great divide of comforter and pillows, Scott slept with his back to her, his breathing slow and regular. A slight wheeze hummed with each breath. Maddie considered waking him. She wanted to talk, to lay awake in the dark and share her excitement about the day. They used to do that all the time . . . that and a lot of other things.

She rolled over onto her back and stared at the ceiling, hugging a pillow to her chest. Her eyes stung and her vision blurred as moonlight spilled in through the skylight overhead. How had they come so far from the days where they could share anything to this place where the joy they found in their kids was their only communication? They never discussed plans for the future, never gave voice to their dreams. Maddie glanced over at Scott. What were his dreams? At one time she had known. But not anymore.

Maddie drew the sheet up to her chin and rolled toward the door. Her eyes brimmed with tears that rolled down her cheek to dampen the pillow. Did they even have a future together? Or had their union become only a matter of convenience as barren as her parents' marriage? Would they physically occupy the same house but never again intersect in any meaningful way?

Maddie squeezed her eyes shut. She couldn't live like that. Wouldn't live like that. But she refused to think about the only other alternative and what that might mean for their family's future.

Ten

Maddie raced around the kitchen ignoring the heat. In the last four weeks, the summer temperatures had soared, and August promised to be more of the same. When they'd renovated the house years ago, Scott had balked at putting air conditioning in a New England home where the thermometer seldom broke eighty. Today, that decision seemed shortsighted.

Maddie swept the counter clean of lunch dishes and loaded them into the dishwasher before glancing at her watch. With only a week until the performance, today's full run-through and final costume fitting would take the whole afternoon and a good part of the evening, and she was going to be late getting Annie if she didn't leave soon.

Maddie added detergent and started the dishwasher. In the family room Shaun lay sprawled on the floor in front of the television. "Shaun, where's Kylie?"

"Out on the deck getting skin cancer." Shaun pointed over his shoulder with a grin. "Someday she'll really be an old bag if she keeps it up."

Maddie nudged him with her toe as she strode by. "You just love to torture her, don't you?"

"Hey, Mom, it's my job."

Maddie stepped over to the screen door. Kylie lay on her stomach on a lounge chair, her skimpy pink bikini covering little of her body. For a moment Maddie just stood and stared, her hand on the screen. How had this beautiful young woman emerged from the pudgy-fingered girl who loved to look for crayfish? It had happened before Maddie's eyes and yet she hadn't seen it coming. As if sensing the appraisal, Kylie looked up.

Maddie pulled the screen open. "Can you unload the dishwasher when it's done?" She was expecting an argument but Kylie just nodded.

She swung her long legs to the ground and sat up. "No problem. Any chance I can go to the coffee house tonight?"

"Sure, why not."

Kylie snapped her mouth closed. "You're not teasing me, right? I can go?"

Maddie nodded. "You've been home for weeks now. I think we can cut you a little slack on the last few days. How are you getting into town?"

"Larkin is picking me up. Can you tell Dad?"

"Sure. Home by midnight, okay?"

Kylie leapt off the lounge and bounded across the deck, planting a kiss on Maddie's cheek. "Thanks, Mom."

Maddie gave her a quick hug, her hands slipping on Kylie's shoulders as the scent of coconut lotion filled the air. "Got to go."

She grabbed her purse and keys by the computer and ducked into Scott's office on her way out. "I'm leaving."

Scott grunted and waved a hand without turning.

"What do you think about letting Kylie go out with Larkin tonight?" Maddie asked, rephrasing her earlier agreement into a question as she realized she'd made the same kind of unilateral decision that made Scott crazy. "She's been housebound most of the summer and pretty good-tempered about it."

"It's okay with me as long as Kevin isn't part of the plans."

"Nope, just Larkin," Maddie said, relieved to have avoided an argument as she sprinted for the door.

On the road a few minutes later, Maddie sang a few bars of the show's opening number. Anticipation made her smile. Today was going to be fun. She'd been looking forward to it all week. Maddie tipped her head back, a chuckle born of pure pleasure sounding loud in the silent car. She was living her dream. Sure, it was just a local production, but she was happy and feeling appreciated for the first time in a long while.

Maddie pulled up in front of the store and turned off the engine. Was there more to her pleasure than a theatrical performance? She snatched her keys from the ignition, knowing that, at least in part, it was true. She and Adam had become close friends over the last few weeks. Maddie looked forward to their time together, and often felt sad when it was over. Well, it would be over for good in another week. Probably a good thing too, because as much as Maddie had scoffed at the idea, Annie had been right. It was hard not to be intrigued by a man who laughed at your jokes, a man whose face lit up when you walked into the room.

One week more. And if Maddie found herself wishing time would slow down and make the week last just a bit longer, she firmly put the thought aside. It would be over soon enough.

The coffee house parking lot was packed. Live music in a town the size of Kerry always drew a crowd especially without a cover charge. Kylie reached for the car door handle.

"What's the rush?" Kevin slid a hand across the back of the seat and pulled her to him. "I've been gone a long time."

Kylie turned to face him. "It felt like months."

Kevin lifted a hand to her hair, pulling loose her ponytail and letting her dark hair fall around her shoulders. "We've got a lot of catching up to do," he said and leaned in to kiss her. "It's been too long."

Kylie met his kiss but then put a hand to his chest and pushed him back. "We'd better go in. I know my mom is going to ask me about this tomorrow, and I'd better know what I'm talking about. She knows one of the guys who plays here."

Kevin's hand drifted from her hair to her collar, where he slipped loose the top button of her shirt.

Kylie shuddered, wondering why she felt so uneasy at his touch. It wasn't like they hadn't done this before, but this time it felt different. Ever since Larkin dropped her off, Kevin had been all over her.

"Come on, Ky. Let's just blow this place and find ourselves a little privacy."

Kylie slid back toward the door. "Like I said I'm going to get the third degree tomorrow, and I need to know what goes on in there. If I get caught in another lie I'll be grounded for the rest of my high school career."

"Okay, we'll go listen for a while," Kevin said, his tone resigned. "But first I want to show you how much I missed you." His hand closed on her upper arm. He pulled her to him just as a knock sounded on the window.

Kylie spun toward the sound and opened the window.

"I thought that was you." Vincent leaned both arms on the frame and peered into the car. "You coming in?"

Flustered by his sudden appearance, Kylie hoped she didn't look as disheveled as she felt. "Sure, we just got here. When are you playing?"

64

Vincent pulled open the car door. "In about half an hour. I just came out to get some music from my car."

With the door open, Kylie stepped from the car. Behind her Kevin grumbled as he threw open the driver's side door.

"Everything okay here?" Vincent asked Kylie, his eyes level with hers.

"Fine," Kylie answered as Kevin rounded the front bumper.

She introduced the two men. Vincent held out a hand and Kevin reluctantly shook it.

"So what do you play?" Kevin asked as he slipped an arm around Kylie and they headed toward the club.

"Piano, jazz mostly, but tonight I'm on keyboard backing up the band. Do you play?"

Kylie felt Kevin tense. He pulled her closer. "No time. I've got to get ready for football."

Vincent nodded. "Your first time here?"

"Yes," Kylie answered for both of them.

"Then I'll get you the best table in the house, right up front where you won't miss a thing." Vincent held the door for them as Kevin steered Kylie into the club, his hand never leaving her side.

Maddie stood offstage as Emily Tuttle put the finishing touches on the curtain call. She called the chorus members out first. Then the supporting players. She and Adam would be last. Maddie spotted him in the wings on the opposite side of the stage as she wiped her dripping face. She must have sweated off five pounds at least. She hoped so because the ankle-length skirts she wore hugged every curve and she had more than her share.

They'd been at this all day, stopping many times for lighting changes as well as fine-tuning the dance numbers. Running through the whole show had taken hours, but it was finally coming together.

"Maddie and Adam," the director called.

Adam extended his hand to her as they met center stage. Maddie slipped her fingers into his as they came downstage and each took a bow. Then they joined the others and the entire ensemble bowed before breaking into a spontaneous round of applause.

Afterward Maddie spotted Annie weaving her way through the throng onstage.

"You sure you're okay getting home by yourself?" Annie asked.

"Fine." Maddie nodded toward the theater where Phil had been waiting for nearly an hour to take Annie out for a late dinner. "I think your date is waiting in the third row."

Annie waved to her husband but then lingered. "So I'll see you on Monday. My turn to drive, right?"

"Right."

Annie crossed the stage but glanced back over her shoulder, as if she were leaving a child at day care for the first time. What on earth was bothering her tonight? Maddie frowned.

"Are you as hungry as I am?" Adam stepped up to her, wiping his face with a towel, his dark hair a mass of damp curls.

Maddie smiled. "You mean that Snickers bar from the vending machine wasn't enough for you?"

"All day? I don't think so. How about we stop at the diner before heading home? And don't tell me you're not hungry. You worked as hard as I did today."

"Actually, I'm starved. Pancakes and eggs would hit the spot. I'll meet you there." The words were out of her mouth before she had time to stop them.

Adam grinned. "Deal."

Minutes later Maddie pulled out of the theater lot, her heart beating too fast and her stomach queasy. She was just having dinner. No big deal, Maddie reasoned, ignoring the eager anticipation that hummed along her nerve endings and made her almost giddy.

The Pathway Diner was a fixture in downtown Kerry, the silver trailer with bright blue trim reminiscent of an earlier time. Maddie pulled into the parking lot. She had to eat, she told herself as she pocketed her keys. Inside, she spotted Adam seated by the window. He waved her over.

Maddie slid into the booth. Her breath caught in her throat as Adam smiled at her in a way she hadn't seen the likes of in years. Her gut told her to walk away, but she didn't budge.

"I'm glad you came," he said, his tone casual though he continued to stare at her as if he couldn't believe she'd agreed to meet him.

"I wouldn't want to pass out from low blood sugar on the drive home," Maddie quipped, feeling excited and uneasy at the same time.

A young teenage waitress appeared and took their order: pancakes and eggs for Maddie and steak and eggs for Adam.

"Just think next week we'll be finished with all our performances. Are you getting nervous yet?" Adam leaned against the vinyl seat and stretched his legs out in the aisle.

"I guess I should be, but I'm not. Not yet, anyway. I'm sure by Thursday I'll be a wreck."

"You're going to be great."

"I hope so." Maddie fingered the spoon on her place mat. "So which night is your dad coming to see the show?"

"All of them."

Maddie grinned. "You're kidding?"

Adam leaned forward as the waitress deposited two mugs of coffee on the table. "It's kind of a family tradition. When I was a kid and my mother was in the summer show, my dad and I would go every night. He hated the idea of her performing with no one there to cheer her on." Adam sipped his coffee. "That first summer after she died, I tried out for the title role in *Oliver*. I was too tall for the lead, but they cast me as the Artful Dodger. My dad was in the front row every night."

"That's a great story."

"So, how about you? What night is your family coming?"

Maddie hadn't even thought about it. "My son, Shaun, will want to come the first night and Kylie too, unless her boyfriend is back in town by then."

"What about your husband?"

"I'm not sure which night he'll be free. He's got a big project at work and that's taking up most of his time." Maddie looked up from her cup to find Adam watching her.

"If he's ever heard you sing, I'm sure he'll want to be front and center on opening night."

Maddie doubted it but kept the thought to herself as the waitress appeared and set down their steaming plates.

But Adam didn't dig in right away. "That voice of yours is a gift, Maddie. When we're done with this show, I'm going to miss hearing you sing."

"Well, there's always next year." Maddie kept her tone light as she met Adam's gaze.

"That's a long way off." Adam reached across the table and covered her hand with his. He flashed her an impish smile. "And next year you'll probably be starring with some other leading man and letting him take you to dinner."

Maddie matched his teasing tone. "I thought Rita told me you had the lead in every show for the last decade. Planning on opting out next year?"

Adam feigned a modest smile. "No chance. Like I said, I'm a ham through and through. So I guess you're stuck with me."

She could think of worse things to be stuck with, Maddie thought and fought the urge to say it aloud. She flushed, her hand resting in his. And though she had every intention of slipping her hand free as she met Adam's gaze, she let her hand rest there, her heart hammering at the thought of seeing Adam again, even if it was next year.

Kylie was ready to die of embarrassment. Sitting in the front seat of Vincent's silver Civic, she stared straight ahead, her eyes filled with unshed tears.

"I'm sorry you have to take me home," she said but didn't turn to look at Vincent in the close interior of the little car.

"Not a problem." Raindrops misted the front windshield and Vincent flicked on the wipers. "I wasn't about to let Kevin drive you, not in the condition he was in."

"I didn't know he had that flask with him." Kylie crossed her arms over her chest. She sunk lower in the seat as Vincent made the right turn onto Market Street.

"He must have spiked his coffee all night to get that loaded." Vincent glanced over at her. "Would you have driven with him?"

"No way." Kylie shook her head and then paused, not quite sure what she would have done if Vincent hadn't intervened. "I guess I would have called my mom. She always says to call her if I don't feel safe."

"Good choice."

"How'd you know . . . about Kevin, I mean?"

"No guy makes that many trips to the bathroom unless he's snorting coke or smoking weed. But the dead giveaway was when he stumbled into the stage and killed the speakers."

Kylie giggled. "He couldn't even get up."

"You deserve better," Vincent said quietly, his eyes on the road as he pulled up to a stoplight. "You should be dating some guy your own age who doesn't forget about his date."

Kylie turned to the window trying to hide her blush. "I know . . . ," she began, but the words suddenly stuck in her throat.

Beyond the window, light streamed from the Pathway Diner, framing its patrons in a perfect still life. Kylie stared, blinked, then stared again. Her mother sat in a front booth holding hands with a man Kylie had never met.

"You okay?" Vincent asked.

"I just want to get home," Kylie murmured, unable to take her eyes from the scene.

The light turned green and Vincent hit the gas. Kylie craned her neck for one last glimpse, already second-guessing what she had seen. It could have been some woman who looked like her mom, Kylie reasoned but didn't believe it, her anger building with each turn of the tires.

Could her mother really be a total hypocrite, lecturing Kylie about waiting to have sex and then cheating on her husband? Kylie didn't know the answer and a part of her didn't want to even bring it up, because knowing for sure would be far worse than a mere suspicion.

Eleven

Scott's eyes drifted closed. His elbow slipped from the drafting table and he caught himself before his head hit the floor plans he'd been working on for the past three hours. He retrieved his pencil from the floor, wishing he'd never heard of the Hingemen project. Sarah Hingemen had changed her mind so many times, Scott was running out of ideas for restructuring the pediatric oncology unit.

Around him the house was quiet. Shaun was in bed, and Kylie and Maddie weren't home yet. Unlike last summer, this year the house had been an ideal place to work. Maddie kept the kids busy on weekends, allowing him to catch up with the work he hadn't finished during the week. And Kylie and Shaun tended to occupy themselves at night with rented movies and video games while Maddie was at play rehearsal.

Except for the blow-up he and Maddie had a month ago over cosigning the Baldwin's' loan, these past few weeks had been trouble-free. Maddie was efficient and cheerful, going out of her way to take care of everything before she left for rehearsal. Even Kylie's grounding hadn't been the source of tension Scott had feared. Kylie had endured the punishment with a grace Scott felt demonstrated her growing maturity.

The back door slammed. Kylie flew by the office doorway.

"Hey, Ky, how about a good night for your dad."

She appeared in the doorway, her face flushed but her features carefully neutral.

"Did you have a good time?" Scott ventured.

"Yeah."

"Where'd you go again?" Talking to his daughter was like pulling taffy, a lot of work that produced a little nugget of sweetness, and that's what kept him coming back for more.

"We went to the coffee house in Kerry."

"You and Larkin?"

"Yeah." She hesitated a moment, then lifted her gaze and actually looked at him. "Mom home yet?"

"Not yet. Rehearsal must have run late."

"Yeah, real late." Kylie leaned against the doorjamb. "Have you met any of the people she's working with on the show?"

Scott leaned back in his chair. "Only Annie. I figure I'll meet them this week when I see the show."

"So, you are going?"

"Of course. I thought maybe you and Shaun could go with me."

"Opening night?"

"Sure, if you want to."

"I'll be glad when this show stuff is over."

Scott leaned forward, curious to hear his daughter's reasoning. "Why? It hasn't been that bad. I mean, I know Mom's been gone a lot, but she's the happiest I've seen her in years."

"There's a reason for that," Kylie murmured under her breath. Before Scott could ask what she meant she turned away. "I'm going to bed." She crossed the study and planted a quick kiss on his cheek. "Good night, Dad."

Scott smiled. "Good night, Bug."

Kylie stopped halfway to the door. "You haven't called me that since our last trip to the Outer Banks when we built that giant lady bug on the beach."

"I remember."

"I like it."

"Me, too."

Scott listened to Kylie's footsteps move up the hall.

He'd just had a conversation with his teenage daughter. Scott grinned. He'd have to try it more often.

Maddie's heart pounded as she stood in the wings Monday night trying to catch her breath and focus on the scene ahead. After Saturday night's dinner with Adam, she knew she needed to keep a tight rein on her emotions for the remainder of the show, a resolution that worked better in theory than in practice as she spotted Adam step onstage for the final scenes of this full dress rehearsal.

Maddie gulped a breath and smoothed the narrow skirt that

reached to her ankles. The restrictive costume made walking difficult, and dancing the Shipoopee was like running a 5K race with ankle weights. Maddie inhaled deeply, waiting for her pulse to slow, but her heart still raced as she heard her cue for the footbridge scene.

As she crossed the stage, Adam turned to smile at her just as he'd done at the diner. For a moment Maddie felt disoriented, like her two worlds had collided. Were they Marion and Harold? Or were they Maddie and Adam? And who was that smile really for? But Maddie had no time to consider the point as she stepped onto the footbridge and Adam took her hand.

Maddie took up the lyrics and lilting melody of "'Til There Was You.'" She lifted her gaze to find Adam staring at her so intently that Maddie felt his character's dilemma in a single glance. Would Harold stay in River City with Marion and reap the consequences of having conned the townspeople out of their money? Or would he be on the next train out of town?

The conflict played across Adam's features, his expression tormented. As the last notes of the verse drifted into the silent theater, Adam leaned in to kiss her. His lips touched hers, and as his arms came around her, Maddie fought the impulse to give in to his touch. This was a stage kiss, not the real thing, she reminded herself, her back stiff and unyielding.

From the depths of the theater, the director's voice invaded Maddie's consciousness.

"Wait, just one minute." Emily Tuttle strode up to the stage as the music broke off in a gaggle of sound. "I know I said we weren't stopping, but I just have to say this." Emily came up the side steps to the stage, her manner brisk. "You two have wonderful chemistry. We've seen it throughout the show. This is the climactic scene for this couple. Now I know this may be an awkward moment for you as an actor, Maddie, but you need to stay in character and remember what Marion is feeling. She is a woman in love for the first time. She's literally been swept off her feet by this man." Emily leaned on the footbridge railing and smiled. "So, put a little passion in it, all right?"

Maddie blushed as a chuckle erupted from those close enough to hear the instructions.

Adam squeezed her hand. "It's just like breathing, easier when you don't think about it and just let it happen."

Maddie nodded.

"Let's take it from the last verse of the song." The director disappeared into the darkness.

The music began and Maddie tried to stifle her embarrassment as she sang. She'd tried so hard to be professional. But this scene hit too close to home, tearing at the thin barrier she'd constructed to wall off her real emotions from those of her character.

A feathery touch on her cheek brought her back to the song. Adam's hand cupped her cheek in an unscripted but purposeful gesture. His gaze held hers, keeping her in the moment and in character. And this time when he kissed her, Maddie didn't hold anything back. For the moment she was Marion Purue, being kissed by the man she loved.

After the final number and curtain call, Emily Tuttle gathered the cast for a review of what needed to be fine-tuned in the final two rehearsals. She had a suggestion or a word of praise for everyone, but her face creased in a smile when she came to Maddie.

"You certainly take direction well," Emily said as a few catcalls peppered the air and good-natured laughter rippled through the group. "Nice job."

Maddie laughed, glancing over at Adam, who winked at her, and then at Annie who seemed preoccupied after a nearly perfect run-through. After climbing out of the constricting costume, Maddie donned her street clothes before joining Annie for the ride home.

"Are you feeling okay?" Maddie asked after they'd ridden in silence for several minutes.

"Fine, just a little tired." Annie tapped the steering wheel with her nails. "I need to ask you something that might overstep the bounds of friendship."

"Sounds serious."

"Do you have feelings for Adam?"

Maddie started to laugh before Annie held up her hand. "Wait, don't just blow it off. Something has happened in the past few weeks and if you can't be honest with me, at least be honest with yourself."

Maddie stared out into the darkness. "He makes me laugh. I don't get a lot of that at home."

"Is there more to it than that?"

With anyone else Maddie would have been annoyed at the question, but with Annie she felt an irresistible urge to talk. "I do look forward to rehearsals, but that's not just Adam. This is the first time in years I've had a chance to do something just for me."

"So, you aren't in love with him?"

Maddie turned toward the window. "No, of course not. He's just a friend. Okay, I'll admit it's been fun having Adam pay attention to me, but it's nothing more than a harmless flirtation."

"So, next week when the show is over, you won't have a problem not seeing him?"

"Out of sight, out of mind. Isn't that how the old saying goes? Anyway, you can't be tempted by what you can't see."

Annie's silence was not lost on Maddie. Clearly she didn't agree. Maddie wondered if she was fooling herself. Maybe walking away from Adam at the end of the show would be harder than she'd thought.

An insidious and tantalizing thought crept into Maddie's mind. Did she have to walk away from Adam? Maddie shook her head in the dark interior of the car. Of course she did.

Didn't she?

"She doesn't see it." Annie wrapped her hands around a mug of hot chocolate and settled on the porch swing beside Phil. Through the trees glimpses of the moonlit lake were just visible. Annie blew on the foamy chocolate and sipped. "If you could see the way Adam looks at her. She may not be in love with him, but he's in love with her. And if he goes after her, there's nothing working in that marriage to keep her there."

"You saw this coming." Phil slipped an arm around her and gently set the swing in motion.

"I wish I'd been wrong." Annie drew her legs up on the seat and propped the hot mug atop them.

"So what do you want to do?"

"Besides pray, you mean?" Annie offered the mug to Phil.

He took it from her and sipped before handing it back. "Prayer is a given. We'll both do that, because it's not in God's plan for this marriage to fail through neglect."

"But one of them has to want to save it, and right now Maddie is too wrapped up in herself to even think about Scott."

"And he's got his head so filled with work he doesn't see what's happening. You know what Scott told me last week? That this summer's been the best their family has had in a long time."

"The man needs a wake-up call." Annie leaned her head on his shoulder.

"Maybe that's exactly what he needs." Phil stuck out his foot and stopped the swing. "We both thought when we moved up here that we were supposed to help your mom and dad by buying the business from them, but maybe God's got more for us to do."

"But how can we help Maddie and Scott without meddling in their marriage?"

"Don't think of it as meddling. Think of it as running interference while God works on their hearts."

"Those are some pretty hard hearts."

"Lucky for us we aren't working alone." Phil sprang up from the swing. "And I think I know just where to start."

Annie swayed at the sudden motion, barely able to hold on to her mug. "I love a man of action."

"That's why you married me." Phil grinned at her from the back door. "We're a team."

The back door swung closed.

"Forever and ever," Annie whispered into the night and sipped her hot chocolate with a contented sigh.

Scott pulled his car into the driveway and cut the engine. Maddie's car was still gone. Good, rehearsal must have run late. He'd promised to be home early tonight, and though ten o'clock didn't qualify as early, at least he'd beat her home. Reaching across the passenger seat, Scott gathered his briefcase and portfolio. He dropped the work in his office and shrugged off his jacket as he came down the hall. "Hey, anybody home?"

"In here, Dad." Shaun looked up from his video game.

"You've been playing that a lot lately, Shaun. Maybe too much? How about you give it a break. So where's Ky?"

"Up in her room." Shaun reluctantly set the video handset aside. "Mom said she couldn't go out until you got home."

Scott groaned. He wasn't going to win any points with his daughter after tonight.

"So which night are we going, Dad?"

Still thinking about Kylie, Scott missed the question. "Go where, Bud?"

"To Mom's show. Can we go opening night?"

"I don't know, Shaun." Scott glanced down the hall, picturing the work in his office. "How about you and Kylie go then. I'll ask Phil if he can give you a ride."

"When are you going?" Shaun crossed over to the counter and stared up at Scott with a suspicious glare.

"I'm not sure yet."

"You're not going at all, are you?"

"I will, just another night."

Shaun backed off a step, then turned toward the stairs, his shoulders rounded. "You say that now, but you won't do it."

"Shaun, listen. When I say I'll do something, I will."

He turned on the bottom step, his lower lip trembling. "Like when you said you'd go to church to hear Kylie play the violin? Or when you said you'd put the float out in the lake, only we did it with Mom because you weren't around?"

Scott recoiled at the accusation in his son's eyes.

"This is important to her, Dad. She's worked hard all summer and she needs us to see what she's done."

"I'm going to try, Bud, but . . ."

Shaun trudged up the stairs. "Yeah, right, I know, you have to work."

Stunned by his son's sarcasm, Scott wondered when Shaun had grown from a boy with no bigger worries than buying a new video game, into a young man who felt the need to defend his mother.

In the silent kitchen, the phone's ring sounded shrill. Kylie would get it, Scott thought. It was always for her anyway.

He glanced at his office, not sure how he was going to get all that work done this week. He was under pressure from Rob Sanders to wrap up the design phase of the Hingemen project. Sarah Hingemen had other ideas though, too many ideas, and her continued indecision would keep them from breaking ground any time in the near future.

"Dad, the phone's for you," Kylie screamed.

Scott picked up the kitchen extension, surprised to hear Phil's voice.

"Scott, sorry to call so late, but I wanted to know if you and the kids are going to the show opening night."

"Actually, I was about to call you." Scott paused. "I was hoping you could do me a favor and take Kylie and Shaun with you."

Phil's silence spoke volumes. "I don't think that's a very good idea."

"It's just one show. What's the big deal? Maddie will be so busy she won't even know I'm there."

"Scott, listen. You need to see your wife."

Phil's tone sounded like Shaun's, only an octave lower, and Scott conceded the point. "Okay, I'll be there. I'm not sure how I'll get out of the office in time to pick the kids up . . ."

"How about I take the kids and you just get yourself there."

"I'd appreciate it," Scott said, mentally figuring what time he would have to leave Boston on Thursday to make it to the show.

"No problem. So I'll see you there at 8:00 p.m.?"

"Sure, save me a seat."

"Will do."

Scott hung up the phone. It was just one night. He'd go in early tomorrow and work through lunch to make up the time. Good thing Maddie didn't do this all the time.

Scott frowned, mentally sizing up the work he had to do over the next two weeks. The sheer volume made him cringe. Maybe he could miss the first act. As long as he made it in time for the curtain call, who would know the difference?

Twelve

The murmur of conversations hummed beyond the closed curtain as the Community Theater filled with patrons.

Maddie felt sick. Standing in the wings, she rubbed her queasy stomach. Dressed in an ankle-length skirt and a lace blouse so high it tickled her chin, she nervously wiped her damp palms on her skirt. At least the skirt wasn't tight. She'd been so nervous the last few days she'd barely eaten a thing. Pacing to the stage door and back, her stomach churned as she went over her first lines. Once she got started she would be all right. At least that's what everyone told her, but the waiting was agony.

One thought made her smile. Somewhere out in the audience Shaun and Kylie were finding their seats along with Phil. Scott had said he would meet them, but Maddie didn't think he'd actually make it. In Scott's mind this ranked right up there with Kylie's playing the violin at church, a nice pastime but hardly a command performance worthy of his presence. Maddie wondered why he couldn't see that life wasn't made up of command performances but of little interludes. Piano recitals, class plays, baseball games, and not the playoff games, just an ordinary Saturday morning game. All of these moments helped to define the family Scott had abdicated in favor of work. And tonight would be no different.

Distracted by such thoughts, Maddie jumped when a yellow rose appeared over her shoulder.

"Break a leg out there tonight. I know you'll be wonderful."

Maddie spun around to find Adam looking ever so natural in a turn-of-the-century suit and bowler hat as he handed her the rose.

Maddie lifted it to her nose, the scent light, sweet and comfortingly familiar. "I thought the leading lady received flowers after the performance, but I'll take what I can get. Thank you." When he didn't reply, Maddie looked up to find him staring at her.

"You are so beautiful," Adam said softly.

"It must be the costume," Maddie joked.

"No, it's you." Adam stepped closer and reached for her hand. "You were born to do this, Maddie. To sing with that beautiful voice while others sit back in awe and listen. I know you're probably a little nervous . . ."

"A little?"

Adam tipped her chin up with one finger. "That's not a bad thing. Use it. Go out there and enjoy it. It's a high like no other." His finger traced the line of her jaw, gently tugging at her pearl earring. "And afterwards say you'll come with me to the cast party so we can celebrate together."

Maddie shivered at his touch. "I don't think . . ."

"Right, don't think. Just come with me."

The tension in his shoulders and the expectant look in his eyes held her attention.

"All right," she said. A surge of pleasure made her blush at Adam's instant grin. Maddie couldn't remember the last time anyone had been so happy just to have her around.

The first strains of the overture began and the male cast members walked quietly to their places for the opening scene.

"I'll see you out there." Adam dropped a kiss on her forehead before stepping out onto the stage.

The warmth of his lips lingered on her skin and Maddie shivered, knowing that in this moment they had crossed the boundary from character to conviction.

Scott rushed through the rear door of the theater as the audience applauded the opening number. He spotted Kylie and Shaun with Phil in the middle of a row down in front. Not wanting to climb over other theatergoers, Scott opted for a seat in the last row. When Shaun turned to look for him, Scott pointed at the seat before falling into it.

He leaned back and stuck his feet out. What a day! Lunch with the Hingemens. A late afternoon board meeting. Then he'd raced out of the office to try and beat the rush-hour traffic headed north. No such luck. He'd barely made it on time.

The orchestra accompanied the cast in a lively musical number. Scott scanned the stage for Maddie. She wasn't there. His thoughts turned to the renderings still to be completed. At least lunch had been productive. The Hingemens had finally settled on a configuration for the outpatient oncology wing. The lobby would be shaped like a starfish with all essential laboratory and outpatient services able to be accessed from the hub.

Scott spotted Maddie as the townspeople exited the stage. She moved against the crowd with a purposeful walk. No nonsense. Just like Maddie. The leading man tried to get her attention. He stepped in front of her, but Maddie just looked down her nose at him before slamming the door in his face. Scott knew that look and for a moment felt a twinge of sympathy for the poor guy playing opposite his wife.

His mind returned to the hospital project. He mentally calculated the angles and dimensions he would need to make the new floor plan work. It would need cubicles where receptionists could discuss private patient information. A play area for the younger children was a must as well as easy access to outside parking and the hospital cafeteria.

A soaring soprano arrested Scott's train of thought. Startled, he focused on the stage where Maddie sat in a window seat singing to the evening stars. For a moment, Scott closed his eyes, the timbre of her voice recalling the way Maddie used to sing around the house. She really did have a beautiful voice. Lilting and unrestrained, Maddie hit the high notes with clarity, the sound floating out into the dark theater.

Scott relaxed in his seat and began to follow the story. He watched the traveling salesman chip away at the frigid veneer of the uptight librarian. Harold Hill wooed her with song, dance, and a good measure of charm until by the end of the first act, the librarian threw away the evidence she'd collected against him. She stared up at him with nervous adoration as the curtain closed, and Scott marveled at his wife's performance as he made his way to the lobby for intermission.

"Isn't she great?" Shaun appeared at Scott's elbow. Kylie hung back a few steps.

Scott turned to his son with a smile. "She is pretty good. What do you think, Ky?"

Kylie wrapped her arms around her waist and glanced back at the theater doors. "I think she's really into the part."

Scott nodded and handed Shaun a twenty for the concession stand. "Share it with your sister," he called after the boy as both kids were lost in the crowd.

"Glad you could make it." Phil clapped him on the shoulder.

"Almost didn't. The traffic was murder."

"Does Maddie know you're here?"

"I don't think so."

"How about we go backstage afterwards and surprise them?"

"Sounds good."

"I'll even give you half the roses I bought for Annie since I know you didn't have time to stop and get some."

Scott flinched. "I'll take you up on that."

Minutes later, the houselights flickered and the second act began. As Scott sat in the dark theater watching Maddie flawlessly portray Marion the librarian, he wished he'd thought to buy her flowers. Her performance was flawless, and as the show neared its close Scott couldn't tell where Maddie stopped and Marion began.

A fast-paced dance number left the audience applauding. The townspeople exited the stage and Maddie hurried through the crowd looking flushed and nervous. Eagerly she stepped onto a footbridge to meet the leading man. The mandatory love scene, Scott realized, his interest piqued. Every show of this vintage had one. But Scott's interest shifted to unease as Maddie looked adoringly up at the guy and began to sing. Her voice tapered off and the final note hung in the air as the leading man took Maddie in his arms and kissed her.

Scott's gut clenched. *It's just a stage kiss.*

But something in the way they held each other, in the set of their mouths, the attitude of their bodies made Scott want to shout at them to stop. The moment passed, but Scott couldn't take his eyes off Maddie for the rest of the show. She was Marion Purue, and in the final scene when she stood up for Harold Hill and made the townspeople see how he had changed their lives, Scott could feel her passion for the man.

The curtain call was lengthy. By the time Maddie and her leading man stepped onstage and joined hands, the crowd was on its feet. Scott jumped up as well. Maddie smiled and took a bow, no longer the love-struck librarian but merely a lovely woman in period costume who didn't have any real feelings for the man whose hand she held.

Scott opened his program and glanced at the name. Adam Slater.

The houselights came up. Scott tried to shrug off the disquiet that tugged at his brain as he waited for the kids in the lobby. It was just a show. Still, he wondered why he'd never known Maddie was such a good actor.

Backstage, chaos reigned behind the closed curtain. Maddie closed her eyes and clasped her hands to her chest. A standing ovation. She couldn't believe it. Enveloped in one joyous hug after another, Maddie congratulated her fellow cast members on a near perfect opening night.

"You were wonderful." Annie hugged her and hooked her arm through Maddie's as they made their way to the stage door.

"So were you." Maddie glanced over her shoulder and spotted Adam being clapped on the back by an older man she assumed must be his father. Quickly, she turned back to Annie. "That library number was a hit. Did you hear the applause? And you said you couldn't dance."

"It was fun, wasn't it?" Annie beamed. "I can't wait to do it again tomorrow."

"So getting through the audition was worth it?"

"Every nervous note. I can see why people do this for a living. The adrenaline rush is addictive."

They stepped through the stage door and out into the adjacent hallway. A sea of bodies blocked their way as cast members met their smiling families.

Maddie spotted Shaun and Kylie in the crowd with Phil and Scott right behind them. Scott? Maddie couldn't believe he'd actually come. Surprised, she moved toward them, steeling herself for a lukewarm response from her husband. Off to one side, Phil lifted Annie off her feet, his smile brimming with pride as he swung her around. A twinge of envy colored Maddie's smile before Shaun threw his arms around her in a hug she hadn't seen the likes of since he'd hit double-digit birthdays.

"I knew you could do it," he whispered. "I'm so proud of you. That's what you always say to me and now I can say it to you."

Tears stung Maddie's eyes at her son's words. "You don't know how much it means to hear you say that."

Maddie glanced up at Scott.

"You were amazing," Scott said, holding her gaze. "For a while you actually had me believing you were someone else."

Maddie blinked. "Really?"

Shaun stepped aside as Scott pulled a bouquet of white roses from behind his back. "I believe this is a theatrical tradition, flowers for the leading lady." He handed them to her and then dropped an awkward kiss on her cheek.

Surprised, Maddie simply stared at him, her hand lifting to her cheek as a blush crept up her neck and heated her face.

"Hey, Mom, he's allowed to kiss you. You are married, remember?" Shaun teased.

Kylie stepped up to the group, parroting her brother's words. "Right, you are married, remember?" She crossed her arms over her chest, her sullen expression in sharp contrast with the smiles around them.

Maddie sighed. Long ago she'd given up trying to figure out her daughter's moods and simply decided to love her through them. Some days that was easier than others.

Phil and Annie joined them. Annie held one white rose, a thoroughly romantic gesture that made Maddie think of the yellow flower she'd received earlier.

"How about we all go to the diner and celebrate with hot fudge sundaes drenched in whipped cream?" Phil proposed.

"Oh, yeah!" Shaun shouted.

Maddie glanced at Scott, prepared for his inevitable frown when family activities took him away from work. But to her surprise he nodded, throwing an arm around their exuberant son. Kylie, however, pursed her lips as if she wanted to bail on this family nonsense.

Annie leaned over and caught her eye. "Come on. It'll be fun."

Even Kylie couldn't resist Annie's grin. "Okay fine, but no whipped cream. Do you know how many calories are in that stuff?"

Scott brushed up against Maddie's arm. "Don't you have to change first—that is, unless you're planning on turning the diner into an old-fashioned soda shop."

Maddie's eyes widened. Her husband had made a joke. Maddie couldn't remember the last time he'd done that.

Annie grabbed her arm. "We'll just be a few minutes."

In the ladies' dressing room, a communal facility with costumes hung on metal racks, they changed into their clothes. Maddie pulled a hairbrush from her makeup bag, knowing she needed to speak to Adam before joining her family. "Why don't you go? I'll just be a minute," she said, meeting Annie's gaze.

Annie glanced at the door. "Just a minute, okay? I'm starving." She grinned, then rescued her black character shoes from the floor before leaving.

Maddie tugged the brush through her hair with long hard strokes, freeing her hair from the stiff hairspray. She wondered what to say to Adam and decided on the truth. She was a woman with a family and if for a moment she'd forgotten, she needed to get her priorities straight. Maddie shouldered her bag and pulled open the dressing room door.

Adam stood in the hallway.

Maddie started to speak, but he cut her off.

"I know. I saw your family. Beautiful kids, by the way."

Relief stole the tension from her shoulders. Perhaps she'd read too much into this. "Thanks for letting me off the hook."

"Another time?"

Maddie hesitated, wondering when this relationship had slipped so close to the edge she couldn't tell whether it was friendship or something more. "How about we settle for the cast party Saturday night after the final show?" she suggested.

"I was hoping for something more private, but I'll take it," Adam said cheerfully. He stepped in closer. "You blew them away tonight, Maddie. I know Harold Hill usually gets top billing, but you stole the show."

A warm tingle worked its way up her back at his proximity.

Adam leaned in but didn't touch her. "You almost had me believing you were in love with me."

Maddie's breath caught in her throat at the longing in his eyes.

"But I know what we have is friendship, and after our final show we won't even have that."

Maddie could hear the resignation in his tone. She opened her mouth to speak, but Adam pressed a finger to her lips.

"I think I can live with it—not happily, but I can." He stepped back and winked at her.

Maddie watched him go, his back straight, his stride easy, but the tenor of his words and the look in his eyes stayed with her. For a moment she had an almost irresistible urge to run after him. A wave of intense longing made her stomach queasy and her foot inch forward before she turned from the fantasy and stepped back into her real life.

Thirteen

S cott didn't want to be here. He had hours of work to do and still he sat in the darkened theater watching a show he'd already seen twice. Why he felt compelled to see this final performance, he didn't know. It was just a gut feeling. He couldn't shake the gnawing unease he'd felt since seeing Maddie kiss Adam Slater on opening night.

Last night's show had been a carbon copy of the first, the looks exchanged, the movements exactly as Scott remembered. Which should have made him feel better, but it didn't. Why did it feel so real? Chemistry, maybe?

Scott crossed one leg over the opposite knee as the second act began. He clenched his fist as Harold took Marion's arm, a wave of pure rage tensing the muscles in his arms and chest. Scott hadn't felt the emotion in years, but he knew it instantly. Jealousy.

Why did he sit here and torture himself? Did he really suspect his wife of having an affair? Ridiculous. Maddie would never do that. But still he couldn't quiet his building rage as he sat in the dark watching his wife fall in love with another man. Last night he'd left immediately after the performance, his anger a slow burn, but when Maddie got home an hour later he'd fumed in silence. All the laughter they'd shared Thursday night had vanished, replaced by a familiar silence fueled not by indifference but by ire.

How had he forgotten how wonderful her voice sounded? He'd lived with Maddie for seventeen years, and somehow he had forgotten how to love her, forgotten how to talk to her, forgotten how good it felt to hear her say she loved him. Sure, she wasn't perfect. Maddie was assertive and bossy. But he'd known that when he married her. He'd admired her strength, her competitive nature, and her ability to find a way to get things done. Her drive to be the world's best mother became her life's work while Scott focused on securing the future for their family. And that shift in priorities, away from each other, had allowed the love to fade from their hearts.

But was it too late?

Onstage the cast gathered for the Fourth of July celebration. Maddie and Adam danced center stage, their feet moving in unison, their cheeks pressed together. Scott leaned forward, anticipating the next scene. Maddie approached the footbridge, her face flushed with exertion. She looked beautiful.

Scott's jaw clenched as they joined hands, sensing a subtle difference. An undercurrent pulsed between them as the music built to a crescendo and they kissed. Having seen the other performances, the difference was unmistakable. Tonight Harold kissed Marion with a quiet desperation as if the idea of leaving her was tearing his soul apart. The audience barely breathed as Maddie and Adam parted to finish the song, the longing in their eyes so real Scott felt it like a blow to the chest.

He bolted to his feet and strode from the theater. He didn't need to see any more. His gut had known the truth all along. Maddie was falling in love with Adam Slater.

Standing in the empty lobby, Scott forced himself to think clearly. Maddie might have feelings for the guy, but that didn't mean she would throw away a seventeen-year marriage. After tonight the show would be over. Maddie would come home to him and she wouldn't see Adam again.

Or would she?

Scott glanced at the theater doors. His marriage was under attack, and he needed to figure out how to save it.

The final curtain descended and the cast broke into a frenzy of embraces and tears. It seemed as natural as breathing. Maddie turned to Adam. His arms slipped around her waist and pulled her close. For a long moment they held each other, her cheek pressed to his shoulder. Around them the cast began to filter offstage and still they held each other.

"I don't think I can let you go," Adam said, his voice hoarse and unsteady.

Maddie rested in his arms for a moment before she drew in a deep breath. "We can't stay like this forever."

"Try me." Adam linked his hands at the base of her spine and looked into her eyes.

"I am going to miss you, Adam." Maddie smoothed his collar before she stepped backward, ending the embrace.

"It doesn't have to be so final. We could still be friends, talk occasionally, maybe get together for coffee."

"I think we both know that won't work."

"I can't believe I'm not going to see you again, not going to hear you sing or watch your face light up when you laugh."

A wave of sadness came over Maddie. "You do make me laugh."

Adam stepped in closer, capturing her hands in his. The anguish in his gaze was so powerful, Maddie couldn't look away. "Never underestimate the power of laughter; it's the thing you miss when it's gone."

Maddie swallowed hard, knowing her commitments and her life lay with a man who hadn't looked at her this way in years. "I have to go."

"You are coming to the cast party," he urged.

"Annie and I are coming, but just for a few minutes. I can't stay."

Maddie's heart raced as Adam lifted her hands to his lips. He kissed her palm then surrounded her fingers with his in a gentle grip.

"Just tell me one thing," he asked. "I've been acting since I was a teenager and I've never fallen for any of my leading ladies . . . until now."

Startled, Maddie looked up from their joined hands to meet his gaze. Guilt assailed her at the desire in his eyes.

"You felt it too. When you kissed me, for just a minute it was real, wasn't it, Maddie?"

Tears stung her eyes as Maddie backed away from him across the empty stage. "Yes," she whispered just loud enough for him to hear before she turned and walked out the stage door.

Steam blanketed the windows of the parked car as Kylie came up for air. She straightened her shirt and pushed up to a sitting position, then wiped the fog from the window.

"Hey, what's up?" Kevin sat up behind her and slipped his arm around her waist.

"Nothing," Kylie said quietly.

She'd thought she could do it, thought she could drown all the mental warnings in one night of passion. Her mother's words were nothing more than lip service anyway. What a hypocrite! She'd preached abstinence while she cheated on her husband. Kylie had almost called her on it too, after seeing them together at the diner, but instead of attempting that awkward conversation, she'd decided to follow her mother's example, not her words. Kylie wasn't a kid, and she wasn't waiting any longer. Why should she? No one else did.

Kevin lifted her hair and kissed her neck. "Hey, I thought you said this was the night."

"It doesn't feel right," Kylie said.

"Feels right to me." Kevin pulled her back against him.

Kylie grimaced at his tone, trying to figure out why this guy who used to make her knees shake no longer did. She'd spent the last hour trying to work up some excitement for what they planned to do.

"This isn't the way I wanted it to be." Kylie waved a hand at the car's interior. "Somehow I thought this night wouldn't include a seat belt jammed in my side."

"What do you want, a motel room?"

"A bed would be nice."

"Why are you messing with me? You made me think this was it, and now you're bailing on me?" Kevin pulled her into his arms. "Come on, Kylie, let's just finish what we started. You can't leave me hanging like this."

"Forget it. This isn't happening. Not tonight."

Kevin sighed loudly. "When then?"

Kylie turned to him. "I want our first time to be special, something we'll always remember."

"I'd remember this," Kevin said and leaned toward her.

Kylie pushed him away. "Be serious."

"Okay, if you're looking for romance, how about my house next weekend?"

"With your parents ready to walk down the basement stairs any minute? I don't think so."

"Hey, Ky, I'm trying here, and my parents won't be home next weekend."

"They're leaving you home?"

"Just for one night, but that's all we'll need. I was going to have a party, but now I can think of a better way to spend the time." He leaned over and kissed her ear.

Kylie smiled. He was trying to be romantic. He hadn't gotten angry with her, and he'd come up with a much better plan.

His warm breath on her neck sent a shiver up Kylie's back before she spoke. "I won't be back from the beach until Friday, but I don't have any plans for Saturday, at least not yet."

Kevin turned her to face him. "So what do you say? I'll bring the protection and you bring, well, you just bring you."

Kylie giggled, liking the sound of that. "You're on."

Fourteen

Maddie awoke Sunday morning to an empty bed. Usually Scott slept like a downed telephone pole, not moving until it was time to hit the snooze button and catch an extra ten minutes sleep. Sunday was his chance to sleep in while she and the kids went to church, but today he was gone. Maddie took in the bunched pillows and tangled sheets. Apparently, she wasn't the only one who'd had trouble sleeping last night. Maddie wondered what had kept him up. Work, most likely.

Sitting up, she grabbed her white robe and threw it on over her shorts and T-shirt. As she trudged into the bathroom, a wave of sadness assailed her. It was over. The rehearsals. The show. Everything.

She flipped on the faucet, letting the water run. She'd done the right thing. The only thing. She knew that. But still a hollowness settled in her chest at the thought of never seeing Adam again.

She splashed water on her face and ran a brush through her hair, determined not to think about him. But the memories came unbidden—memories of the desire in his eyes last night onstage before he'd kissed her, of the tremor in his voice as he held her behind the closed curtain and told her he couldn't let her go. Maddie's hand rested over her queasy stomach, the memory so intense her fingers trembled.

She shook her head and grabbed a towel, drying her face with brisk pats. *Don't think about it. It's over.* She tossed the towel aside and hurried downstairs, seeking the distraction of a strong cup of coffee.

The gurgle of the percolator met her halfway down the stairs.

"You started the coffee?" Maddie spotted Scott in the family room. "Thanks."

He stood by the French doors staring out at the lake, dressed in khakis and a navy golf shirt.

Maddie grabbed a mug from behind the glass cabinet doors. "Phil and Annie are coming for lunch after church, remember?"

"I didn't forget. We just talked about it Thursday." He didn't turn.

His tone was as frosty as the day was fine.

"Steaks on the grill, okay?"

"Sure."

Whatever had him up last night must still be worrying him. Maddie poured a cup of coffee and added a splash of milk. Scott wasn't likely to be good company this afternoon if he had work on the brain.

"So, what did you do last night after you dropped Shaun at Mark's house?" Maddie sipped her coffee as she opened the refrigerator.

"I got some work done."

Maddie's hand closed on a cantaloupe. "Is the end of the Hingemen job in sight?"

"Not even close." Scott dismissed the subject with a wave of his hand and joined her in the kitchen. "I thought you'd sleep in after the cast party last night."

"I didn't stay long. Annie wanted to get home and she was driving."

"You could have gotten a ride from someone else if you wanted to stay."

"I guess so." Maddie juggled the cantaloupe and a basket of strawberries as she closed the refrigerator with her foot.

"So the party went on without the leading lady?"

"Sure, why not?" What was that funny tone in his voice? Sarcasm? No, but he wasn't just making conversation either. "Scott, I wanted to thank you for coming to the show opening night."

"I'm glad I got a chance to see it."

"It meant a lot to Shaun since he's leaving for camp soon."

"When is that again?"

Maddie suppressed a sigh and looked up from slicing the fruit. "I'm taking him tomorrow, and Kylie's leaving on Tuesday to go to the beach with Larkin and her parents. She'll be back Friday."

"And what will you do while they're gone?" He picked up a strawberry and tossed it in his mouth though the hard edge to his tone belied his casual pose.

"I don't know. Same thing as last summer, I guess. Clean a few closets, take the boat for a sail, meet a few friends for lunch."

"Friends?"

Maddie glanced up from the fruit she was spooning onto her plate. "Yes, Scott, I actually do have friends."

What was with all the questions? He seemed agitated, his usual indifference replaced by a high-energy restlessness. "Did you get much work done last night?"

"Not enough."

"The house was quiet."

"It takes more than quiet, Maddie. It takes time and imagination to get those floor plans right. And now I'm going to lose the afternoon because we've got guests coming." Scott crossed the room, headed for his office. The door closed behind him with a thud.

Why was he so angry? He'd invited Phil and Annie to dinner, not her. But that was in the high spirits of the other night. Maddie refilled her coffee cup, a twinge of guilt making her wonder if Scott's mood had anything to do with her. She'd been distracted lately with thoughts of Adam and the show. Maybe Scott had noticed.

"What did you say to Dad?" Kylie asked as she cruised into the kitchen, her dark hair still matted from sleep. "He sounds pissed."

"Language, Ky."

Kylie shot her an angry glance. "Fine. He sounds mad. So what did you do?"

"I didn't do anything. Your dad's venting about work." Kylie opened the refrigerator, turning her back on Maddie. "He was fine Thursday night."

"He was, wasn't he?" Maddie recalled Scott's easy smile, the gentle paternal ribbing he'd given Kylie and Shaun. "Now that the show is over I'll have to pay more attention to all of you."

Kylie didn't respond, but when she shut the door with nothing in her hands, Maddie was reminded of the little girl who'd been afraid to ask if the Easter Bunny was real for fear she'd learn the truth. "So it's over right? You and that guy, Adam?"

Startled, Maddie slowly lowered her mug to the counter. "Adam and I are friends. We worked on the show together, that's all."

"So you never saw him outside rehearsals?" Kylie's eyes narrowed.

Maddie met her daughter's accusing stare, dismayed by the irony of their role reversal. Usually she was asking the questions instead of dodging them. "Once. We stopped at the diner after last week's rehearsal ran late."

"So, you won't be seeing him again?" she repeated.

Maddie's queasiness returned. "No, I won't be seeing him."

"Good," Kylie said forcefully, but Maddie heard a touch of relief in her tone.

Maddie sensed she should pursue the subject, but she didn't want to think about Adam, much less talk about him. "How was your date with Kevin last night?"

"Okay."

"Just okay? Used to be you couldn't wait to see him."

"I'm over that infatuation stage. Now we're ready to take our relationship to the next level."

Maddie didn't like the sound of that. "Sounds clinical. Aren't you going to miss him while you're away this week?"

"It's only for a few days. Besides we've made plans to get together Saturday night."

Something in her tone as she flipped on the faucet made Maddie push a bit further. "You're planning something special?"

Kylie leaned over, pulling her hair back with one hand, and drank from the running faucet. Water dripped from her chin as she stood. "Nothing special. Just dinner and maybe a walk by the lake."

"Minus the stop at the boathouse, right?"

Kylie grabbed a paper towel and wiped her mouth. "I promise, no boathouse."

"Good, especially since it seems you're not as keen on this guy as you used to be. Feelings change, and the boathouse would make for a big regret later."

Kylie stilled, her hand poised over a bunch of bananas before she tore one off and headed upstairs. "Don't you have to get dressed for church?" she said over her shoulder as Maddie tried to quiet her rising unease.

Fifteen

S cott ran his hand over the flaking paint of the weathered hull. "So what do you think? Can we save her?"

In the dim light of the boathouse, the old Blue Jay rested upside down on a pair of sawhorses. Phil cast a practiced eye over the old craft as he walked a full circuit around it.

Scott watched his friend and tried to figure out how to ask the question that had been gnawing at him since last night.

Phil tapped the beer can he held with one finger before pulling the tab. "Why do I get the feeling we're out here to talk about more than this boat?"

Scott nodded. "Smart man. I wanted to ask you something out of earshot of Maddie and the kids."

"Shoot."

"Have you ever seen your wife kiss another man?" Scott asked.

"Can't say as I have. I take it we're talking about Maddie and the show." Phil raised the can and took a slow swig. "It was in the script. She had to do it."

"She didn't have to like it."

"And did she?"

"Oh, yeah." Scott stepped to the window and gazed out at the smooth water of the lake. Over on the dock he could see Maddie and Annie sipping lemonade while the kids took a swim. "I know what it's like to be on the other side of that kiss. I think she's in love with him."

"Do you care?" Phil asked pointedly.

Scott spun around, his jaw clenched. "Of course I care; she's my wife."

"But do you care about Maddie, or is it your pride that's hurt?"

Scott opened his mouth and then snapped it shut, taking a moment to answer. "I care about Maddie."

"So when's the last time you kissed her?"

"A long time ago," Scott admitted as he leaned both hands back against the sill.

Phil squatted down next to the Blue Jay and cocked his head to get a good look underneath. "You know the day you were married I'm sure they read that Scripture about how a man leaves his mother and father and clings to his wife and they become one flesh."

"We're a long way from that."

Phil rapped the underside with his knuckles before standing. "That reading was more than just words on a page. It was a part of the plan for your marriage and your life."

"If there's a plan, I'd say we're way off track."

"When you don't stay connected physically and emotionally, it's just too easy for your marriage to unravel."

Scott studied his friend. "You've been married what? Ten years? And it's obvious that you and Annie are crazy about each other. How do you do it?"

Phil met his gaze. "You really want to know?"

"Yeah, I do."

"Okay, but remember, you asked," Phil said with a smile. "Our marriage works because we've asked God to be a part of it."

The mention of God made Scott uncomfortable. But he was curious enough to follow up. "And that made a difference?"

"You tell me? Are we like most couples you know?"

"No way."

"There you go. We're different because we've put our trust in Him to guide our lives and help us grow more in love with each other each day."

"So how do I get that?" Scott asked, his practical side wanting to get this process in motion.

"First, you have to want God in your life and you have to accept by faith what Jesus told us."

"About being God's son and about rising from the dead? I've known that since I was in second grade."

"But did you ever really believe it, not just in your head but in your heart? Did you ever think of yourself as a sinner saved by grace?"

Scott pushed off the windowsill, dusting his hands off on his pants. "Not really. I mean I know I'm not perfect, but I'm not a sinner."

Phil nodded. "I used to think that too. I figured as long as I followed the big ten, you know the Ten Commandments, then I was safe. I mean compared to the people around me I was a pretty good guy. I hadn't murdered anyone or cheated on my wife. I even paid my taxes without shaving the truth. But God doesn't compare us to others, He compares us to the only perfect person who ever lived, His Son. And up against that standard we all fall short, even those we admire the most." Phil ran a hand over his jaw where a day's growth of beard shadowed his jaw. "I know I've told you about my brother."

Scott nodded.

"Cam died right after Annie and I were married. On the surface he was the perfect guy with the perfect life. Great wife, beautiful kids, a great job, and college accounts paid in full before his kids were in kindergarten. He had it all, which made me wonder why he always seemed so unhappy. It was only after the heart attack that he realized he'd invested his time and energy in things that wouldn't last. I mean when you die and you stand before God, do you think He's going to ask you how many houses you designed or how much money you made?"

Scott shrugged. "Probably not."

"Right, he's going to ask you how you cared for what he gave you. Did you love your wife and kids? Did you tell your children about him? Did you use your talents for Him or only for yourself? Because when we use what God gave us exclusively for ourselves, that's sin. The sin of pride. Cam got a wake-up call. He ended up in intensive care and he knew he needed to make some changes in his life." Phil met his gaze. "Maybe this is your wake-up call, Scott."

"I wouldn't even know how to start making things right with Maddie."

"Just spend time with her. No grand gestures. Just listen to her."

"I've never been a good listener. Buying her jewelry was always more my style." Scott's laugh sounded hollow. "Think a diamond necklace will make her fall in love with me again?"

"You tell me."

Scott shrugged. "You're right. She'd take one look at it and think I was trying to soften the blow before I told her I was missing the family vacation again this year."

"Right, so no grand gifts. Just start small. How about taking her out to dinner at her favorite restaurant?"

"I could do that," Scott said, mentally figuring how he was going to shift his workload to accommodate this new project.

"The thing is," Phil said, leading the way out into the sunlight, "you have to be the man Maddie fell in love with, not just pretend to make things right. And to do that you're going to need some help."

"You're talking about God?"

Phil tossed his can in the air, easily catching it between his two palms and flattening it. "Asking for His help with something He wants for you anyway is a slam dunk."

"I like the sound of that."

Outside, splashing water and squealing laughter filtered through the trees. Scott smiled. Earlier he'd been floundering and now he had a direction to take, but one last question. "I don't know about this prayer thing. I don't think I remember the words."

"Just talk to God. Praying isn't complicated. It's just words from the heart."

Scott studied the ex-linebacker, admiring Phil's ease with the subject of God. Scott had always thought of those athletes who professed their faith in the locker room as holdouts for God's help on the field. But clearly there was more to it than that. Scott followed Phil back down the path to join their families.

Just talk to God? He could do that.

Maddie was always a little weepy when she dropped Shaun off at camp each year. But on the ride home Monday night, her streaming eyes made it difficult to see the road. Exhausted from the six-hour-round trip to Maine, she was smart enough to know her tears were not just for Shaun. Her son wasn't the only man missing from her life this week.

She had pushed thoughts of Adam aside yesterday with everyone gathered round the picnic table and vying to get a word in edgewise. If Maddie had been a little quieter than usual no one seemed to notice. Even Scott managed to shake off his work worries and join in the cannon ball contest as the men and kids competed for the last piece of chocolate cake.

Relief flooded Maddie's tired senses as she pulled down the driveway. Kylie's CD player greeted Maddie as she climbed from the car. It blasted the latest Dave Matthews hit from her bedroom window. Inside the house, it was almost as loud. Tomorrow when Kylie left for the beach, the house would be quiet—too quiet. Maddie tossed her keys on the counter and tried to ignore the music.

Wandering around the kitchen, she opened cabinets, the bread drawer, the refrigerator, but nothing appealed. She was hungry, but didn't feel like cooking. Defeated, she sank onto a stool and rested her head in her hand closing her eyes.

Thoughts of Adam came without warning. A smile touched her lips as she let her mind linger on the memories: the way he held her as if she were the most precious thing in the world, the way he looked at her with undisguised desire. Maddie gave in to the imagery and pictured herself walking across the stage to him. Adam's hand grasped hers in a possessive hold as she stared up at him. He leaned toward her, his arms pulling her close as his lips met hers in a mutual kiss.

The garage door banged against the wall.

Startled, Maddie opened her eyes and turned toward the noise. Scott kicked the door closed with his foot and then backed down the hallway trying to juggle his portfolio case and a large grocery bag.

Heat flooded Maddie's face, guilt driving her to hurry over and rescue the bag. "You bought dinner?"

"Not exactly."

The bag in her hands felt cold as she set it down on the counter. "I'm not all that hungry. How about something light, like a salad?"

"I was thinking of something a little more substantial." Scott headed down the hall to his office with his portfolio case.

Maddie groaned. The man hadn't made it home for dinner in weeks and now he wanted a gourmet meal. She yanked open the refrigerator door. "Let me see what I have."

"All you'll need is in that bag." Scott reappeared in the kitchen and rolled up his shirt sleeves.

He opened the cabinet over the dishwasher and pulled down three oversized pasta bowls. Then he reached into the utensil drawer and pulled out three large spoons.

Standing in a cool draft from the open refrigerator, Maddie watched him. What was he doing?

He unpacked the bag, laying each item on the counter.

Bananas, cherries, nuts, sprinkles, fudge sauce, butterscotch, whipped cream and three different flavors of ice cream. He folded the bag and turned to her with a smile. "It's too hot for dinner. I thought we'd go straight to dessert."

"You thought of this?"

Scott glanced at her over his shoulder. "Guess I can still surprise you."

Stunned, Maddie stared as he flipped the tops off the ice cream and opened the jars. He'd done all this for her?

"Great idea, Dad," Kylie said as she breezed into the kitchen and grabbed a bowl.

Maddie closed the refrigerator.

"I remembered you were leaving tomorrow, Bug, and I wanted your last meal to be a memorable one."

"I'm only going for four days, Dad."

Maddie sagged against the counter. No, he hadn't gone to all this trouble for her but for Kylie. How like Scott to try and make up for months of neglect with one grand gesture.

"Maddie, you having some?" Scott held out a bowl to her.

"No, thanks. I'm tired after driving all day. I'm going to take a bath and go to bed."

Scott let the bowl clatter onto the countertop, a peculiar look in his eyes. He almost looked disappointed. "Suit yourself," he said adding nuts and cherries to his already ample helping.

Maddie started up the stairs, the conversation between father and daughter continuing behind her.

"Want some whipped cream, Ky?" Scott asked. "I bought two cans."

Kylie laughed. "You know I hate whipped cream, Dad. You and Mom are the ones who like to bury a perfectly good sundae in all that foam."

Maddie stopped halfway up the stairs. Whipped cream? She turned, tempted by the treat, then thought better of it. No, too many calories and too much work. A cool bath sounded like a lot less stress.

Sixteen

Maddie hugged the oversized pillow to her chest as she sank onto the sofa. What was she going to do while the kids were gone? She'd already tackled the laundry and the ironing, and she hadn't the energy to start in on the hall closet.

The dreary day beyond the window did nothing to lift her spirits. Maddie shivered and considered lighting a fire in the family room to stave off the late afternoon chill, but decided it was too much work.

Beyond the window, choppy white water churned the lake into a frothy foam. The Sunfish bobbed madly at its mooring. Leaves scuttled across the lawn, swirling down to the dock while rain pelted the roof.

Silent tears slipped down Maddie's cheeks. She stared at the perfectly decorated family room with its natural beamed ceiling and wide board floors. Scott had designed the room, but she had designed the space. The open floor plan. The overstuffed furniture in crimson plaid. The Persian rugs and decorative molding. The room, elegant and yet comfortable, now felt sterile and too precise. Even the books surrounding the entertainment center were shelved according to height.

Was she really like that? So rigid and controlling she couldn't do something spontaneous? Hadn't that been what the show was about? She'd spent the last seventeen years worrying about Scott and the kids. Until she'd met Annie, and later Adam, even her friends weren't really her own. They were acquaintances she'd met through the kids. So Sunday night when Adam had asked if they could still be friends why had she cut him off? And what would she do if he called and asked her to reconsider? Maddie's heart beat faster at the thought.

The doorbell's musical chime echoed in the hallway. Startled, Maddie jumped to her feet and wiped her eyes as she hurried into the foyer and flung open the front door.

Annie stood on the porch, juggling an umbrella and two gooey cinnamon rolls. "I brought you an afternoon treat." She managed to close the umbrella without dropping anything. "Some hot coffee would be great on a day like . . ." Her words trailed off as she caught sight of Maddie's tearstained face. "Maddie, what is it?"

Maddie grabbed her arm and pulled her inside. "Nothing a little coffee and five hundred calories' worth of pastry won't cure. Hang your coat up and I'll make a pot."

Annie threw her slicker over the antique coatrack and followed Maddie into the kitchen.

"Regular or decaf?" Maddie rounded the counter and reached for two plates, handing them to Annie.

"High test, please."

Maddie filled the pot with cold water and poured coffee beans through a grinder. As the whir of the blades faded, Maddie met Annie's expectant gaze.

"Going to tell me about it?"

Maddie measured the grounds and plugged the coffeemaker in. "Just feeling a little blue now that the show is over and the kids are gone for the week."

"Is it the kids you're missing or Adam?" Annie asked.

"I do miss him." Maddie sank onto the stool and hooked one foot around the lowest rung. The faint gurgle of the coffeemaker filled the silence before she spoke. "Adam is a good friend, and I was just wondering what would be the harm in seeing him again. Isn't that what friends do?"

"But you're more than friends."

"We don't have to be."

"You won't be able to help yourself. It's like being on a diet with chocolate cake in the middle of your kitchen." Annie waved a hand at the empty counter.

"Just because it's there doesn't mean you have to eat it," Maddie joked, trying to make light of the temptation.

"But you can only look for so long before you just have to have some." Annie leaned her forearms on the counter. "Seriously, Maddie, can you tell me you only want Adam as a friend, that you never want him to touch you again? Because if you've thought about it, maybe even fantasized about it, then you've already crossed the line."

"Oh, come on. I haven't done anything." Maddie slipped off the stool and grabbed two mugs. She poured the coffee.

"Not yet, but you will. Put temptation in your path long enough and it'll wear down your resistance." Annie accepted the mug, wrapping her hands around the warm porcelain.

"But aren't those women's magazines always telling us that a little fantasy can spice up a marriage?"

"I don't buy that for a minute. Daydreaming about kissing Adam isn't going to bring you any closer to Scott. In fact, it'll start you making comparisons that have no place in your marriage."

"So what should I do?"

"You already know the answer to that; you just don't want to hear it."

Maddie's shoulders sagged. "Stay away from Adam."

Annie nodded. "Right now you want him in your life. In fact, after this summer you're probably wondering what you'll do without him."

Maddie reached for the cinnamon roll, picking at the edges. "I don't want to live without love in my life, not anymore."

"You weren't meant to."

"So what's the alternative—divorce?" Just saying the word sent a shiver of apprehension up Maddie's spine.

"Divorce isn't an option," Annie said, her gaze urgent. "You might consider seeing a marriage counselor, though, someone who can help you work through your problems and help you to remember why you fell in love in the first place."

"I can't remember that far back," Maddie quipped. "Besides, Scott would never agree to see a counselor. Not without a little divine intervention."

"Now there's a good idea."

Maddie suppressed a groan. Annie had her faith and it worked for her, but the answer to every question wasn't always found at God's doorstep.

Annie must have sensed her withdrawal because she changed the subject. "One of the reasons I came by today was to thank you for offering to cosign our loan. Phil and I have decided after a lot of prayer that we're not ready to put ourselves any further into debt so we're not going to pursue adopting overseas."

Maddie was startled. "You're not giving up on being parents?"

Annie sipped her coffee and popped a piece of cinnamon roll into her mouth, chewing with relish. "You know me better than that. We've decided to go back to our original plan and complete the foster parent work-up in New Hampshire. But what we're going to tell them is that we'll take a child of any age, not just a baby."

"And you're okay with that?"

"More than okay. I feel like I'm finally in the place I'm supposed to be. This won't happen overnight. It'll probably take months, but in the end we'll make a wonderful home for some child no one else wants."

"Annie, I'm glad for you."

"So you'll hold my hand when the paperwork and the red tape have me ready to pull my hair out," she joked.

"You bet."

Two cups of coffee later Annie tilted her mug for a final sip and got to her feet. She stood for a moment in silence and then cocked her head to one side. "Can I say one thing before I go?"

Maddie nodded. "Of course, anything."

"Okay, so I know you're not comfortable talking about God . . ."

Maddie forced herself to relax. Annie was a good friend, and if she had something to say Maddie was going to listen.

". . . but when it comes to healing, especially healing a marriage, He is the man to turn to. Think about it: who designed men and women for each other? And who is the biggest miracle worker you know? Put the two together with a little prayer and you'll have the marriage you've always wanted."

Maddie hugged her. "You make a good point. I promise I'll think about it."

"If you want to talk you know where to find me." Annie grabbed her slicker from the coatrack and pulled up the hood before making a dash for her car. Droplets pelted her slicker as she waved one last time before jumping in.

Maddie closed the door, considering Annie's parting words. Her faith was so real, so much a part of who she was, yet Maddie appreciated her sensitivity to those without her insight. She never pushed too hard. Annie believed in God's power to change lives, but she didn't try and defend her viewpoint with biblical arguments. She just put it out there and let her life speak what words could not. How had she developed such a strong faith? There must be a story behind it. Maddie had never asked the question because she hadn't wanted to hear the answer. Now, she was curious.

The phone's ring drew her into the kitchen. Still thinking about Annie, Maddie picked up the portable. "Hello."

"Hello, Maddie."

Her fingers gripped the receiver and her heart raced. Adam?

"I told myself I wasn't going to do this," Adam said, his tone tentative. "But one minute I'm editing an article on septic systems and the next I've punched in your number."

Maddie laughed. "How flattering to think that septic systems make you think of me."

"Everything makes me think of you." His tone was measured but with an intensity that made Maddie's eyes close with pleasure at the sound of his voice. "I miss you, Maddie. I miss talking to you and hearing you laugh at my lame jokes."

Maddie swallowed her eager response. She wanted to tell him she missed him too, but Annie's warning still echoed in the room and she bit back the words. "How are you?"

"A little depressed. I get this way after a show closes."

"I know what you mean and the weather isn't helping," Maddie said, making small talk, anything to keep him on the phone a little while longer.

"Did your family like the show?" Adam asked.

"They did. How about your dad?"

"He loved it, as usual. He's my biggest fan. Though he did say he thought I'd added a layer of realism to this performance."

"Because you're really a con man at heart?" Maddie teased, loving the feeling that bubbled up inside her as a chuckle rolled past her lips.

"Is that what you think of me? That I'm just out to get what I want?"

"And what do you want?"

A prolonged pause met her question. "Do you really want to know?"

Maddie nodded, though she made no sound.

"I want us, Maddie."

Maddie's eyes stung. Her pulse raced and her breath seemed to catch in her throat. "That's probably not a good idea."

"Probably not, but—"

Maddie wished she could see his face.

When he spoke his tone was urgent. "Maddie, meet me at the diner, just for a cup of coffee, please."

His words hummed in her ear as a wave of desire flooded her brain. And before a rational thought could penetrate, she answered, "Yes."

Excitement tinged his tone. "Fifteen minutes."

"I'll be there."

Maddie hung up the phone knowing she should call him back and say she'd made a mistake. But instead, she grabbed her coat and keys, anticipation driving her out into the rain.

Seventeen

Maddie parked her Jeep in the diner's back lot. A gust of wind pelted her with rain as she dashed out from under an overhanging fir and sprinted for the door. Anticipation and guilt made her stomach churn. What was she doing here, she asked herself as she stepped inside. She glanced to the right, half expecting to find Adam seated in the front booth, but caught sight of him in the rear dining room. He stood, a worried frown replaced by a growing smile as she started toward him.

He wore khaki pants and a striped shirt open at the collar with sleeves rolled up. He was so handsome, his dark hair as untamed as the day's rain.

Maddie's hands shook and she stuffed them in her coat pockets. Now that she was here, she didn't have any idea what to say.

"I was afraid you'd changed your mind," Adam said quietly. He seemed to sense her unease and sat back down. "I'm glad you're here."

Maddie sank onto the seat opposite his, fumbling with the buttons on her raincoat. But when she lifted her gaze to meet his, his smile stole what was left of her composure. Her hands fell to the tabletop, her coat forgotten. "I drove over here half expecting to have coffee alone."

"Did you really think I wouldn't come?" Adam asked.

"I didn't know."

"Yes, you did, Maddie. You knew I would do anything to see you."

A hot flush flooded her cheeks.

"I miss you." Adam leaned across the table and captured her hand in his.

Maddie said nothing, simply stared at their joined hands, savoring the warmth of his touch. This is what she had missed, the simple gestures of affection Adam gave so easily without even thinking about it. She let her hand rest in his for a moment and then slowly pulled it back.

"All the way over in the car, I wondered just what I would say if you did show up." Her words poured forth in a rush of sound that made him smile. "And now that I'm here I still haven't any idea."

"How about telling me you missed me, too?"

Maddie clasped her hands in her lap as her thoughts vacillated between glee and guilt. "I have thought about you."

"I'll take that for a start."

"Which is why I think we'd better leave this alone."

"You could have told me that on the phone, but you didn't. You wanted to see me."

"Because we're friends."

"Maddie, if that's all we are to each other this would be just another cup of coffee, but it's not."

"That's the problem, Adam. I want what we had this summer, but it can't be anything more."

The waitress approached and Adam waved her away with an impatient hand. "Why not, Maddie? I think if you let yourself you'd want a future as much as I do."

She looked into his eyes. Pain radiated from their steely depths, deepening the crow's feet at the corners.

Quickly, she slid from her seat. "This was a mistake. I don't know what I expected, that I could see you and that would be enough. Or that you could see me and want nothing more. I was fooling myself. I'm sorry."

She spun on her heels and pulled her hood up. Hurrying to the door, she wrenched it open and ran out into the downpour.

Rain whipped her face. Her sneakers crashed into puddles, soaking her lower legs and feet. A gust of wind threw back her hood as she ran to her car. Beneath the overhanging tree, she fumbled for her keys. A sob burst from her throat as she snatched them from her pocket. Gritting her teeth, she unlocked the door and reached for the handle.

An outstretched hand encircled her arm. "Maddie, wait. We can be whatever you want but don't run away." He spun her around, pulling her against him as rain melded his dark hair to his head. "Don't leave, not now," he whispered, his lips close to her ear.

Maddie leaned against him and his arms encircled her in a possessive hold. "Don't you see, it's too hard to be near you."

"Hard for who?"

"For me," she answered with an exasperated sigh.

"Which only means that you want me as much as I want you."

"Even if I did, I have other people to consider here. My children, my . . ." She leaned back and met his gaze.

106

"Your husband?" Adam finished for her, an edge of anger in his tone. "Maddie, why are you trying to save a marriage that makes you miserable?" Adam traced the line of her jaw with his knuckle. "You deserve better and I want to give it to you."

Wind whipped the branches, showering them with a deluge of rain. "Let me try, Maddie. Let me love you."

She shivered as Adam's lips closed over hers in a kiss so familiar and yet so frightening.

Maddie responded with pure instinct. Her arms slipped around him and her hands slid over the shirt now plastered to his back. It was so easy to give in, to just let her body go where her mind had already been. For a moment pleasure overrode that small voice in her head sounding a note of caution, a small voice that sounded remarkably like Annie. 'You won't be able to help yourself,' Annie had said. And she'd been right.

Maddie pulled away, her breath coming in ragged gasps.

Adam cupped her face in his hands, forcing her to look at him. "I know you felt that."

Maddie couldn't deny the truth. "Feeling it and giving in to it are two different things."

"Maddie, please come with me to my office. We'll talk. Nothing more, I promise." His hands squeezed her shoulders in a gentle hold as if willing her to give in to his words.

Slowly Maddie stepped back, out of his reach. Her fingers longed to smooth the anguish from his brow but she knew better. Instead she stuffed her hands into her pockets to keep them still.

"Think about it, Maddie." Rain dripped from Adam's hair as he stared at her. "I'm not going anywhere. You know where to find me."

Maddie drove out of the diner lot, her emotions at war with her good sense. The battle for her integrity was being waged by emotions she barely recognized much less condoned. Self-interest versus family. Excitement versus routine. Sensuality versus celibacy.

Maddie hit the gas, her heart beating as fast as the windshield wipers dispersing the rain. Her hand rose to her lips. Without conscious thought her fingers rested there as if she could hold on to Adam's kiss with a mere touch.

She shouldn't have come. She'd known it driving over, but nothing could have stopped her from seeing Adam, not after she'd heard his voice on the phone. And now?

Anguish made her queasy. She would never see him again. She'd made that decision when she got into her car, her mind choosing what her body could not. And yet where was she going? Home? To an empty house? To Annie's maybe? No, much as she liked Annie, confessing her infidelity would be too embarrassing. Besides it was just a kiss. It's not like she'd let it go any further.

Still, guilt needled her conscience. She vacillated between shrugging off the whole event as meaningless and turning her car around and driving to Adam's office.

Was it really so wrong to want someone to love her? She'd spent her life seeing to the needs of others, always putting her family first. And now in a wave of pure selfishness she wanted something for herself. She wanted to be loved and cherished, to be the most important person in someone's life. In Adam's life.

Beyond the car windows clouds darkened the sky. An early twilight deepened the gloom as the rain tapered off. Maddie flipped on the car lights. She knew she was trying to rationalize her own desires. Palming the wheel with one hand, she turned onto the highway stifling a tired chuckle at the irony. If it wasn't so painful, it would be laughable.

Up until this summer Maddie truly believed she'd outgrown her youthful passions. Those bouts of pure physical longing never even entered her thoughts. She figured she and Scott had broken the bank as newlyweds. They'd used up their share and hadn't stored any away for the lean years of later marriage when job stress and parenting had taken the place of desire.

Truth be told, she barely missed the physical passion . . . or so she'd thought until she met Adam. And it wasn't lust that had drawn her to Adam, but his openness. He listened and laughed. He thought about her when they weren't together and told her so when they were. It would be too easy to fall in love with a man who met her every emotional need, and too easy to let those emotions spiral into a passionate act she could never take back.

No, Annie had been right. The division between thought, fantasy, and actual behavior was as thin as tissue paper. Hold one up to the light and you could see right through it to the next and the one beyond. Maddie hadn't wanted to believe it, but she knew better now.

Reluctantly, she flipped on the blinker for her exit. She didn't want to go home. She didn't want to spend the evening thinking about Adam or second guessing her decision not to see him again. The kids were away, and Scott was undoubtedly working late. She needed something to do.

Pulling onto Lake Shore Drive, Maddie drove past the drive-in theater. Recently renovated, its specialty was double features, one old and one new movie just like in years past when the drive-in was the hot place to be on a cool summer night. Maddie scanned the features. This week the oldie was *Fantastic Voyage*. Maddie remembered loving that movie as a kid. She hit the brakes. A movie, a hot dog, and a big bag of popcorn sounded like just the ticket for a night of mindless entertainment. Sure, she'd be the only one sitting alone in her car when the place filled with couples. Maddie shrugged, pulling into the parking lot. After all these years she was used to being alone.

Eighteen

A car door slammed. Scott glanced at the clock in the kitchen: 11:40 p.m. He'd given up on dinner hours ago, held out for dessert, and finally settled in front of the Sox game with a beer to watch the end of the game.

Scott scowled at the metallic scrape of a key in the door. He'd gone out of his way to make tonight a special evening. All Maddie had to do was show up. And she couldn't even do that.

Spying his blue sports coat hung over a chair, Scott bounded to his feet. He caught up the jacket, the gift-wrapped box peeking out of the pocket, as Maddie appeared in the kitchen.

She tossed her hand bag on the counter. "I didn't think you'd be home tonight."

"Obviously," Scott said. And though anger made his fists clench and his voice tight, he purposely chose a milder approach. He knew Maddie. Yell at her and she would yell back. A shouting match wasn't likely to get him what he wanted, his wife's undivided attention. "Where were you?"

She looked surprised at the question and uneasy as well. Scott's hands gripped the jacket, feeling the edges of the box he'd slipped into his pocket hours earlier.

Maddie crossed the kitchen and filled the kettle, placing it on the stove. "I went to the drive-in."

"By yourself?" Doubt blistered his words, though he kept a firm hold on his temper.

"Of course by myself, who else would I go with? The kids are gone and you weren't here." Maddie turned to get a mug and a tea bag from the cabinet, her shoulders tense, her face in profile.

Scott's eyes narrowed. She wasn't lying, but she wasn't telling the whole truth either. He'd lived with Maddie long enough to know the difference between a blatant lie and one of omission.

Scott tossed his jacket on the stair railing, his anger now tempered by fear. In the hours he'd waited for her to come home he'd wondered if Maddie was with Adam Slater, never quite believing it. Now he wasn't so sure. "Funny thing, I was here. I got home at six and we had dinner reservations at the Riverboat at eight."

Maddie's eyes widened as she spun toward him. "I love that place. We celebrated our tenth anniversary there."

"I know."

"Why didn't you tell me?"

"It was supposed to be a surprise."

"You could have called me on my cell phone."

Scott heard the defensiveness in her tone and true foreboding sent a tremor up his back. "Like I said, I wanted to surprise you. Turns out the surprise was on me."

"I'm sorry, Scott. If I'd known . . ." She turned her back to him and snatched the kettle off the burner before it whistled.

Scott strode around the counter, covering the distance between them in a few strides. He pulled up short just inches behind Maddie, so close her ponytail tickled his chin. "If you'd known I was here, would you have come home?" he asked quietly.

Maddie stilled. "Of course."

Scott sensed no conviction in her words. "Earlier this summer you tried to surprise me with dinner."

Maddie nodded, pouring water into her mug. "That didn't work out so well either."

"I think it's safe to say that we're no good at surprises."

"I agree."

Scott wished she would turn around so he could see her face. Instead he stretched his arms out and leaned on the counter, effectively caging Maddie in, though he did not touch her. "So how about we forget about surprises and make a plan to go out."

"You mean like a date?"

"Exactly."

"What did you have in mind?" Her hands clutched the mug as she turned around and leaned back against the counter.

Scott stared down at her. How had he forgotten how good it felt to be this close to her? *Slow. Go slow.* Phil's words echoed in his head. "I was thinking we might get away. Kylie won't be back until Saturday."

"And Shaun's in Maine until the end of the month."

"How about we surprise him," Scott said, knowing anything that included Shaun would sell the idea for Maddie. "We could head up to

Maine tomorrow, spent a day in Kennebunkport and then visit him on Friday."

"You would do that?" Maddie studied the edge of her cup before taking a sip.

"Sure, I'll call in the morning and tell them I'm taking a few personal days. I have some coming to me."

Maddie bit her lip as if squelching a remark.

Scott took a step back. "So, what do you think?"

"It sounds great."

He thought he heard a note of cautious enthusiasm in her tone as her finger absently traced a pattern on her lower lip.

Scott's pulse raced at the peculiar and yet somehow sensual gesture. "Good, well then, I think I'll head upstairs." He grabbed his jacket. "Are you coming?"

"In a while. I'm just going to finish my tea. Maybe read a little."

Scott nodded and started up the stairs. The box in his jacket jabbed his thigh with each step. One vacation trip wouldn't fix what was wrong in their marriage, but it was a start. Scott smiled, thinking ahead to tomorrow. Maybe he should go on the Internet and look for a place to stay. Tossing his jacket over the upper railing, he headed back downstairs, his feet silent on the carpeted treads.

Halfway down, one look at Maddie stopped him cold.

She sat at the island, her tea forgotten, one finger still pressed to her lips as silent tears rolled down her cheeks.

Scott turned and deliberately retraced his steps, hoping for the sake of their family that his best intentions weren't too late.

Maddie pulled her overnight bag from the closet shelf. Sunlight streamed through the skylight above the bed as she tossed the bag on the comforter. Marriage was a lifetime commitment. The day they'd said their vows Maddie thought that meant enduring through the tough times. Now she knew the routine of everyday life had its own destructive abilities. Boredom could deafen and monotony could mute the communication vital to lasting love. But last night she'd seen a chance to more than endure, to build a new relationship with Scott on the crumbled foundations of the old one.

Maddie gathered up a pair of pants, white shorts, and a few brightly colored shirts. On impulse she grabbed a sundress and threw it in the bag, too.

She couldn't remember the last time she and Scott had gone away without the kids. The prospect of hours alone produced a wide palette of emotions, not the least of which was fear. What would they talk about? But other emotions tugged at her as well. Interest. Curiosity. Even a touch of suspicion. Why had Scott planned a dinner last night and this getaway today? Why had he paid more attention to her in the last few days than he had in years? Guilt drove her to the obvious conclusion. Did he suspect she had feelings for Adam?

Sitting downstairs last night, Maddie had to admit her husband was making an effort. A few months ago she'd wanted nothing more. Now it left her feeling hopeful, and a little trapped too. If Scott chose to make their marriage work, she belonged here with him. But love again? She didn't think she could ever love Scott the way she had years ago.

Maddie zipped the bag closed. Glancing in the full-length mirror, she studied her khaki shorts and pink T-shirt. A few months ago she would have flinched at her ample curves; now she merely shrugged. She wasn't much thinner, perhaps a few pounds from all the dancing in the show, but more than actual weight she was more comfortable with her appearance. She didn't need to be a size eight to make someone interested in her. Adam had taught her that. And that newfound confidence made her smile as she shouldered her overnight bag and headed downstairs.

In the kitchen, Scott held the phone with one hand as he handed Maddie a cup of coffee. "We've got a great day for the drive. Are you packed?"

Maddie nodded before sipping the coffee. A little sweet. She'd stopped using sugar years ago, but Scott didn't know that.

"How about I make us some breakfast?" Maddie opened the refrigerator as Scott smiled and stepped around the counter to finish his phone call.

Maddie had the melon sliced, the bacon crisp, and the eggs scrambled before she noticed the increased volume of Scott's conversation as he stood by the window overlooking the lake.

"Mrs. Hingemen doesn't need me to make those changes. Have her fax over the new ideas and I'll incorporate them into the waiting room."

Maddie plucked a bagel from the toaster with two fingers and tossed it on a plate as a prolonged silence ensued.

"Everything all right?" she asked.

Scott glanced over his shoulder as he slapped the phone against his palm. "Should be. I just have to run one thing by Rob."

Rob Sanders, the company's founding partner. Maddie frowned. She stabbed the butter with a knife and spread some on the bagel.

Scott turned toward the window, his shoulders tense. "That's impossible, Rob. She approved the final plans last week."

Maddie glanced up, not liking the sound of that.

Scott tapped the glass door with his foot. "She'll have to wait then. I'll be away for the next few days with my wife. I'll see her when I get back."

Maddie smiled and set the plates in the warming oven.

"Memphis? What is she doing there?" Scott pulled the deck door open. A cool breeze off the lake filled the room. "Two hours. Why?"

His tone grew softer as Maddie strained to hear.

"I can't do it today. She'll have to wait until Monday."

Above his shirt collar, his neck reddened. "No, I . . . I know how much this project means to the firm. Yes, I do, but . . . fine, fine. I got it."

Scott slammed the deck door closed. Phone in hand he turned to Maddie. His brow furrowed and jaw clenched, he looked angry but resigned. "I'm sure you heard most of that; I'm afraid we'll have to postpone the trip for a day."

Maddie stiffened, the glimmer of hope she'd harbored upstairs fading away. She should have seen this coming.

Scott strode into the kitchen and took her hand. "Just for a day, Maddie. I have to fly to Memphis and meet Mrs. Hingemen. She wants me to see what they've done at St. Jude's Children's Hospital so we can include some of their ideas into our plans. I'll be back first thing tomorrow."

And what would it be tomorrow? A board meeting? A partner's review of the project? Maddie couldn't even find it in herself to be angry. Disappointed, maybe, but mostly with herself for falling so easily into this fantasy trip. Maddie studied her husband. He seemed concerned about her reaction to this change in plans, but then he always did. Last summer, he'd waited until the night before vacation to tell her she was making the trip to the Outer Banks without him. He'd apologized profusely, giving her all the reasons she would have a better time without him. Her screaming had drawn the kids to the top of the stairs, where they stood wide eyed with fright. Maddie had looked at their faces and vowed never to raise her voice again.

Even with the kids gone this morning, she wasn't tempted to scream, though. Somewhere inside, she'd known this was coming. Maddie picked up the orange juice and poured herself a glass. "When are you leaving?"

"Right now. Rob booked me on the noon flight out of Logan. I'll be back on the 8:00 a.m. flight tomorrow and we can drive up to Kennebunkport." Scott lifted her chin with one finger. "Maddie, I'm sorry. There was nothing I could do to get out of this trip."

"It doesn't matter." Maddie turned from him and caught up an oven mitt. "Do you have time for breakfast?"

Scott glanced at his watch and shook his head. "Not if I'm going to make the flight."

"Then you'd better get going." She pulled a single plate from the warming oven.

Scott started toward the stairs and then stopped. "If you talk to Shaun today, don't tell him we're coming Friday. Let's make it a surprise."

Maddie nodded and slipped onto the island stool setting her breakfast in front of her. She opened the morning paper, folded it, and laid the page beside her plate. Glancing over her shoulder at the empty stairway, she reached for her coffee.

Tell Shaun? Not a chance. She wasn't about to let Scott break her son's heart ever again.

Nineteen

Scott left his car running outside the general store and dashed inside. The door squeaked at his touch and Phil emerged from the back room, his sizable frame dwarfing the counter. Wearing blue jeans and a paint-spattered work shirt, he looked about as comfortable as a man could get.

"Hey, what can I get for you?" Phil asked.

"Just coffee to go. I've got a flight to Tennessee out of Logan in less than four hours."

"Last-minute trip?"

"Very last minute, and it blew my plans to take Maddie away for a few days."

Phil grabbed a large cup from the stack beside the coffeemaker. Steam rose from the cup as he filled it. "Glad to see you two are getting back on track."

"Or we were until this trip came up."

"How'd Maddie take it?"

Scott grabbed a Snickers bar from the counter display and tossed it on the counter. "Funny thing, she wasn't even mad."

Phil frowned. He capped off the coffee. "Disappointed then?"

Scott shook his head. "Not really, and when I said we'd do the trip tomorrow I didn't get much of a response. It was like she didn't care one way or the other." A shiver of apprehension raised the hair on Scott's neck. Maybe Maddie was just going through the motions so she could say she'd given their marriage her best shot.

Phil put the coffee in a bag. "Do you know the biggest enemy of any good marriage?"

Scott shrugged. "Lack of communication?"

"Nope. The biggest enemy of a good marriage is apathy. When one partner stops caring enough to make it work."

"I can't make her care," Scott said, retrieving a few bills from his pocket and tossing them on the counter.

"Let me ask you something." Phil's eyes narrowed in a questioning glance. "You've been trying to win your wife back on your own, right? Maybe you planned a few surprises, even bought her a gift or two, knowing you."

Scott flinched. He'd hidden the jewelry box he'd planned to give Maddie under his old baseball uniform intending to give it to her when they came home from the trip.

Phil nodded. "I can see I'm right, and I give you credit for wanting to fix what's wrong in your marriage. The problem is you'll never be able to fix it on your own. You need some help."

Scott groaned. "Not a marriage counselor."

"Those have their place, but that's not what I'm talking about."

Recalling their conversation at the boathouse, Scott said, "You're talking about God, right?"

"Exactly. God doesn't just want to be the guy you call on in a crisis and then forget about until the next one comes along. God wants to make you a better husband, a better father, a better man every day. But here's the catch; He can only do that if you want Him to."

"So, let's just say I wanted His help. What do I have to do?"

"Just tell Him so. Tell Him you know you've messed up in the past, but you believe in His Son, Jesus, and you want His help in your marriage and in your life."

"Sounds easy enough."

"The trick is you have to mean it. God knows your heart. When you're ready He'll be listening, and the good part is He never turns away anyone who loves His Son." Phil handed the coffee across the counter. "Do me a favor?"

Scott took the bag. "Name it."

"Let me know if you decide to try things God's way."

"Will do."

Back in his car, Scott marveled at his friend. Phil wasn't like all the guys Scott knew in college or saw at the office. Phil didn't have big dreams about making a lot of money or an inflated ego that drove him to seek recognition for his talents. He didn't tell off-color jokes about women, and he talked about God like other guys talked about football. Down to earth. And with an ease that came from living what he believed every day.

Could God really make a difference? And more basic than that: did he really believe in God at all?

Scott palmed the wheel as he switched lanes. Oh, he'd learned the doctrine. His father had seen to that before he ran out on his family. Scott had learned the prayers, but it hadn't made a difference. He remembered begging God to send his father home. And when his prayer went unanswered, Scott decided that God didn't exist—or worse, that He did exist and didn't care. Either way, the result was the same; he was on his own.

Phil's life and his words bore witness to a God Scott had never considered. A God who cared so much He sent His Son to die for us, a God who wanted to be involved in the day-to-day workings of Scott's life.

Scott didn't know if he believed that yet. But he was a man who liked to hedge his bets. He decided to send up an experimental prayer, the first he'd prayed in years, like a weather balloon and a test flight all rolled into one.

I don't know if all Phil told me about You is true, but I'm starting to think he might be right. So Lord, keep me safe today. It would be ironic if I died in a plane crash on the very day I'm starting to figure this out with Maddie. So please bring me home safely to my wife.

It wasn't much of a prayer, but it met Phil's criteria.

It was from the heart.

Maddie's apathy lasted as long as it took to clean the kitchen and dive into a project she'd been putting off for too long. Sitting on the foyer floor, her coffee cup beside her, Maddie eyed the half-empty closet with despair. Around her boxes of wrapping paper, old raincoats, mismatched mittens, and outgrown snow boots littered the floor. She sighed and reached for her cup. If this was to be her life's work, she'd go crazy. Her kids were growing up. One day soon they'd move out and she'd be left here alone. Or alone with Scott, which amounted to the same thing.

Maddie grimaced at the chilled coffee and set it aside. She was back where she'd started. The summer show had been a temporary reprieve from her restlessness, but now it was over and she was still stuck in a loveless marriage with a husband who made promises he never kept.

A horn sounded in the driveway. Maddie looked at the mess around her and gladly abandoned the task in favor of her visitor. She dusted off her shorts, glad Annie had such good radar for Maddie's bouts of self-pity. Grabbing the front door, she threw it open. "I hope you brought more of those—"

She froze. The car in the driveway wasn't Annie's. With a sharp intake of breath Maddie recognized the black Volvo even before the driver emerged and leaned on the roof.

Adam.

His smile was broad, but with a touch of apology. He rounded the car and started up the path to the house. "Now I know I said I wasn't going anywhere, but today I'm playing hooky from work. And on the off chance you might be looking for me, I thought I'd see if you wanted to take this beautiful day and play hooky with me." He leaned one foot on the bottom step and looked up at her expectantly. "Your kids are gone for the week, so say yes."

"How do you know that?" she asked, staring down at him, hardly able to believe he was standing in her yard.

"Because you told me."

"That was weeks ago."

"Yes, it was, but when you talk I listen. And I thought you might be missing your kids as much as I miss you." He stepped onto the porch and reached for her hand. "Come with me, Maddie. Just for today. It will be our getaway day."

Maddie's mouth quivered and she bit her lip. Adam studied her expectantly. He wasn't pleading with her to come, but clearly he wanted her to say yes.

One day. What could one day matter? With an ease she wouldn't have thought possible yesterday, she embraced the idea, eager for the adventure. Just one day out of a whole lifetime. Guilt brushed at the edges of her mind, but she mentally waved it away like the annoying strands of a spider's web.

She grinned and pulled the door closed behind her. "I'd say it's a perfect day for a getaway."

Twenty

In the boarding area, Scott watched the flight departure change on the screen for the third time in as many hours. What had been a noon flight was now scheduled for early evening. Equipment trouble, he'd been told an hour ago. He paced to the window, kneading a knot in his neck, his mood sour.

He'd wasted the whole day sitting here when he could have been driving up the Maine coast with Maddie. Maybe they'd have stopped for ice cream and then found a quiet place overlooking the ocean to have dinner. Scott clenched his fist, his frustration growing.

The public-address system crackled. A pretty airline employee with a practiced smile spoke into a handset from behind the counter. "We are sorry for the delay getting you folks to Tennessee this afternoon."

Her accent reminded Scott of Maddie's when they'd first met, before years of living in the North had hardened the vowels and blunted her soft drawl. "We've reassigned the aircraft for your trip and it should be arriving within the hour. Again, we are sorry for the delay, but the safety of our passengers is our first concern."

Scott stifled a groan. Another hour. By the time he got to Memphis Mrs. Hingemen would undoubtedly put off their tour of the hospital until tomorrow and he'd end up losing another day.

He couldn't believe his bad luck. Or was it really luck at all? If Phil were here, he'd say things happen for a reason. Scott frowned. When was the last time he'd been delayed three times for a flight?

He took a seat by the window, stretching his legs in front of him. Was there a reason he was still at Logan? Had he made the wrong choice this morning when he'd talked to Rob?

For years he'd put his work ahead of his wife and family, appeasing his guilt with assurances about future times together. But Kylie would be off to college in two years, the same year Shaun entered high school. Scott had missed their childhood while he worked to insure their financial future. Maddie had the memories of lazy summer afternoons

120

sailing on the lake or swinging in the hammock reading books. Scott's memories existed only on videotape. Pictures taken by Maddie of Kylie riding horses or Shaun playing T-ball.

He'd chosen his career over his kids, and done the same thing this morning with Maddie, assuming she would be there when he got home. But if Phil was right, if apathy sounded the death toll in a marriage, then that choice might be more costly than he'd realized.

Scott glanced at his watch. Was it too late? If he left right now, he could make it home in time to leave tonight for Maine. Would Maddie agree to go after he'd let her down? What had she spent the day doing? Had she even given him a thought?

Scott leaned forward, his head in his hands as he recalled the look on Maddie's face as she'd sat alone in the kitchen this morning, hope fading from her eyes like a storm cloud eclipses the sun, changing her eyes from soft blue to muted gray.

Scott winced at the memory. He needed to find a way back to his wife, back into her head and her heart, and he couldn't do it alone. A silent prayer born of equal parts desperation and blind, untested faith, poured from his heart.

Lord, I've messed up. With Maddie. With Kylie and Shaun. And I need Your help. I know I'm ambitious and proud, and I'm sorry for that. You didn't make me a husband and a father so I could spend all my time ignoring my family. I thought I was doing it for them, but really I was doing it for me. Well, I'm done with that. Please forgive me, Lord. I know You are a father too, that You sent Your Son here to save us. I didn't always want to believe it, but that kind of love is hard to ignore. Your Son changed the world forever. So Lord, change me and help me to be the husband and the father You want me to be.

Around him the airport hummed with activity. Scott looked up. Was that what Phil had meant? Could an honest plea change his life? Scott hoped it could as he gathered his overnight bag and headed home.

Maddie hugged her knees to her chest and stared out over the treetops. Adam's idea of a getaway had obviously taken some planning, and included a gondola ride and a picnic lunch at the top of the world. She hadn't been here in years. Not since her kids were little and first learning to ski. The view from the mountaintop was still magnificent even without snow.

Adam was propped up on his elbows beside her. She could feel his gaze linger, not on the scenery, but on her.

Maddie glanced over her shoulder. "You're staring."

"Just taking in the view." Adam smiled. "For most of the summer I got to see you every day and this past week I've gone through withdrawal."

"I'm hardly that addictive." Maddie laughed.

"I beg to differ. You're like nicotine, only there isn't a patch that will help me quit."

Maddie chuckled. "You'll get over it."

Adam pushed himself up to sit beside her, all his good-natured humor falling away like a coat shed on a spring afternoon. His shoulder gently brushed hers as his gaze settled on the horizon. "No, actually I don't think I will."

Maddie's smile faded, the change in Adam's tone stealing the mirth from her mood.

Throughout the drive up here Adam had kept the conversation light, their getaway day just a chance for two friends to share an afternoon. But now, his shoulder resting against hers, the tenor of his tone upped the ante on their adventure.

Adam's eyes narrowed as he squinted in the late afternoon sun. "It isn't easy being single in a town the size of Kerry. I'm thirty-five and people assume I'm either divorced or gay."

"I'm sure you don't lack for companionship," Maddie offered, trying to lighten the mood even as she disliked the thought.

"I've dated my share of women, but I've never met anyone I wanted to spend my life with . . . until now." Adam turned to her and captured her hand, drawing her around to face him.

Maddie's nerves tingled with equal parts anticipation and fear. If she were honest, she'd known this was coming, had wanted it to come. Annie had been right. Maddie would never be able to see Adam and not want what they'd already shared. His touch. His words of admiration and endearment.

Maddie met his gaze, ready to say all the proper words any married woman should say in this circumstance. But when Adam lifted his hand and brushed one finger along her cheek, the words never made it past her lips.

"I love you, Maddie." His gaze never wavered.

Maddie eyes stung with unshed tears. How could he love her? They'd known each other such a short time. Sometimes she thought they were more Harold and Marion than Adam and Maddie. And yet her heart bounded at his words. She fought the impulse to lean forward and kiss him and echo his words with her own.

But did she love him? Or did she love being admired and desired by a man who wasn't afraid to tell her so? If she was honest with herself, her feelings were more infatuation than love.

One tear slipped down Maddie's cheek, her churning stomach a mixture of exhilaration and guilt. "I wish . . ."

"What do you wish, Maddie?" Adam took both her hands, squeezing gently. "And please don't tell me that you wish we'd never met."

Maddie shook her head. "No, not that. I loved this summer. Meeting you, acting with you. I love the way you make me feel, like I'm important and interesting and worth spending time with."

Adam lifted her chin with his finger. "You are all those things."

"You make me almost believe it."

"Because it's true."

Maddie closed her eyes, searching for the words. "Don't you see, I wish we could go back to where we were, to where we liked each other but could still walk away without pain or regrets."

"We're long past that now." Adam studied her in silence for a moment. An eagle screeched, its soaring cry the only sound on the mountain. "Can we talk about Scott?"

Maddie bristled at the name. "He doesn't belong here."

"But he does. He's right here between us and he has been all along. The question is, do you love him, Maddie?"

Maddie's gaze shifted to the trees along the horizon, buying time to come up with an honest answer. "When I married Scott, I promised to love him forever . . ."

"You didn't answer my question," Adam said softly. He ran his hand gently up her forearm, drawing her gaze back to his with nothing more than the power of his words. "Do you love him?"

"It's not that simple."

"But it is." The moment lingered, the silence electric with unvoiced expectations and possibilities.

Then Adam abruptly got to his feet. He held out a hand to her. "I want to show you something. Will you come with me?"

Maddie placed her hand in his and let him pull her up. "Where are we going?"

Adam began to gather up the picnic basket and blanket. "To a place where they know a thing or two about love."

Scott exited the interstate at Kerry. It had taken him over three hours, but he was almost home. Relaxing a bit, he turned onto the two-lane road that would take him to Whitefish Lake.

The glaring afternoon sun had faded into the purple tones of twilight. Scott flipped up his visor. Probably too late to leave tonight, he calculated, but if Maddie agreed they could be on the road at daybreak. They'd be halfway to Maine before Scott called the office and told them he wasn't coming in. He'd catch heat from Rob. A lot of heat. Standing Mrs. Hingemen up would jeopardize his position with the firm, but he'd simply explain that while he waited at the airport he'd gotten word of a family emergency. Scott flipped open the glove box and tossed his sunglasses inside. A family emergency. That was no lie. He hoped he'd gotten a clue in time to save his marriage.

Twilight beckoned, its shadows closing around the car. Scott flipped on the headlights. Nearing the outskirts of Kerry, the houses were fewer, the traffic light. The largest tract of land was an old Catholic cemetery. In the fading light, the homes he passed were cloaked in gray shadows, their secrets hidden behind decorative doors and picture windows. How many of those houses with their newly cut lawns and flowered walkways hid family secrets the world would never know about until they exploded onto the front page of the local paper? Abuse. Infidelity. Divorce. Depression. All hidden behind pristine facades.

Was that what had happened to their family? Had the magnificent house he'd designed for Maddie become nothing more than a facade empty of love? Scott had to admit he'd had a part in that, but still he was optimistic about the outcome of this weekend. He'd placed this problem in hands bigger than his own, and in doing so had found an unexpected peace. He wasn't so naïve as to think it would be easy to rebuild what years of neglect had wrought. Regaining Maddie's trust and love would take time, but he hoped that, unlike Phil's brother, who realized too late the price of his neglect, he would have years to make up the difference.

The roadway paralleled the old cemetery for half a mile. Gray stones against a gray sky reaching out into the dusk. Scott shivered. Cemeteries had always unnerved him. He had no fears about restless souls wandering the earth, but he found the whole concept of death unimaginable. All those stones marked the lives of people who had once eaten and laughed and worked and made love and now they were gone. Gone to a better place, some would say. Scott had never found much comfort in that trite expression, especially when the whole idea of eternity anywhere was one he couldn't get his mind around.

The thought of his nonexistence terrified him and always made him break out in a cold sweat. His heart raced, and he felt like his skin couldn't contain his panic. So when all his friends in high school had taken to smoking cigarettes and drinking rockgut wine in the cemetery, Scott had always found a reason not to join them. The thought of hanging out in a place where mortality stared you right in the face seemed like inviting the inevitable.

But Scott wasn't that young man anymore. As if to prove it, he forced himself to take a final look at the cemetery. In the deepening twilight he spotted a couple sitting on a stone bench, their heads close together and their hands clasped as they studied a gravestone. Scott returned his gaze to the road, but a faint stirring of familiarity made him glance back. But they were gone, lost in the darkness. A sudden shiver convulsed the muscles of Scott's back as he hit the gas hard, longing for home.

Twenty-one

Why had he brought her here? To a cemetery of all places. Seated beside Adam on the stone bench, her hand warm in his, Maddie was content to wait. She had nowhere to go, no reason to go home. The twilight closed around them, sealing them into its quiet. An occasional car went by on the road, its headlights quickly changing to a reddish glow as it disappeared into the summer evening.

"I promised to take you to a place where they know a thing or two about love," Adam began. "I'll bet this wasn't what you had in mind."

Maddie smiled. "You're right. But I bet you know someone here, probably someone very special."

Adam lifted his hand and pointed at a large, simple gravestone flanked by two urns of fresh flowers. "My mother. It seemed a fitting place to tell you her story."

Adam glanced at the gravestone and then at Maddie. "My dad is a simple guy. Hardworking, blue-collar, do-anything-for-you kind of guy. He was well into his thirties and working for the road department in Quincy when a buddy of his who worked backstage at a Boston theater offered him front row seats to a show making quite a stir at the time. Ever hear of *Hair*?"

Maddie chuckled. "What did he think of all that bare skin?"

"My dad's the unflappable type. He didn't really get what all the fuss was about. But one thing in the show did catch his eye."

"Your mom."

Adam smiled. "I wish you could have heard her tell the story of this tall, lanky man she met backstage one night after the performance. She was wearing a bathrobe, but when she shook my father's hand and he looked into her eyes, she said she felt like a giddy teenager on prom night. One look and he made her feel that beautiful."

Maddie smiled, knowing just what that felt like. Like father, like son.

"They were married three months later and moved up here to Kerry shortly after I was born. My mom never acted professionally again. She traded in her career for life as a housewife and mother," Adam continued, his voice tinged with a mixture of affection and nostalgia. "When I was about seven I remember asking her if she missed it."

"What did she say?"

"That all she ever wanted was a man who would love her forever and a mischievous little boy she could teach to sing and dance and spoil rotten." Adam squeezed Maddie's hand. "She died when I was twelve, but I like to think she got exactly what she wanted. A child who adored her and a man who would love her forever, and he's never stopped. See those flowers?"

"They're beautiful."

"My dad's doing. Every week from spring thaw to the first snowfall, he makes the two-hour trip to bring fresh flowers to her grave. He couldn't bear to live in Kerry after I went to college so he moved north but he still comes here every week." Adam brought Maddie's hand to his mouth and kissed it. "That's the only kind of love I know, Maddie. The only kind I want."

The longing in his eyes stole her breath away as he leaned in closer. "I've been holding out for years, waiting for the kind of love that survives no matter what you throw at it. Job loss. Financial worries. Even cancer. I didn't think I'd ever find it . . . until I met you." Adam cupped her face in his hands. "So I want to ask you again what I asked you up on the mountain. Do you love him, Maddie?"

The single word seeped from her soul in a whisper. "No."

Adam gently pulled her into his arms. "Then come home with me, Maddie. Stay with me tonight and let's plan a future together."

The urge was overwhelming. Annie had never felt anything like it. She set aside the rag she'd been using to wipe down the coffeemaker, glancing around for a reason for her sudden distress. But she was alone in the store, closing up for the night just as she had been for the last half hour. So why did she feel this urgent need to pray for Maddie? She had no idea where Maddie was today or what she was doing, but Annie didn't question the particulars. She'd been a Christian just a few years, but she knew the power of prayer. Annie closed her eyes and focused her attention on God.

Heavenly Father, wherever Maddie is, she's in trouble. Only you know what kind. Only you know what she needs. Guard her and protect her, Father. Be a lamp to her feet and lead her out of the darkness. Help her resist the temptation that is so much a part of this world, and bring her home safely to her family tonight. And I ask this in Jesus' name, Amen.

Annie opened her eyes to the familiar surroundings of the store she'd grown up in. She picked up the rag and finished cleaning the coffee machine, its stainless-steel surface shining in the overhead light. She might never know what had happened tonight. Maybe Maddie would tell her and maybe not. But Annie knew she'd done what she could and the peace she felt was as pervasive as the earlier anxiety had been upsetting.

Earlier in her life she'd doubted that prayer made a difference. But since she'd given her heart to Christ not long after Phil had done so, Annie had witnessed the power of prayer. The power to comfort and calm. The power to change lives. Her own and many others.

Annie turned off the store lights and locked the door. She might never know what happened tonight but she wanted to tell Phil about her little part in the plan.

Maddie's stomach fluttered as Adam held her in his arms, his hands moving over her back. This was what she wanted, what in some small corner of her brain she'd known would happen when she stepped off the porch this morning and got into Adam's car. She couldn't see Adam without wanting more—much more. Still a peculiar thought inserted its way into her mind. Annie had been right about the chocolate cake.

A slow rumble of laughter sneaked past Maddie's lips.

Adam drew back and held her at arm's length, a question in his tone. "You know if I were a less secure man, that reaction might make me question my manhood. Now, what's so funny?"

"Chocolate cake."

"I'm about to kiss you and you're thinking about chocolate cake." A smile touched his lips. "How am I supposed to take that?"

"It was just something Annie said when I first realized I had feelings for you."

Adam visibly relaxed. "I'm liking the sound of this."

"She said I'd never be able to spend time with you without wanting more. That one touch, one kiss would lead inevitably to wanting something more intimate."

"Like chocolate cake. You can never have it in your house without finishing the whole thing."

"Exactly."

"So you do have feelings for me?"

"That was never the issue."

"It was for me." Adam captured both her hands and held them like a fragile gift. "I didn't set out to fall in love with you, Maddie. I knew you were married, but I also sensed what you just told me. You haven't been in love with Scott for a long time."

Maddie flinched, hearing her own words from his mouth. "Maybe so, but marriage is about more than love."

"That's news to me."

"No, it isn't. You said so yourself. Your mom and dad knew that marriage is about commitment, about making a promise and sticking to it. It would be so easy for me to go home with you tonight, to give in to the temptation to just live for myself. But the bottom line is whose life I'd be destroying in the process." Maddie met his gaze squarely. "I can't do that to my kids. It would be different if Scott was cruel or abusive, but he's not. He's a good man who works too hard and has forgotten what's important. I may never love him again, but I can't let myself love you."

Adam's shoulders sagged, his gaze on their joined hands. "Sounds like you've thought this through."

Maddie's eyes welled with tears. "No, not really. If I had, I never would have come today and put us both through this. It's maternal instinct pure and simple. I can't choose my own happiness over my kids. Shaun and Kylie are the most important things in my life."

"So you're willing to live a life without love to what . . . protect them?"

"I'm willing to show them what commitment means, what it means to love someone more than yourself."

Maddie's words faded into the darkness as Adam got to his feet and pulled her up beside him. "Then I think we'd better get you home."

Scott drove down the lane. Moonlight shone on the lake, turning it a silvery white. It framed the dark house, creating a haunting silhouette. Scott clutched the steering wheel as he pulled into the garage. Where was Maddie?

His keys clutched in one fist, Scott flipped on lights as he walked from room to room. The foyer stopped him cold, the closet contents strewn across the floor like a job started but abandoned mid-task. A coffee mug caught Scott's eye and he picked it up, his hand closing around the cool porcelain.

Scott's suspicions erupted into fiery anger. The keys bit into his palm as he strode to the phone. He could think of only one legitimate reason Maddie wasn't here.

Phil answered on the first ring. "Hey Scott, don't tell me you're calling from Tennessee?"

Scott barely held his fury in check. "Is Maddie there?"

"Not that I know of. Why, is something wrong?"

"I need to speak to Annie."

"Hold on. Let me get her."

Moments later Annie came on the line and Scott struggled to find a more civil tone. "Was Maddie with you today?"

"No, I worked at the store all day."

"Do you know where she is or who she's with?" A slight pause confirmed Scott's suspicions. "She's with Adam, isn't she?"

"Wait, Scott, don't go jumping to any conclusions—" Annie injected.

Scott didn't hear any more as he hurled the phone across the room. It hit the wall with a sharp thud and crashed to the floor as blood dripped from his hand.

Twenty-two

Maddie cringed at the sight of the house ablaze with lights. The sheer wattage cast the surrounding yard in darkness. And if the lights weren't enough of a giveaway, the open garage door and the BMW inside made the obvious a certainty.

Scott was home.

Adam drove down the lane, his jaw set in a grim line. "You didn't leave those lights on."

"No."

To his credit Adam stood his ground. "Do you want me to walk you in?"

"I don't think that's a good idea. It's likely to make things worse."

Adam shifted the car into park and turned off the engine. He opened the glove box and withdrew a small white card. His movements were slow and deliberate. Clearly he wasn't nervous about a confrontation with Scott.

"I want you to have this." He slipped the card into her hand. "I'm not saying you'll ever need it, but I'll feel better knowing you have it."

Maddie glanced down at the printed business card with Adam's home phone as well as his cell number. "I won't be using this," she said softly.

"I don't expect you will. Just hold on to it." Adam's hands clutched the steering wheel with an intensity appropriate for a near miss collision and not a parked vehicle.

Maddie slipped the card into her pocket and reached for the door handle. "Adam, I'm—"

He cut her off. "Don't say you're sorry, Maddie. I'm not." His voice was a husky whisper. "You know where to find me. Now just go."

Maddie stepped from the car and closed the door. She turned toward the house as the engine started up. The Volvo's tires spun against the dirt, but Maddie refused to look back.

Every action had a reaction. And every choice had consequences.

How many times had she told her kids that? Hundreds? The house drew her forward.

Maddie squared her shoulders, ready to tell the truth and deal with the consequences.

Maddie slipped her key into the front door and turned the knob. Scott was waiting for her in the cluttered foyer.

"I heard the car," he said, his tone measured. Standing amid the cast-off clutter from the closet, his hand wrapped in gauze, anger radiated from him like a downed power line electrifies the ground around it. "Who drove you home?"

Maddie steeled herself for the onslaught, knowing that only the truth had any chance of saving this night from complete disaster. "Adam drove me home."

"The guy from the play."

Maddie nodded. "Yes."

"You spent the day with him?"

"Yes."

"Our little trip to Maine would have shot a hole in your plans. Lucky my boss bailed you out of that one."

"We didn't have any plans."

"Really." Scott's words, heavy with sarcasm, matched his look of disbelief.

Maddie cringed. "Adam dropped by after you left."

"What's he doing dropping by at all?"

"We got to be friends during the show." Maddie began gathering up the scarves and hats strewn on the floor.

"Yeah, I saw what kind of friends you are. I was there, Maddie. Every night. That was no stage kiss."

Maddie stopped midreach. Scott had been at the show every night? Why?

"You two are more than friends." Scott kicked aside a bag of wrapping paper. Reels of ribbon rolled across the floor as he advanced on her. "So did you sleep with him?"

Outraged at the question and yet flustered because she'd thought about it, Maddie's face flushed with heat. "I didn't sleep with him."

Scott loomed over her. "You've never been a good liar, Maddie."

"I'm not lying to you. I wouldn't do that."

"Well, you sure aren't sleeping with me. You must be getting it somewhere."

Maddie's eyes widened in disbelief. She'd expected Scott to be angry, but the cruelty in his tone was something she'd never considered. She literally couldn't speak.

But Scott had enough steam for both of them. "How long has it been, Maddie? Do you know how many times I wanted you and you turned away?"

Was that true? Maddie couldn't remember the last time Scott touched her. "Not all the time . . ."

"No, but even when we did make love, you made me feel like you were doing me a favor. I don't want a partner in bed who spends the whole time wishing it was over. I want a wife!" Scott shouted so loudly the chandelier above their heads swayed. Light danced across the foyer, giving the room an eerie glow.

"Then try coming home in time to be a husband," Maddie exploded. "Try giving me something besides the leftover minutes in your day before you collapse on the couch and fall asleep watching the ball game. You spend more time watching TV than you do talking to me." Maddie couldn't stop herself. "This isn't about sex, Scott. It's about time. You give the kids a few minutes each week and figure a little quality should make up for no quantity at all. Well, you aren't giving either one."

"So I'm not only a bad husband, but a bad father?" Scott's words hissed from between clenched teeth.

Maddie fired back. "Ask yourself: when was the last time you gave our kids your undivided attention? You've always got one eye on the door when they're talking to you, like you're thinking about all the work in your briefcase."

"So my neglect makes it okay for you to have an affair. Hey, then maybe this guy Adam isn't the first." Scott spit the words at her, the veins in his forehead bulging.

Maddie hurled the clothes in her arms at him, fury searing her tone. "You are a small man, Scott. Why would I ever choose to stay with you when there's a man out there who actually loves me?"

Maddie snatched up her keys and ran from the house. Sprinting for her car, she threw open the Jeep's door and started the engine. She floored the gas as Scott raced from the house. Maddie didn't even acknowledge his shouts as the Jeep sped by him and raced down the lane.

Her eyes stung with unshed tears, her nerves so hot-wired that if she didn't move she would explode.

Fury coursed through Maddie. How had she ever believed she could spend the rest of her life with Scott? She whipped the wheel left and spun out onto Shore Drive, her knuckles white as the Jeep took the turn on two wheels.

She'd been wrong, so wrong. That speech she'd given Adam about commitment and sacrificing for her family sounded great, but Maddie couldn't live under the same roof with Scott for another night, much less the rest of her life.

The undulating road dipped around a dark bend, the moonlit lake laid out in full view as Maddie sped around the corner.

A small rational thought tried to rein in her anger. Maybe she hadn't slept with Adam, not in the physical sense, but their affair had been one of the heart. She wanted Adam and she'd gone out of her way to meet him. She'd touched him and kissed him and allowed him to touch her in ways no man except Scott had done. An affair? Perhaps Scott had been right, but that was no excuse for his cruelty.

She didn't have to take that from him. Any man capable of that kind of cruelty was capable of unleashing the same on his children, and she would never let that happen to Kylie and Shaun.

Darkness surrounded her and Maddie flipped on the brights.

She wasn't going back to the house. Not tonight. And maybe not ever. So where was she going?

Maddie fumbled in her pocket.

A gust of wind buffeted the Jeep, pushing it over into the center of the roadway.

Her fingers closed over the edge of Adam's business card. She glanced down at it and then back up to the roadway.

Two shining eyes met her gaze.

Maddie threw the wheel right, avoiding the deer.

The Jeep veered onto two tires, still barreling forward.

With a flash of déjà vu Maddie saw the giant tree stump before the Jeep hit it head-on.

Twenty-three

Annie spotted the wreck. Her hands shook as she grabbed her cell phone and dialed 911. She grabbed Phil's arm as he veered over into the left lane and parked on the grass. "That's Maddie's Jeep."

Phil threw open the door. "We knew they were in trouble. It's just a different kind of trouble. Let's go."

Annie raced toward the vehicle, horrified by the crushed metal and broken glass. The front of the Jeep, crumpled like an accordion, rested against a huge tree stump. The front windshield had shattered and a starlike pattern obscured the driver's side window. The opaque nature of the glass kept Annie from getting a good look inside. All she could see was the deployed air bag and a lot of blood.

Lord, let her be alive, Annie prayed.

Phil grabbed the door handle. It wouldn't budge. The front and side fender had bent the door panel inward.

"We need to get in there." Annie tried to peer into the car and see if Maddie was breathing.

Wedged up against two small trees, the passenger side was inaccessible.

Annie could think of only one way inside. Racing to the back of the Jeep, she reached for the tailgate. It yielded under her hand and swung upward. She scrambled inside and over the backseat before she got her first look at the devastation.

Maddie lay slumped over the collapsed air bag, a steady stream of blood flowing from her forehead.

Annie placed two fingers on Maddie's neck and felt a pulse bounding rapidly under her fingers. "Maddie, it's Annie. Can you hear me?"

No response.

Phil appeared at the back door. "The fire department is on the way. They're going to need to cut her out. How is she?"

"Unconscious, but she's got a pulse."

"Good. You need to keep her spine from moving. Put one hand on either side of her head and hold it still. Keep talking to her. Help's on the way."

Annie held her friend's head immobile, chiding her gently. "Where were you going in such a hurry anyway?"

She thought she heard a low groan. "Maddie, don't move. We're going to get you to the hospital as soon as we can." Annie twisted backward. "How long until they get here?"

Phil leaned in. "Could be fifteen minutes. Since they closed the firehouse in the village, the ambulance and rescue truck have to come from Kerry."

Panic prickled Annie's spine. "And what are we supposed to do in the meantime?"

"Pray, Annie. We're supposed to give the care we can and pray."

Scott had never felt so helpless in his life. Standing on the roadside well back from the accident scene, he watched as firemen used the jaws of life to cut Maddie's Jeep apart. After what seemed an eternity they eased her out onto a backboard and strapped her to a stretcher.

Scott rushed toward the stretcher but Phil grabbed his arm, holding him fast.

"She's in good hands and you're with me." Phil grabbed the keys from Scott's hand and spun him toward the car.

Scott twisted back toward the wreck. "You said on the phone that she was okay."

"I said she was alive. Let's get going. Annie's going to follow in our car."

A siren's wail split the night. Flashing lights tainted the dark night, distorting images into fearful shadows. The ambulance pulled away, gaining speed as Phil bundled Scott into the passenger seat of his own car.

Phil didn't try to catch up with the ambulance.

Scott gripped the seat. "Can't we go any faster?"

"She's getting the care she needs and they'll need to examine her in the ER before they can tell us anything."

Scott's head lolled backward onto the headrest. His hand gripped the seat; his eyes focused on what stars he could see out the window. How had he let this happen? He'd let his anger eclipse his good sense. When Maddie had raced from the house he'd hesitated about going after her. He needed some time to cool off and so did she. But when it dawned on him just where she was going, Scott ran after her. Too late. Maddie's Jeep peeled down the drive. He should have gotten in his car and gone after her, but his pride wouldn't let him.

"This is my fault," Scott said aloud. "She was driving too fast because of me."

"You two had a fight?"

"Oh, yeah." Scott flattened his hands on his thighs as if urging the car to go faster. "I thought it would be different now."

Phil shot him a sober glance. "What would?"

"I tried what we talked about this morning." Was it only this morning? It seemed like a week ago.

"Tried what?"

"Asking God to help me put my marriage back together. So much for answered prayer because if this is it, I'm not talking to that guy ever again." A rough edge of anger crept into Scott's voice.

"God didn't do this to you, Scott. He may have allowed it to happen but he didn't do it to punish you."

"Kind of splitting hairs, aren't we?"

"God loves you, Scott, but he gave you free will. You made a decision to trust him this afternoon, but then what happened?"

"I came home and found my wife had spent the day with another guy."

"And you were mad?"

"Wouldn't you be?"

"What did you do with that anger?"

Scott flinched. "Okay, I may have said some things I didn't mean, but she's sleeping with the guy."

"Do you know that for a fact?"

"No." Scott hunkered down in the bucket seat. "So, you're saying this is my fault."

"No, I'm not. What happened today is the result of a thousand different choices you and Maddie made over the past few months, and all those choices came together tonight to produce a terrible accident."

"God could have stopped it."

Phil gripped the steering wheel, accelerating onto the highway where the faint lights of the ambulance flashed in the distance. "Yes, he could have, but God doesn't go around usurping your free will. Actions have consequences, Scott. God is ready to love you through them, but the physical consequences of our decisions are unavoidable. You and Maddie started down this road a long time ago."

Scott's shoulders sagged. "I know. So what do I do?"

Phil glanced over at him. "You had it right this afternoon. You have to trust God with your life, to help you make different choices."

"You think he'll hear the prayers of a screw-up like me?"

"He hears them all and he answers them all."

"But sometimes the answer isn't what we want."

"Not always," Phil admitted.

"I couldn't take that."

"Don't tell me; tell Him," Phil said.

Scott fell silent, the eerie yelp of the siren in the distance the only sound on the road. He knew he wasn't in any position to bargain with God. He'd ignored the Almighty for so many years he figured God didn't owe him anything. He could have prayed for God to save Maddie and promised he'd be the perfect husband in exchange, but somehow he knew that wasn't the right prayer for this moment. A week ago he would have raged at heaven with words and deals, but now his mind stilled and all his thoughts came together in one simple but desperate plea.

Lord, I trust you. Please save my wife.

Maddie awoke in a haze of pain. Her chest felt like she'd stepped into a pitcher's fastball and caught the full brunt on her sternum. Her shoulder burned and her head pulsed with pain. Still woozy, Maddie tried to talk, but though her lips moved, no sound came out.

Maddie's eyes flew open. Panic assailed her as she realized she had a tube down her throat. Her heart raced as she lifted a hand to pull it out, but her brain wasn't sending the right signals to her hand.

"She's awake, folks."

Maddie turned toward the voice, flinching at the searing pain that shot through her head at the simple movement. An older nurse with graying red hair and a nose full of freckles leaned into Maddie's sight line. "Welcome back. I'm Shirlie, and you're in Green Mountain Regional Hospital in the emergency room."

Maddie lifted her chin, trying to speak.

"We needed that tube to help you breathe while you were unconscious, but I think maybe we can take it out now. What do you think, Dr. Shin?"

An Asian woman with short black hair stepped to the bedside. "Her O2 sat is 100 percent. We can discontinue the endotracheal tube." Dr. Shin pulled on a pair of gloves. "I want you to cough very hard for me and we can take this out."

Maddie attempted a cough, and as she did so the doctor pulled the tube out in one swift motion.

"Better?" Dr. Shin asked.

Maddie nodded. "What happened to me?" Her voice, even at a whisper, sounded hoarse and barely discernible.

But Dr. Shin understood. "You were in a car accident. You took a pretty bad blow to the head when you hit the window, but since you were wearing your seat belt and the air bag deployed, you don't have any internal bleeding or other serious injuries from the crash."

"So I'll be all right?" Maddie whispered.

Dr. Shin paused just a fraction of a second. "I believe your husband is waiting outside. I'm going to bring him in to discuss your follow-up care."

"Follow-up?"

"You can expect significant bruising to the chest and shoulder as well as the abdomen from the seat belt and the air bag. But why don't we talk about the rest of it when your husband gets here."

The rest of what? Maddie tried to concentrate on the doctor's words, but every muscle in her body hurt and her thoughts felt distant. It reminded Maddie of being a kid in the bathtub with her head under water while her mother was calling to her to get out. She could hear the words but they sounded distorted and far away. And what was that about follow-up care?

Maddie closed her eyes. Hopefully Scott would have better recall than she did when the doctor explained her discharge instructions. She drifted off in a fitful doze but opened her eyes when she heard Scott's voice.

"Thank God you're all right."

Maddie opened her eyes and stared up at her anxious husband. He captured her hand and leaned down close to her ear. "I'm sorry, Maddie, for everything I said, all the—"

"Mr. Alexander, please take a seat," Dr. Shin interrupted his apology. "We need to talk."

Even through the haze of painkillers, Maddie didn't like the sound of that.

Scott's hand covered hers, and he remained standing as he turned to give the doctor his attention.

"We did a chest X-ray when Maddie first came in to rule out any injury to the thoracic cavity, but what we found wasn't trauma induced. The X-ray revealed a small growth in her left lung."

Maddie's hand creased the white sheets in a death grip as a hoarse whisper escaped her lips. "Cancer?"

The doctor's dark eyes filled with sympathy though her words were frank. "Most likely, yes. It will take a biopsy to confirm the diagnosis. I've set it up for day after tomorrow. We need to observe you for the next twenty-four hours due to the nature of the head injury you sustained." Dr. Shin flipped through the chart. "9:00 a.m. on Friday, but I want you to know there's a very good chance that the growth is malignant."

Maddie cringed away from the one word she'd feared all her life. *Cancer.* Panic assailed her.

"But I never smoked," Maddie whispered, her throat sore and voice still raspy.

Dr. Shin nodded. "Though we all think of the direct link between cigarettes and lung cancer, we also find the disease in people with no history of smoking. So neither of you smoke?"

Scott shook his head. "I did for a while back in college but gave it up years ago."

"How about your family, Maddie? Did your parents smoke?"

Maddie nodded, remembering all the cocktail parties her parents had given when she'd sit on the stairs listening to drunken laughter and trying to peer through the haze of smoke that stopped just shy of the ceiling. "Secondhand smoke caused this?"

"It may have been a contributing factor. We'll know more tomorrow after we get the biopsy back. But I wanted you to be aware of what we're looking at here."

"Which is what exactly?" Scott hooked a stool with his foot and pulled it up close to the bed and sat down all without letting go of Maddie's hand.

"The tumor appears to be quite small, but if it is malignant, it will have to be removed along with a good deal of normal lung tissue to make sure it hasn't spread."

"Will I need chemotherapy?" Maddie glanced over at Scott and waited for the inevitable distance he usually managed to put between himself and any health crisis. To her surprise, she found all his attention riveted on the young doctor and her answer to the question.

Dr. Shin nodded. "Even if the closest lymph nodes are clear, a round of chemo may be in order in a patient your age, Maddie. But that won't be decided until the tumor is removed and staged."

"Did the accident make the situation with the tumor any worse?" Scott asked, leaning forward.

"On the contrary," Dr. Shin said. "The accident may have saved her life. These kinds of tumors can grow undetected until they are quite large and the prospect of a total removal very difficult. The chest X-ray revealed a small but significant lesion. Without that test it might have been years before the tumor grew large enough to produce symptoms that would have sent you to a doctor."

Maddie shivered, just wanting to be rid of the growth in her chest. Panic tightened her throat as a cold sweat drenched her body. It was growing inside her, getting bigger by the day and she would die if it didn't come out soon. Anger surged through her and for a disjointed moment Maddie felt at odds with her own body.

Much like she felt at odds with the man who held her hand.

"We'll get through this together, Maddie," Scott said. "Thank God we found it in time."

He was here now, handling the crisis with just the right measure of attentiveness and concern. And though Maddie didn't doubt his sincerity, she doubted Scott's ability to weather the long haul. The bloody dressings, the pain management, the throwing up.

Maddie's life was falling apart around her, her body racked with pain and her mind flooded with worry about herself, her future, her kids. What she needed was a lifeline to cling to, someone who would be with her no matter how ugly it got.

And despite his words, she wasn't sure Scott was up to the task.

Twenty-four

S till dazed, Scott stared at the doors leading out to the waiting room. Maddie was on her way upstairs for the night, where they would observe her for complications from the head injury.

Scott sagged against the wall. *Cancer.* How was he going to get through this?

The double doors in front of him swung open and a stretcher surrounded by paramedics rushed into the ER.

Scott waited for them to pass, then straightened his shoulders and walked on through.

"Is she all right?" Annie asked, getting to her feet when she spotted Scott.

Scott didn't know how to tell them, didn't know how he would tell Maddie's folks or the kids. Scott closed his eyes in pain. Kylie and Shaun. This was going to tear them apart.

A hand touched his shoulder, steering him over to a nearby chair. Scott collapsed into it, looking into the worried faces of these two wonderful friends.

"She's banged up from the accident but no serious injuries." Scott's hand shook. He gripped the arm of the chair. "But she's got cancer, they think. In one lung. They found it when they did a chest X-ray."

Annie sank onto the seat next to him. "But it's treatable, right?"

Scott nodded. "They think they caught it early. She'll need surgery and then chemotherapy, though they won't know for sure until they see exactly what kind of cancer it is."

"How's Maddie doing?"

"She's in shock. She didn't even ask her usual barrage of questions. The pediatrician used to say he was going to charge us for an extra appointment because Maddie asked so many questions." Scott tried to smile but couldn't.

"Think I could sneak up and see her?" Annie asked.

"You could try. She's on the fourth floor, but I have no idea how to

142

get there."

Annie dropped a quick kiss on his cheek. "Don't worry. I know the way." And with that she was gone, a woman on a mission to see her friend.

Scott leaned back and straightened his legs out in front of him, his head falling backward in weary repose. "Thanks for waiting, Phil."

"No problem," Phil said, taking the seat next to him.

Scott closed his eyes, the weight of the day a burden that pinned him to the chair. Was it only this morning he and Maddie had been headed to Maine? It seemed eons ago. Even the fight they'd had just hours ago seemed a distant memory in light of the news.

"How are you doing?" Phil asked quietly.

"The truth? I'm reeling." Scott stared up at the ceiling tiles. "I love her. I think I've only realized how much in the last few days, but this chemo scares me. I don't know if I can handle it. I know that sounds shallow and selfish . . ."

"It sounds real to me. You wouldn't be human if you weren't scared."

Scott turned to his friend. "No, you don't get it. I mean I literally lose my lunch whenever I have to deal with any kind of illness. Just the sound of someone throwing up makes me puke. I don't know if I can do this."

"You can. It just won't be easy."

"Maybe I could hire nurses to take care of Maddie after her surgery?"

"How do you think Maddie would like that?"

"She'd hate it. She won't even have a cleaning lady once a week because she doesn't want strangers in the house."

"Kind of lets out the nurse idea then, wouldn't you say? Maddie needs to be as comfortable as possible during this process because it's going to be brutal." Phil didn't mince words as he continued. "If you want to show her you love her, you'll do the tough jobs no matter what it takes. This is your family. Maddie's taken care of you for years; now it's your turn." Phil clapped a hand to his shoulder. "And we're here to help."

"I know that, thanks." Scott straightened in his chair, craning his neck to release the cramped muscle at the base of his skull. "And thanks for not hitting me with the God talk. Any other Christian would be spouting the gospel trying to convert me right about now."

"I don't have to." Phil smiled, a brief upward turn of his lips though his eyes were serious. "God's already got a claim on your heart and he's never going to let you go."

"When did that happen?"

"When you asked him in."

Scott glanced over at Phil, massaging the back of his neck with one hand. "And then I went right back to my old ways."

"Maybe so. We all mess up. But when you prayed, you truly wanted God to change you, right?"

"Yes."

"And God never refuses a prayer like that. I'd say you're stuck with Him now and the good part is you'll never be alone again."

Phil's words settled into Scott's brain, and a wave of relief washed over him. He wasn't alone. He'd prayed that prayer out of desperation, not knowing how truly desperate his life would become just hours later. But desperate or not, if sincerity mattered he'd committed himself to making a change. For the first time in hours Scott felt the load lighten just a bit. He wasn't alone. Maybe with God's help he could do this.

Annie stepped off the elevator as a familiar figure exited the stairwell and started down the fourth floor hallway.

Annie sprinted after him and grabbed his arm. "Adam, you can't go in there."

He shook off her grip, his angry expression laced with fear. "She'll want to see me."

"Not tonight. I'll tell her you were here, and if she wants to see you I'm sure she'll call." Annie stopped short. "How did you know she was here?"

Adam glanced at the nurses' station and then down the hallway. "I have a receiver tuned to the police band in my car so I don't miss anything newsworthy. When I heard the call go out for the extrication unit to respond to Lake Shore Road, I drove out to see what kind of story it might make."

Annie had seen the wreck and she knew just how he must have felt when he realized the car was Maddie's.

Adam took a step back, a tight-lipped frown sharpening the angle of

144

his jaw. "I knew she didn't walk away from that accident, so I came here. A friend in admission gave me the room number."

"She's all right, Adam."

He tensed, glancing down the hall again, clearly impatient to be on his way but wanting as much information as he could get before walking into Maddie's room. "Then why is she still here?"

"They're keeping her for observation. She hit her head pretty bad."

"So she'll be going home tomorrow—all the more reason I need to see her tonight."

Annie knew she couldn't physically prevent him from seeing Maddie, but she felt as compelled to intervene now as earlier she had felt compelled to pray. "She won't be going home tomorrow, and right now she needs to rest."

"I won't stay long."

"I thought you two already said your good-byes."

"We did, but that doesn't mean I can stop caring about her. I love her, Annie, and I think there's a very good chance she loves me too."

Annie flinched. Was that what Maddie and Scott had fought about? Was she leaving Scott for Adam?

Adam started down the hall and then turned abruptly. "Why won't she be going home tomorrow?"

"Because the doctor needs to run a few more tests. They found something they weren't expecting."

"What did they find?"

"I can't tell you that, Adam." Annie approached him, willing to plead if that's what it took to get him to leave Maddie alone. "Maddie needs her family right now, and you are no part of that family. You say you love her, and I believe you because I know how easy she is to love, but her husband is right downstairs and her children will be coming soon and none of them need you here to make a hard situation even worse."

"Maddie needs me."

"No, she doesn't. You want her to need you but she doesn't. She has all she'll ever need this side of heaven right here in her family and if she forgot for a few weeks just how precious it is, that car accident tonight just reminded her. Go home, Adam."

His shoulders sagged, his handsome face an agony of pain. "Will you tell her I was here?"

Annie nodded. "I don't make Maddie's decisions for her, and I will tell her, but then you need to let this be her decision. If she wants to be in touch with you she will, and if not then you need to let her go."

"All right, I won't call her, but I'm betting she calls me."

"Maybe she will. But let me ask you something," Annie said quietly. "I've heard a little about your family from some of the people in the show . . ."

"Rita, right?"

Annie smiled. "Right. She does love to talk." Her smile faded. "How would you have felt as a young boy if some man had tried to come between your father and your mother?"

"I would have wanted to kill him."

"Then why would you want to put some other child through that. Maddie's family is not so different than the one you grew up in. Don't try and take that away from them."

Annie watched the parallel take root in his mind and the realization of its truth dawn in his eyes before he turned and walked back the way he had come.

Twenty-five

Scott met Kylie at the door Friday afternoon. She breezed into the house, her face tan and her mood upbeat. "Did Kevin call?" she asked, dumping her bags in the hallway and heading for the phone. "No, he didn't."

"Then I'd better call him. We had kind of said we might get together tomorrow night. Just movies and maybe some pizza afterwards."

Something in her breezy chatter made Scott pause. He didn't know if she was lying. He couldn't tell, but right now he had bigger problems to deal with.

"Kylie, sit down for a minute."

"Can't, Dad, I've got a hundred things to do today. I need to stop by school and get my last paycheck from the camp director and then I need a ride to the mall. Where's Mom?" Kylie stopped short and turned on him with a questioning glance. "And what are you doing home on Friday?"

Scott followed her into the kitchen and took a seat at the counter, nudging the stool closest with his foot. "Kylie, sit."

She did, sitting on the edge of the stool like a horse at the starting gate, ever muscle primed to run.

Scott searched for a good way to tell her the news and finding no such eloquence, he just laid it out. "Kylie, Mom's in the hospital."

All the energy of moments earlier seemed to drain from her body as she gingerly leaned on the counter, her eyes wide. "What happened?"

"She was in a car accident."

Kylie's hands clutched the edge of the stool. "But she's all right?"

"She's pretty banged up. Her injuries weren't serious, but there's—"

Kylie splayed her hands on the countertop. "She hit that big old tree trunk on Lake Shore, didn't she? I saw it on the way home. There's still tire marks on the road. Larkin's mom said it must have been some tourist who doesn't know the road because anyone who lives here never would have been going so fast." Kylie stared at him, her eyes growing wide. "Why was she going so fast? Did you two have another fight?"

"Hold on, Bug—"

"Don't treat me like I'm some little kid. Do you think I don't hear you two fighting all the time?"

"Whoa, hold on, Kylie. I know you must be scared, but you don't need to go looking for someone to blame . . . ."

"Do you know what it feels like to live in this house and hear you two fight or worse, not talk to each other at all?"

Scott felt like he'd opened a floodgate. Where was all this coming from?

But Kylie was on a roll. "I'm sick of hearing you fight over why you never come home. Why don't you stop hurting each other and just go ahead and get a divorce?"

"Well, you almost got your wish," Scott snapped, wishing as soon as the words were out that he could take them back. He shouldn't play into her anger. He needed to be the parent here, the calm role model. How did Maddie deal with Kylie every day? Her moods ran to polar extremes, and their gravitational force just sucked you in.

Kylie's anger drained away, taking with it the color from her face. "You fought about Adam, didn't you?"

Scott froze.

Her hollow voice was more a plea than a whisper. "She swore to me that she wouldn't see him again."

Scott reeled backward at her words. "You knew about Adam?"

"I saw them together once."

"What were they doing?"

Kylie straightened, her eyes taking on a hooded appearance. "Just eating at the diner."

Scott's face flushed with rage and embarrassment that his daughter would have witnessed this. The accident and the subsequent diagnosis had driven from his mind all the rage about Maddie and Adam, but now it returned full throttle.

"I'm sure she meant it when she told me it was over," Kylie whispered, her eyes brimming with tears. "She wouldn't lie to me. She never lies."

"It's okay, Kylie. You don't have to defend her."

"I didn't mean what I said before about getting a divorce."

"I know that, Ky. But you should think before you let that stuff fly out of your mouth because sometimes you can't take it back."

148

"I'm sorry." Where moments ago she had let her teenage outrage rain down on him, now with her legs dangling and her head bent forward, her dark hair not quite covering the tears that slipped from her eyes, she looked like a scared little girl.

Drawn to her, Scott stood and slipped an arm around her trembling shoulders. "It'll be all right, Bug. I'm not going anywhere."

"What about Mom?"

The word *cancer* flashed like a neon sign in his mind, its brightness blotting out his rage. Scott didn't know what the future held for them, but he knew what his daughter needed to hear.

"Mom's not going anywhere either. We'll work through it together," Scott said.

Kylie threw her arms around him and buried her face in his chest. "Do you know what Shaun prays for at night, Dad?"

Scott kissed the top of her head. "No, what?"

Kylie wiped her nose with the back of her hand. "He asks God to keep us all together and to make you and Mom love each other again."

Scott's heart ached at her words as he held his daughter and offered up his own version of that same prayer.

Lord, I know You don't want this marriage to fail through my neglect or my anger. Show me how to love my wife again. Show me how to love and protect my kids through Maddie's illness. Make her well, Lord, and restore us as a family. Amen.

All Maddie wanted was to go home. She had been poked and X-rayed, had IVs started and blood drawn. They'd given her drugs before the biopsy, and she remembered little of the procedure, which was a good thing because she was starting to feel like her body wasn't her own. Every muscle in her back and chest ached from the crash, and she couldn't even make it across the room by herself. Pushing the head of her bed up with the controller, Maddie swung her feet to the floor, determined to make it to the bathroom and at least brush her teeth. A wave of dizziness made the room spin.

"Whoa, I'm sure you're not allowed to be walking alone," Annie said, breezing into the room. "Where's Scott?"

"Gone home to meet Kylie." Maddie gulped in a breath and blew it out slowly. "She's due home from the beach this afternoon but we decided to only mention the accident and not the biopsy, at least until we hear the results."

"Any word yet?" Annie asked, setting down two coffee cups on the bedside table.

"Not yet. The surgeon said he should have it back by the end of the day and then we'd meet and discuss possible options."

"Sounds clinical. How are you doing?"

"Scared. Terrified, actually. The only time I've ever been in the hospital was to have my kids, and they kicked you out the door after forty-eight hours. This seems like an eternity to me, and if I have to have surgery I'll be here even longer."

Annie patted her arm. "Slow down."

"What if it is cancer?"

"It's a diagnosis, not a death sentence. Remember that."

"But if it's cancer . . ."

"Not all cancers kill," Annie said, taking a seat on the bed next to Maddie. "They change your life, make you look at things differently, but they don't always take your life; in fact, sometimes they give it back to you."

Her voice was so small, Maddie had to strain to hear the last words and when she did, she could hardly believe them. How could cancer be life giving? But something in the set of Annie's shoulders and the slight quiver in her tone gave Maddie a sudden insight.

"Sounds like you're talking from experience."

Annie nodded. "I am."

"You've had cancer?"

"A precancerous condition actually, and of a very strange kind." Annie brought her knee up on the bed, turning to Maddie. "I'll tell you about it sometime when you're feeling better."

"I'd like to hear about it now if you want to tell me. I could use something to think about besides myself."

"Okay." Annie reached for her coffee cup and handed one to Maddie. "I've never told anyone this story before."

Maddie nodded, curiosity overcoming her earlier terror as she settled back against the raised bed.

"You know that the reason Phil and I are trying to adopt a baby is because we can't have one of our own."

Maddie nodded, sipping her coffee. Annie's infertility wasn't a secret, but she had never wanted to talk about the underlying cause.

"It probably didn't help that we married late. We both knew we wanted kids, and we thought all we'd have to do was stop the birth control, but it didn't work out that way." Annie fiddled with the plastic cover on her cup.

Maddie couldn't help but think about how she and Scott hadn't even been trying to get pregnant when they found out Kylie was on the way.

"We tried on our own for a few months," Annie continued, "and then we started seeing an infertility specialist. She did the usual work-ups and then tried me on Clomid, which was popular at the time, but nothing worked. We'd wait every month, praying my period wouldn't come. I even went so far as to make a deal with God, promising I'd become a strict churchgoer if he'd give us a child."

"You did?"

Annie smiled a crooked grin. "You've only known me as a Christian, but back then I had only a passing acquaintance with the Almighty. Anyway, we were talking about trying in vitro fertilization and wondering where we would get the money to pay for it when we found out I was pregnant."

Maddie knew this story didn't have a happy ending. "Did you miscarry?"

Annie shook her head, her red hair falling around her face and lending a touch of color to her pale cheeks. "We were so excited, making all kinds of plans like all couples do for their first baby. I was even starting to show early. It was all going so well until I started getting sick."

"Like morning sickness?"

"Worse, much worse. I literally couldn't hold anything down and then I started bleeding. When they admitted me to the hospital I was severely dehydrated and my blood pressure was very high."

"What kind of tests did they do?"

"They scheduled me for a sonogram. I'll never forget that morning. The lab tech put this gel on my belly and ran the scanner across it, and we could tell by the look on her face that something was wrong." Annie shivered at the memory. "She told us she needed another opinion and she left to get a doctor, who then called in another colleague to confirm his diagnosis. The second doctor they brought in was an oncologist."

Maddie suspected the pregnancy had to be terminated but an oncologist? "What happened?"

"What was growing inside me was called a hydatidiform mole. I wasn't pregnant at all, but I had a precancerous growth in my uterus that

151

needed to be removed and quickly. Twenty percent of such cases develop into a full-blown cancer, some with metastasis to other areas of the body."

"Oh, Annie." Maddie reached out and covered Annie's hand with her own.

"They scheduled a D&C for later that day, a routine procedure that should have had me out of the hospital the next morning, but I had a very rare complication and bled heavily on the table during the procedure. So heavily that they had to perform a hysterectomy."

Maddie didn't know what to say. "Annie, I'm so sorry."

Annie looked up at her. "Thank you, but I'm not sorry it happened. That event, gruesome as it was, changed my life."

How could she be grateful for the loss of her uterus and the end to her dreams of having a child? Maddie couldn't imagine gratitude, even in retrospect, to such a heart-wrenching event. And yet Annie looked perfectly serene, as if she meant every word.

"At the time, though, you must have been so angry."

"Angry? I was furious. I couldn't understand why this had happened to us. And I blamed God, big-time. He didn't give us the baby we'd been praying for. I decided that God couldn't possibly love us if he allowed all this suffering in our lives."

"And how did Phil handle it?"

"Better than I did. He didn't blame God for our troubles, and he had a kind of peace that made me want to kill him. At first I thought he didn't care that we'd lost our only chance at ever having a child." Annie picked at the nubby cotton blanket on the bed. "It wasn't that he didn't care, but all his attention was focused on me and making sure I got well. It put a huge strain on our relationship. I was still mourning the future we would never have, and he was just trying to get me through each day."

Maddie flashed back to the conversation she and Annie had earlier in the week about God's ability to save shattered marriages. Maddie had wondered then how Annie had come to have such strong faith and it looked like she was about to find out. "So what happened to change your mind because I know you don't feel like that now? I've never met anyone who loves God as much as you do."

Annie smiled. "I'm glad it shows, but after the hysterectomy I blamed God for everything. I was recovering from major surgery and add to that the terrible anxiety of waiting to see if I'd be part of the 20 percent who develop cancer. I had to go for blood work every two weeks and the waiting for the results was agony. I felt like I had a time bomb planted inside me, and all I wanted was to get it out."

Maddie nodded. She knew that feeling.

"All that worry took its toll. I fell into a deep depression after the surgery. There were some days I barely made it out of bed, and most days I didn't even bother to shower. I was on medical leave from my teaching job and I decided I was never going back to teach other people's kids when I would never have one of my own. I was so bitter and my life was so dark. It was like living deep underwater beyond where the sun reaches. Every movement was such an effort, from walking downstairs to doing a simple thing like making breakfast."

"Phil must have been crazy with worry about you."

"He was, and I didn't care. He tried to get me to see a doctor but I refused. Later he brought me information on support groups for women who had miscarried, but I screamed at him and told him I didn't belong there because I'd never even been pregnant."

Maddie couldn't imagine Annie screaming at anyone, much less the man she adored.

Annie grimaced. "I'll never forget the look on his face. It was like I'd slapped him. All he was trying to do was help me and I was pushing him away with both hands. But when I saw the look on his face, saw the pain I was causing him, something in me wanted to fight to get my life back. But the darkness doesn't go away just because you want it to. I was still spiraling down and I couldn't seem to make it stop. I wanted my life back, not the life I'd dreamed of having with a baby but the life I'd already had with Phil. Finally, I even agreed to see a psychiatrist, who put me on medication for depression. But still I couldn't manage to even get out of bed most days."

Outside the room, a laundry cart trundled by the door and the overhead pager sounded, but Maddie barely noticed as Annie lifted her head and met Maddie's gaze.

"Finally, out of desperation I turned to God and prayed. I had seen the difference he had made in Phil's life and I wanted that for myself."

"So you made a deal with God and asked Him to heal you?"

"No, I literally got down on my knees and told Him I was sorry," Annie said.

"Sorry for what?" Maddie couldn't see where, in that scenario, other than screaming at her husband, Annie had done anything wrong. She was the victim.

"I told God I was sorry for living my life without giving Him a second thought, for only calling on Him in times of trouble. I'd sat in church with Phil for years and heard all about the love of God and I'd never let it into my heart." Annie's hand closed in a fist. She gently struck her chest as if illustrating the point. "I'd heard how Christ died for my sins, yet I had never accepted the gift of salvation He died to give me. And so that day I did. I accepted the gift. I thanked Him for it and opened my heart to Him. It says in the Bible, 'I stand at the door and knock; if anyone hears my voice and opens the door I will come in and dine with him and he with me.' "

"And did you get better after that?"

"No, not for quite a while afterward, but I clung to the trust I had placed in the Lord that day, knowing He was with me through it all. And after many months and several different medications the darkness began to lift."

Maddie leaned forward. "And weren't you ever tempted to go back to your old ways?"

"Sure, I still am sometimes, but what I had learned in the darkness was that God was the only light I needed. He healed my spirit and eventually my body and gave me back the man I loved. I could never walk away from that, not then and not now."

The hallway door swung open. A Middle Eastern man with coffee skin and a balding head advanced into the room. "Mrs. Alexander?"

Maddie recognized Dr. Akmed from the morning's procedure.

"Is your husband available? I have the results of your biopsy."

Maddie's voice was just above a whisper. "He's gone home to my daughter."

Annie reached for her hand and Maddie held on tight.

"I'm afraid the results are as we suspected. The growth is malignant. We'll need to schedule you for surgery as soon as possible."

Twenty-six

Maddie pressed her hand to her incision site as Scott held the door open for her. Had she only been gone a week? It seemed like so much longer. But the house looked the same, maybe a bit cleaner, but all Maddie could think about was sitting down. Her side ached from the incision, and she wondered if it was time for another painkiller.

But sitting wasn't an option as Shaun and Kylie skidded to a stop in the foyer with Annie right behind them.

Shaun ran to Maddie and would have hugged her had Scott not stepped in front and gone down on one knee to greet their son. "Shaun, how about you take Mom in the family room and help her get settled on the couch," Scott said.

Shaun blinked, his eyes filled with tears. "Are you okay?"

Maddie held out her hand, and Shaun grasped it like a lifeline. "I'm doing fine, Bud, but a little pampering and a pillow wouldn't hurt."

Shaun grinned. "I've got just the one to make you feel better." He squeezed her hand and dashed up the stairs.

Maddie watched him go. Her eyes stung as her gaze shifted to Kylie. She hung back, unsure what to do; then she hurried forward and kissed Maddie on the cheek.

"I'm glad you're home," Kylie whispered.

"Me, too." Maddie wrapped an arm around her as they walked into the family room.

Kylie eased her down onto the couch. Maddie managed to stifle a gasp as she sank into the soft surface. Shaun came racing down the stairs with something hidden behind his back. Pulling up short, he revealed his surprise with a shy smile.

"Try this for your side, Mom." He held out a blue-and-white pillow with swimming fishes and dancing crabs embroidered on the front. Maddie instantly recognized the pillow as part of the infant crib set in Shaun's room the day they'd brought him home from the hospital. He'd had it with him ever since and he never went to sleep without that pillow.

"Thank you." Maddie patted the couch beside her.

Shaun perched carefully on the seat while Kylie sank to the floor by her feet.

After an awkward silence, Kylie asked the question on all their minds. "So, Mom, did they get it all?"

Maddie ran a hand over Kylie's hair. "The doctor told your dad and me that the operation was a complete success. They removed the growth and a wide margin of clean tissue around it."

"So, if they got it all, do you still need chemo?" Kylie asked.

Maddie nodded. "I need to do it just to be sure."

"Will your hair fall out?" Shaun's chin quivered.

"I think so, Bud. Maybe I could borrow your Sox cap."

"Or maybe we could go shopping for a wig," Kylie suggested with a smile.

"And stop for a few pair of shoes on the way home." Maddie loved her daughter's answering grin, feeling like they were conspirators in a plot to max out her credit cards.

"Are you hungry?" Kylie bounded to her feet.

"A little, but I don't think I could move right now." Maddie shifted on the couch.

"You're fine just where you are. Come on, Shaun."

He slipped off the couch and raced after his sister.

Maddie threw Annie a questioning glance.

Annie smiled. "They've been planning this all week. It's a surprise."

"Thanks."

"Don't thank me. I'm not the one who thought it up, but I enjoyed helping out," Annie said.

Shaun and Kylie returned to the family room moments later. He carried an old patchwork quilt they used to use on vacation at the beach and she held a large wicker picnic basket.

Looking at the basket, Maddie couldn't help but recall her picnic with Adam. But watching her children fuss over the arrangement of the blanket and the filling of the plates, Maddie pushed aside the guilt and concentrated all her attention on her kids.

"What a great idea," Maddie exclaimed as Kylie handed her a plate with fried chicken, potato salad, and coleslaw. The menu seemed familiar. Maddie wondered if it was a coincidence that she was about to eat the same dinner she had prepared for Scott earlier in the summer and never had the chance to eat. "Who came up with the menu?"

156

"Dad did," Shaun piped in. Maddie met Scott's gaze, but he merely shrugged and smiled, then continued to pile food on his plate.

"And wait'll you see what's for dessert—brownies smothered in chocolate sauce and whipped cream."

"You weren't supposed to tell her," Kylie said, swatting his head.

Shaun ducked. "Sorreeee. I didn't think it was a secret."

Maddie smiled, feeling right at home amidst the squabbling.

Scott appeared at her side and handed her a glass of apple juice. "Should I get the Percocet?"

Maddie shook her head and took a sip. "I'm okay for now. Maybe after we eat. So, this was your idea?"

Scott nodded, taking the glass from her and setting it on the table. "I had a little help with the cooking." He inclined his head toward Annie, who was quizzing the kids about the start of school next week.

"She's a good friend." Maddie tried a forkful of potato salad. "And she can cook too."

"Personally I like yours better but don't tell her." Scott eased down to sit with his back against the arm of the couch, his head just inches from Maddie's knee.

Maddie started in on the chicken. "So when do you have to go back to work?"

"The beginning of next week."

"I'm surprised they're not demanding you come in today."

"Actually Rob's been okay about my taking off once I explained the situation."

Maddie stared down at the top of Scott's head. "That doesn't sound like Rob."

"People surprise you sometimes."

Maddie frowned. Not Rob Sanders. That guy was as close to a workaholic as Maddie had ever seen, and he'd been leading Scott down the same road. Maddie wondered if Scott was putting on a good face because of her diagnosis. He certainly had been attentive to her every need lately, but Maddie was sure he must be champing at the bit to get back to work and leave the housework behind.

They ate in silence for a minute. Maddie tried to think of something to say but couldn't come up with something that the setting didn't rule out. She couldn't talk about how the kids were doing emotionally, not with them sitting a few feet away, and Scott wasn't likely to have the answer in any case. It was doubtful he'd done more than gloss over the whole situation with them. He wasn't exactly a feelings kind of guy.

"Anybody ready for dessert?" Shaun leaned over to inspect their plates.

"We will be in a minute," Scott answered. "You and Kylie could bring it in if you want."

"Just don't make me touch the whipped cream," Kylie said, getting to her feet. "I hate that stuff."

"Don't worry; that's my department." Annie joined the kids in the kitchen.

Maddie watched her go. "I don't know how we would have gotten through this without her."

Scott nodded, setting his empty plate aside. "She's been so great about helping out. But she can't do it much longer. She needs to get back to the store."

"I know. I should be fine in a few days."

Scott glanced over his shoulder. "I was thinking we could hire someone to help out for a while."

Maddie stiffened. "I don't think that's necessary. I can do it, maybe with a little extra help from the kids."

"This is a big house, Maddie. Once you start on the chemo you won't have the energy to do it, even with the kids' help."

"I don't like the idea of some stranger washing our clothes and cleaning up after us."

"Don't you think these are extraordinary circumstances? We might have to think about trying something different for a few months."

Maddie fought down a wave of tears. Maybe it was the anesthesia but ever since the surgery the least little thing could set her off. "We've talked about this before. No one is going to be able to do things the way I like them done."

"So maybe you'll relax your standards a little, just for a while." Scott got to his feet, his jaw set and a hint of exasperation coloring his tone. He reached for her plate. "And let's face it; we're going to need help with the kids. Driving them around like you usually do every fall isn't going to work this year."

Sitting on the couch staring up at him, Maddie felt small and vulnerable, but instead of reacting with tears, anger seeped from her pores and out of her mouth. "What's the real reason you want to hire a housekeeper? So you can go back to spending three nights a week in Boston and not have to worry about what's going on here?"

Scott stiffened at her attack. "I've been home for more than a week now. What more do you want?"

"I want you to be here for the kids."

"I will be."

"Not if there's someone here to do the job for you."

"Come on, Maddie, give me a little credit. I'm trying here."

"For now," Maddie whispered under her breath.

Scott scowled at her. "You'll say anything to get your way. Fine, I won't hire anyone to help. You can do it all yourself."

"Fine, that's all I wanted."

"Mom?" Shaun stood in the family room, his brow furrowed, his hands filled with two plates heaped high with brownies and whipped cream. "You aren't mad at Dad, are you? This whole thing was his idea."

Maddie felt like a shrew. "No, Shaun, of course I'm not mad. Your Dad and I are just trying to work out . . ."

Kylie rounded the counter and banged two dessert plates down on the counter. "Nothing ever changes around here. I should have known better than to think it would." She stalked upstairs.

Maddie stared after her, knowing she had ruined her own homecoming.

Shaun stepped up beside her, extending the hand that held one gooey desert. His lower lip trembled. "I don't want things to change around here. I like them fine just the way they are."

Scott walked Annie to her car. "Listen, thanks for everything you've done this week. I really appreciate your help."

"My pleasure." Annie reached into her pocket for her keys. "Would you mind if I made an observation?"

"Go ahead." Scott knew she'd overheard the earlier argument but supposed Annie had earned the right to take him down a peg for getting angry with his sick wife.

"She's scared, Scott." Annie unlocked her car and pulled open the door, leaning on the door frame between them. "Underneath all that anger is a woman so scared of needing anyone that she's pushing you away. and she doesn't even know she's doing it."

Annie's remark floored him with its simplicity. Scott leaned against the car's hood. "I get that, Annie. I'd be scared too, but even knowing that, I still react. Maddie has always known just what button to push to get me riled."

"You two have a long history together, and not all of it positive, but remember, Scott, that you're a new man now. When you chose to ask God into your life, you became a new creation, and that means you need to ask Him to help you find new ways of reacting to old situations."

Scott stuck his hands into the front pockets of his jeans. "I'm trying, but what do I get for it? A lot of lip. I was just trying to hire a housekeeper to make it easier on her."

"And on you."

"Okay, you're right. It would be easier for me if I knew the kids and the house were okay when I go back to work. But the way she talks you'd think I was never planning on coming home again."

"Because she's scared of being sick and alone. Have you ever been scared of being alone, Scott?"

Scott flinched, grinding the gravel with the heel of his shoe. "Yeah, when my dad left. I used to lay awake at night and wonder what would happen to my sister and me if my mom left us like my dad had."

"And if he'd come back, would you have trusted him right away?"

"No way." Scott shook his head emphatically. "I would have wondered when he'd do it again."

"Exactly. Maddie needs you now, Scott, but she's afraid to trust you."

"So what do I do?"

"Respect her wishes and prove her wrong. Show her she can trust you. Be here every night, no matter what."

"And what about the kids and the house? Who'll take of them?"

"You leave that to me."

"She won't let a stranger into the house."

"I know that. She won't have a stranger; she'll have me."

Scott met her determined gaze. "Annie, you can't do that; it's too much."

"I want to do it for her." Annie met his gaze. "Do you know what it means to have a servant's heart, Scott?"

"No clue."

"It means to serve another out of love, not duty or obligation. I think I'm just starting to understand what that means. So let me do this for Maddie."

"How could I refuse an offer like that?"

"You can't. See, Maddie's not the only one who gets what she wants." Annie ducked into the car with a grin.

She was halfway down the driveway before the smile faded from Scott's face. A servant's heart. Did he have it? No. He knew he loved Maddie, but caring for her with that kind of unselfish love was new to him. Could he even do it?

Not on his own. But with God's grace it might be possible.

Twenty-seven

Kylie curled up on her bed, the phone to her ear. She hadn't seen Kevin since her mom's accident had put a hold on their plans for a night together at Kevin's house.

"It's like they don't even like each other," Kylie said, venting her frustrations. "We put together this whole picnic to welcome her home. It was a great idea. Dad's idea really. Who knew he could think of romantic stuff like that? And then they still end up fighting."

"Tough break. So since the picnic was a bomb, does that mean you can sneak out for a while?" Kevin asked.

Kylie kicked off her shoes. "I don't know. Maybe."

"I've missed you, Ky. It's been a long time. I need to see you."

"I don't know if I can get away. I'll have to ask my dad. What did you have in mind?"

"How about I drive over and you meet me down at the boathouse?"

The boathouse. She should have seen that coming.

"How about you just come over here and we'll watch a movie or something?" she suggested.

"I don't want to butt in on your family when your mom just got home from the hospital."

It sounded logical, but Kylie wondered why she felt uneasy. "Like I said, I don't know if I can get out."

A knock sounded on the door. "Kylie, I need to talk to you."

What did her dad want? She didn't think he'd been in her room in years. Not since she outgrew the bedtime stories he used to read using all these weird voices that made her laugh.

"Hey, Ky, you going to meet me or not?" Kevin asked.

"Hold on. Can it wait, Dad? I'm on the phone."

The door swung open. "Who are you talking to?"

"Kevin."

Her father's eyes narrowed. "Well, I need to talk to you now so you can call him back."

Kylie sighed, picking up the phone. "I gotta go."

"Try and meet me. Say in an hour."

"I'll try." She punched the off button, trying to figure how to get out of the house. By the look on her dad's face the truth wasn't an option. "So what's up?"

Her dad came through the door, standing in the middle of the room. "You still seeing that guy?"

"Yeah."

He frowned. "I've never met him. He doesn't come around here much."

"He does sometimes but you're not here." Which wasn't exactly true. Kevin did stop by to pick her up, but they never hung out here. They always went to Kevin's house, where his parents never paid them much attention.

"How long have you two been going out?"

"We don't call it going out; we're just together."

"So how long have you been together?"

"Three months." It made Kylie feel older to hang out with a guy who had his license and drove a cool car. None of her friends were dating a senior.

"So you're pretty serious?"

"I guess." Kylie picked at chipped polish on her thumbnail.

"And he cares about what you care about?" Scott leaned back against her desk, crossing one foot over the other.

"I guess so."

"So he must have known how upset you were about your mom being in the hospital."

"Oh, yeah."

"But he never came by this week or offered to drive you to the hospital."

Kylie's hand stilled, dropping to the floral comforter. "He's busy with football. Practice started last week."

"I guess that explains it."

Kylie knew he was trying to make a point in his not-so-subtle dad kind of way, but what he'd said was true. She'd gotten a ride to the hospital with Annie and Phil, and a lot of her friends had sent cards and their parents had sent flowers, but she hadn't heard from Kevin until today.

"You deserve better, Bug," Scott said quietly.

"I think I've heard that before," she murmured.

"From your mother?"

"No, from a friend who gave me a ride home the other night."

"Sounds like someone you might want to listen to."

Kylie smoothed the comforter, but didn't bother to respond.

"Anyway, that wasn't why I came up here. I wanted your help with something." He pushed off the desk and took a step toward her.

Kylie looked up suspiciously. "My help?"

"You're old enough to know that things are going to be different around here for a while. When your mom starts her chemo, she's probably going to be real sick for at least a week after each treatment. She's going to be so tired she won't be able to do much but sleep." He looked right at her. "And that's where you come in."

"What do you want me to do?"

"Annie's going to be helping out around here, but she can't do it alone. She's going to need your help. Shaun, too."

"Sure."

"Annie won't ask for your help, so I want you to ask what she needs and I want you to be in charge of doing the laundry."

"All of it?"

"I know it's a lot. Your mom's always complaining about all of us wearing our clothes one time and then tossing them on the floor . . ." He smiled, a sad kind of grin.

"Or using a towel once and then hanging it on the door with the five other towels I used that week." Kylie frowned. "Nobody better do that while I'm in charge."

"See, you're into the job already. Now you have to stay with it for the long haul, okay?"

"I can do it, but how long do you think?"

"Could be six months. The chemo's going to be tough."

"But she'll be okay, right, Dad?"

"That's what I'm praying for, Bug."

Kylie sat up straight. "You're praying?"

"Lately, yes."

"Because of what happened to Mom?"

"That's part of it, but I started even before that. Prayer is just talking to God, and I hear he's a good listener. Anyway, I was thinking of taking you and Shaun to church this week."

"Really?"

"Sure, I think it's about time I check it out." Scott started toward the door and then turned back. "Ky, I really appreciate you helping out.

164

Have I told you lately how proud I am of you?"

"Not lately," Kylie said softly.

He stood awkwardly at the door with his hand on the knob. "Well, I am." He pulled the door open, and Kylie had to smile when he did this weird kind of wave thing with his hand. She stood staring at the door and then reached for her phone.

She'd forgotten to ask if she could go out. Kylie shrugged. Her dad would never let her. And she didn't want to concoct a story and lie to a man who had just told her, for the first time in forever, that he was proud of her.

Kevin would just have to wait.

Maddie perched on the kitchen stool and reached for the mail. Scott had sorted through the junk mail and thrown it out, but Maddie had insisted on paying the bills as usual. There wasn't much she could do for her family right now but this she could handle.

Behind her the sharp rev of floored engines and shifting gears peppered the air as Shaun took up his favorite pastime, video games. Maddie smiled. It was too loud, but she didn't care. She was just glad to be home.

Maddie quickly sorted through the substantial pile. Scattered in amongst the utility bills and credit card statements, Maddie discovered a number of get-well cards. She set these aside, saving them for after she'd opened everything else, like a fancy dessert after a hum-drum meal.

Many of the cards were from members of the choir at church. One was from Vincent, asking her to hurry back because they were lost without a soloist. She didn't recognize the handwriting on the last envelope, but her nerve endings tingled when she opened the card and glanced at the name.

Adam.

Maddie's hands trembled as she ran the tips of her fingers over the signature. Her heart raced as she turned her attention to the handwritten message.

Dear Maddie,

I hope you open your own mail because what I want to say is for your eyes only. I love you, Maddie. And the cancer doesn't change that. Yes, like any good reporter I have my sources. I know what you're going through. I've lived through it once and I'll do it again, but this time I won't let this disease take another woman I love. I'm in this for the long haul if you'll let me. Call me. Write. E-mail. Just let me know how you are and what I can do. It's going to take a lot of love to get you through this, to make you feel in the midst of it all that you are still the most beautiful, most desirable woman on earth. You always will be to me.
Adam

Maddie closed the card and laid it on the counter, her fingers splayed over its scenic cover as if she could absorb the love and energy it contained through the palm of her hand.

She'd thought about him often in the last week, and here was tangible proof that he'd been thinking about her too. But like the rest of her life, Adam had been eclipsed by her illness. She wondered what would have happened if the accident had not taken place, if she had made it to Adam's house that night? Would she have cooled off and changed her mind before she got over there? Or would she have thrown herself into his arms the moment he opened the door? More likely the latter. She'd been so mad at Scott that night she'd have done the one thing she knew would hurt him the most.

Maddie pressed her hand to her lips. If she'd made it to Adam's house that night, her happiness would have been short-lived. The doctors wouldn't have found the cancer. She might have walked around for a year without it producing any symptoms. And by then it would have been too late for successful treatment.

Maddie's heart beat hard and her breath came in short gasps. If she'd made it to Adam's house that night, she'd have died.

"Mom, you okay?" Shaun stood beside her, his eyes wide and voice anxious. "You're breathing really weird."

"No, I'm fine, Shaun, really."

"Maddie?" Scott came down the stairs at a run. "You okay?"

"Just a little tired is all," Maddie said, suddenly very conscious of the card beneath her hand.

"Then why don't you go up and take a nap? I'll take care of this later."

"You haven't paid a bill around here since we bought the house."

"I can learn. I have a college degree. It may not be in accounting, but I'm sure it'll get me through household budgeting." He held out a hand to her. "Hand them over."

Maddie froze, her face flushed with guilt before she realized he was talking about the bills piled high in front of her.

Maddie placed the other cards over Adam's and slipped them in her sweater pocket then picked up the bills, setting them on Scott's outstretched palm.

"You're sure about this?" She opened her mouth to say more and then clamped it shut.

"Yes, I'm sure and I promise we won't go bankrupt in the process."

Maddie's eyes widened.

"Read your mind, didn't I?" Scott laughed. "You are a control freak, you know that?"

Any other day Maddie might have taken offense at this remark, but today she heard his light joking tone and she responded in kind.

"Chapter Eleven is on your credit report for seven years. If you destroy our credit rating I'm going to be on your back for a lot longer than that."

"I hope so, Maddie."

Maddie glanced up at the sincerity in his tone. His gaze held hers and Maddie found she had to look away. Here she'd been daydreaming about Adam while Scott was trying his best to hold their family together. She owed him more than that.

"Scott, I'm sorry about before. I know you were just trying to help by hiring a housekeeper . . ."

"Don't worry; it's all taken care of."

Maddie squelched an annoyed response, striving for a calm she didn't feel. "I thought we were going to talk about this before you did anything."

"Don't worry. You won't have a stranger traipsing around here. Annie's going to help us out."

"Scott, we can't let her do that."

"That's just what I said, but she really wants to do this for you. She loves you and she knows you'll be crazy if the house is a mess and you can't do anything about it."

"So Annie's going to clean our house, scrub the bathrooms, and do the laundry?" Maddie said, her tone doubtful.

"Close. Kylie has agreed to take on the laundry and Shaun's going to be in charge of the garbage, getting it out of the house and bagged correctly and out to the curb for pickup."

"Really?"

"I think they even liked the idea of helping out. Like they were doing their part to help you get well." Scott set the bills down next to the computer.

"You think it'll work?"

"I do, and I'll be around to pick up the slack. Do the grocery shopping, make the dentist appointments, all that other stuff."

"You will?" Maddie said, unable to keep the doubt from her tone.

Scott stepped up to her chair and placed a hand under her elbow. "Yes, Maddie, I will. You can trust me. Now let's get you upstairs."

Maddie let Scott ease her off the stool. She had to admit it was easier with help.

"I can manage from here," she said, expecting Scott to agree wholeheartedly and move on into his office.

"You can, but it'll be easier and safer with a little help." Scott tucked his arm under hers and walked her to the stairway. "Hey, Shaun, how about you turn that down. Your mom's going to take a nap."

"Sure thing."

Upstairs Maddie sank onto the bed and gingerly lifted her legs onto the comforter, ready to admit the trip had taken more out of her than she'd thought. "Thanks."

"No problem." He stepped to the blanket chest, lifted the lid, and pulled out a soft fleece blanket. "Here try this. I'll wake you for dinner." And with that he was gone.

Maddie sank back into the pillows and slipped the card from her pocket. Staring down at it, she knew she couldn't do this. She couldn't deceive Scott anymore. She had made her choice that night in the cemetery and fate or God or destiny had intervened to keep her from making a mistake that would have cost her her life.

She owed the man she had married better than her divided heart. Scott was trying hard to do the right thing even if he didn't always know what that was. She owed him her fidelity: body, mind, and soul. She might never love him again. Once this crisis was past he would likely go back to his old ways and work until he dropped, but Maddie wouldn't cheat on him in her head or in her heart.

She tore the card in half and then in half again. And then, as if doubting her own fidelity in the days and weeks ahead, she tore the card into tiny pieces and tossed them in the trash can beside the bed.

Twenty-eight

Maddie had never felt so sick in her life. Lying in bed, she pulled her knees to her chest, hoping to ease the overwhelming nausea. She'd had her first chemo two days ago. They'd given her just enough time to heal from the surgery and then hit her with the potent drugs. Maddie had felt fine the first day but yesterday the overwhelming fatigue set in and the nausea made its debut. She knew the drugs were designed to kill the cancer, but today she felt like they were killing her.

From the bathroom a whiff of chlorine cleaner singed her nose and made Maddie's stomach clench in rebellion. She spotted Annie on her hands and knees cleaning around the base of the toilet. A wave of humiliation swept over Maddie. How could she let her friend do this? Maddie bit her lip. How could she not was a better question. She'd overestimated her recuperative powers. Sure she'd read the stories, the personal accounts of others who'd undergone chemo, but nothing in those graphic accounts prepared her for the sheer weight of the fatigue.

"How you doing?" Annie asked, coming into the room and closing the door behind her. Wisps of red hair poked out from beneath the white bandanna around her head. "Can I get you anything? Something to read or listen to? Maybe one of those books on tape?"

Maddie shook her head. "No, thanks."

"Scott's downstairs and he's going to pick Shaun up after school and take him over to watch Kylie's field hockey game. Will you be okay by yourself?"

Maddie nodded. "Fine. It's easier not to talk."

"Okay, then I'll see you later this week." Annie started toward the door and then came back and knelt by Maddie's bed, taking her hand. "I'm praying for you every night."

Maddie's eyes welled with tears. "I can use all the prayers I can get."

Annie patted her hand. "Rest easy, and remember Phil and I love you very much."

Maddie forced her cheek muscles into a smile. "Thanks."

Moments later, a wave of nausea gripped her belly. Maddie's mouth began to water. She rolled from the bed and stumbled toward the bathroom. Her shoulder hit the closed door as she reached for the knob. Covering her mouth with her free hand, she tried to stop the inevitable.

The door flew open under her weight and Maddie fell to her knees in front of the toilet, barely managing to lift the lid before what little she'd eaten for breakfast made its reappearance. With a stomach flu when you threw up, you actually felt better. But this was different. Maddie clutched the cold porcelain as wave after wave of nausea made her retch long after there was anything there to come up.

A cool hand on the side of her face pulled her hair back into a ponytail. The fresh air on her cheek felt like a blessing, and Maddie thanked God for Annie's kindness.

A large hand rubbed her back. Maddie stiffened, her humiliation complete when she heard his words. "It's okay, Maddie."

Scott? What was he doing here? Maddie cringed. She would have asked him to leave if not for the spasm that ripped through her chest, making her retch yet again.

And she couldn't stop. But the firm hand gently rubbing her back kept her centered. He didn't say another word, but his solid presence reminded her that this wouldn't last forever. A few more minutes maybe. Then she'd be back in bed. And just as if wishing could make it so, the nausea began to subside.

Maddie sank back, sitting on her heels. Scott handed her a damp face cloth. She took it in both hands and wiped the sweat from her face. The coolness was sheer bliss.

Without a word, he lifted her to her feet and tucked her under his arm, leading her back to bed.

Safely back under the covers, Maddie didn't know what to say. But she didn't have to. Scott brushed her forehead with his lips and turned toward the door.

Maddie tried to watch him go, but her eyelids felt heavy and she closed them, giving in to exhaustion. As sleep drew her in, a peculiar thought drifted through her mind. In all their seventeen years of marriage this was a first. Scott was the caretaker and she was the patient. She had nursed him through many minor ailments, but this was the first time he'd done the same for her.

Scott barely made it to the bathroom in his office, his stomach heaving. Moments later, his breakfast gone, he flushed the toilet, sucking in great gulps of air. He'd nearly lost it upstairs. He still wasn't sure how he'd held it together. But he'd stuck it out despite the awful sound of retching that had turned his stomach as sour as milk left to sit in the summer sun.

He hadn't been able to talk, however. He knew if he opened his mouth, he would have been right down on his knees beside her. But he figured talking wasn't really necessary, opting instead for physical reassurance.

Scott splashed cold water on his face and vigorously brushed his teeth, offering up a silent prayer.

Thank You, Lord, for helping me out up there. I know that had to be Your doing because I couldn't have done it on my own. And shallow as this makes me, Lord, I'm scared of what Maddie will look like when the chemo really kicks in and she starts losing her hair. Give me eyes to see Maddie as You see her, Lord, and give me the strength to be the husband and the father You want me to be.

Scott dried his face with a towel, feeling more like himself. The phone in this office rang, and he stepped through the doorway and grabbed it before it could wake Maddie.

"Scott, it's Rob. How's Maddie doing?"

Scott tensed, his shoulders rigid and his hand tight on the phone. Despite the pleasantries, he knew this wasn't a personal call. "It's a rough time for her right now."

"I'm sure it is." Rob gave the appropriate pause. "I was wondering when you'll be back to work."

"The beginning of next week," Scott said, knowing Maddie should be through the worst of the side effects by then.

"That's five days from now," Rob said, stating the obvious. "I thought you might make it in later this week. Mrs. Hingemen specifically asked for you."

"Give her my best and have Michelle go over any changes she still needs."

"Michelle doesn't have your rapport with Mrs. Hingemen, who was gracious enough to forgive you after you left her hanging in Tennessee."

"I told you I had a family emergency."

"You seem to have a lot of those lately."

Scott bristled at the implied slight. "You're going to have to cut me some slack here, Rob. I'm going to need some time off in the next six months. I can work from home and keep in touch with the office by e-mail and fax."

"How much time are we talking about?"

"Well, this week . . ."

"In addition to the two weeks you took earlier this month?" Rob's tone was terse.

"And I'm going to need a week every month until the spring."

"And you think that's going to fly around here? I'll have every staffer in the office asking for time off to care for their mother or their kid if I say yes to you."

"Why don't we give it a try for a month or so and see how it goes. If you find I'm not able to keep up with the work from home, then we'll discuss it again," Scott said. "I've worked for this firm for seventeen years, Rob. I think I've earned a little leeway here. I've made the firm a lot of money with my designs . . ."

"And been well compensated for it."

"I agree. You've been more than generous with money, but time is what I need now."

"All right. We'll try it for a few months and see how it goes," Rob said, though Scott could hear the reluctance in his voice.

"Thank you. Tell Mrs. Hingemen I'll be in touch."

"Will do, and I'll see you first thing Monday morning."

"I'll be there."

Scott hung up. He probably should have pled his case using a soft-sell approach. But Rob was a managing partner and the only way to make him back down was to be more obstinate than he was. Still, Scott couldn't afford to lose this job. Right now he needed the insurance coverage more than he needed the salary. Maddie's medical bills were going to be huge. Just her stay in the hospital with the surgery and anesthesia had already racked up a bill in the tens of thousands. No, Scott had to tread lightly with Rob. His job was a necessary evil right now.

Scott stopped abruptly, about to scoop up his car keys and go get Shaun. A necessary evil? When had that happened? He'd always loved his job for how it made him feel about himself. But in the past month his priorities had changed. No longer was his work the most important thing in his life. Taking care of Maddie and the kids was his first priority.

172

And the funny thing was he liked it. He liked working in the bedroom while Maddie slept. He liked going to Kylie's field hockey games and watching her tear up the turf and then shoot the ball into the goal. He liked helping Shaun with math and driving him around.

This was what he'd missed. And he hadn't even known it. And he thanked God every day for opening his eyes before it was too late. Too late for him and Maddie, and too late for the beautiful family they had created together. He'd been given a second chance, and with God's help he was going to make the most of it.

Twenty-nine

"How's Maddie doing?" Phil asked as Annie pushed past the store's squeaky door.

"Not so good today. She looked like she was going to throw up all morning."

"How's Scott managing?"

Annie came around the counter, dragging the bandanna from her head and combing her hair with her hands. "Pretty well. He's getting the stay-at-home dad thing down. He's even made a few of Maddie's favorite foods to coax her into eating."

Phil brushed an errant strand of hair behind her ear. "Sounds like he's doing just fine. With your help, of course."

"I'll be glad when Maddie's well again. And then we can concentrate on starting our family. With all that's going on, is it so selfish of me to want that?" Annie asked, bowing her forehead against Phil's chest.

He pulled her to him, tucking her head under his chin. "I wanted to talk to you about that."

Annie looked up at him. "I'm listening."

He took a deep breath. "We both felt led to be foster parents, remember? And then all that assurance about how God wanted to use us got lost in all the paperwork and the endless waiting time to get a child. We've been trying to make it work on our timetable . . ."

"And God's timing is not our timing," Annie said, her shoulders sagging. "I know that, but I'm just so tired of waiting."

Phil tipped her chin up. "I was thinking maybe we wouldn't have to wait so long."

"But you just said . . ."

"Annie, we want a long-term placement, right? Hopefully a child we may someday be able to adopt."

"Right."

"I've been praying about this, and God is putting on my heart that all His children aren't perfect. They may be perfect to Him but not to us."

Annie took a deep breath. "You want us to be foster parents to a special-needs child?"

Phil slowly shook his head. "I want us to talk about taking in the kind of child no one else wants, an HIV positive child with nowhere else to go."

Annie turned her head to the side and kissed his hand. "You are a kind and gentle man, you know that? But I don't know if I can do that, Phil. I mean, I was never looking for a perfect child, but the thought of raising a child knowing you were going to lose her . . ." Annie shook her head. "It would be so hard."

"Yes, it would, but do we want a child for what they will become when we're through raising them, or do we want a child to love and nurture each day?"

"It's just such an open-ended situation, knowing they could get sick or die at any time."

"Isn't that true of all families? We could have a child who contracts meningitis and dies in a day or raise a healthy child for years who dies in a car accident. That part isn't in our hands, Annie."

"I know." Annie leaned up and kissed her husband. "I need to think about it and pray about it for a while, okay?"

"Sure thing."

"Mind if I talk to Maddie about it? It might help her to think about something other than what's happening to her right now."

"Fine by me. I was thinking of inviting Scott to the men's Bible study on Thursday night. What do you think?"

"I think your mind has been very busy this morning." Annie laughed, knocking him on the forehead with her knuckles. "It's a great idea. I don't know as he'll go, but all he can say is no."

"My thoughts exactly."

Scott stood in the pew between Kylie and Shaun, thinking how weird it was to be here without Maddie. When it came to religion, she was the knowledgeable one in their family. After all her years of going to church every Sunday, she must have a better understanding of the readings than he did. He just hoped Kylie and Shaun wouldn't ask him anything he didn't have the answer to, which was just about anything to do with the church.

Maybe if he read the Bible he might have a better idea what was going on. Did they even own a Bible? Scott shook his head. If they did, he sure didn't know where it was. And if they didn't own one, where would he get one? Did Barnes and Noble carry Bibles or did you have to go to one of those religious stores to get one?

The choir took up the communion hymn and Scott glanced at the choir loft, half expecting to see Maddie. He frowned. Of course she wasn't there. She was home in bed still wiped out from the chemo last Monday.

Outside after the service, Scott realized he'd done what he always did when he came to church. He'd sat and stood and knelt in the right places, but he'd barely heard a word of what was said. And as for worshiping God, he didn't think he'd done much of that.

In the car Shaun punched Kylie on the arm. "Hey, nobody even noticed Dad's shirt."

Kylie blushed.

Shaun leaned around the backseat with a grin. "Hey, I was just kidding, but you have to admit it's funny. Dad's wearing a pink T-shirt under that sweater."

"It's still wearable," Scott said, wrapping an arm around Kylie's shoulders. He tipped her chin up. "You're doing a great job on the laundry, Ky."

"Thanks, Dad." Kylie smiled. "But I kind of wish you'd warned me about that sorting thing."

"Who knew?" Scott laughed. "Hey, we're just working it out as we go along."

They lapsed into silence as they drove along Lake Shore Road, all three of them glancing at the marred tree stump Maddie had hit. This morning the gnarled wood was covered with yellow and red leaves, a cheerful covering that belied its solid ability to stop a two-ton vehicle in its tracks.

God had been at work that night. Of that much Scott was sure. Maddie could easily have died, but she hadn't. She could have missed the tree and kept right on driving and they never would have found the cancer.

Scott could see God working in his life. He'd been praying every day. Apparently, God liked a good conversation. And Scott found that he liked it too. This should have been the most trying, most stressful time of his life with Maddie being sick and all the responsibility for the kids and the house thrown onto his shoulders in addition to his job. The funny thing was he didn't feel stressed out. Sure, he worried about Maddie and her long-term prognosis. And he worried about what her illness was doing to the kids, but even in the midst of his skirmish with Rob Sanders the other day, Scott had felt a strange ease. He knew without a doubt that he wasn't in charge of this situation and knowing that gave him license not to try to be. He was doing what he needed to do for his family, and for the first time in a long while Scott knew he was exactly where he needed to be.

Maddie leaned on the open refrigerator door and stared at the packed shelves. Scott had gone to the supermarket yesterday afternoon and stocked up on everything. But when Maddie looked at the food, her nausea returned and the idea of actually getting it out of the package and cooking it sent her out onto the deck for a breath of cool autumn air. Late afternoon sunlight glimmered on the water like yellow topaz miraculously floating on the waves. A sharp breeze tossed Maddie's curls into her face and she brushed them back. The wind gust sent leaves skittering across the green lawn in a race to the water's edge.

Maddie inhaled deeply and closed her eyes. The scent of dry leaves and pine mingled as the sun shone against her closed lids in an explosion of orange light. This had to be the most beautiful place on earth, Maddie thought as her eyes slowly opened and she dropped her hand from her hair.

A tuft of blonde hair rested in her hand.

Maddie looked at it and her eyes filled with tears. She choked back a sob. She'd known she would lose her hair, but not this soon. The nausea, the vomiting, the fatigue had been awful, but it was behind her now, at least for this month. But she didn't know how she would deal with this. She'd never been one of those ditsy girls who spent a lot of time on her hair; she'd always taken it for granted. But the idea of losing it terrified her.

The back door slammed. Maddie whirred and without thinking stuffed the hair in her pocket. She swiped at her eyes and forced a smile as she pulled open the door. "I don't know what you guys were thinking about dinner . . ."

"We've got it right here," Shaun said, holding aloft two bags of food in plastic sacks.

Kylie dropped her book bag and field hockey stick by the computer and helped Scott set an impromptu meal at the counter.

Scott filled two glasses with water and poured milk for the kids. "I hope you're a little hungry."

"Looks like more than pizza. Where's it from?"

"The Riverboat," Kylie said, folding a napkin in half and setting it beside each plate.

Scott stepped over to her. "We missed our meal a few weeks ago so I thought we might try take-out this time."

"I didn't know a place like that did take-out," Maddie said, glancing up at him.

"They don't, not usually, but the chef did me a favor."

"Really?" Maddie inched forward to peek at what was in the bags. "What did you get?"

"A little bit of everything and all your favorites." Kylie said with a smile. "Dad asked us what you liked best and since none of us could agree we got one of everything."

Maddie peered into the bag, surprised the heady smell of garlic wasn't sending her stomach into an uproar. She lifted out a black plastic tray with a clear lid to keep the food warm. There were five containers in all. Shrimp scampi. Chicken Marsala. Beef tenderloin with a horseradish sauce. Pasta primavera. And the last container held a dozen French crepes with dipping sauces for dessert.

Maddie looked at her family. "I sure hope you're all going to help me eat this."

"No problem, Mom." Shaun dug a large spoon into the pasta and scooped it onto his plate.

Maddie stepped closer to Scott, all the while watching their children indulge in this impromptu feast. "Thank you. I hope it tastes as good as it smells. The crepes look delicious."

"So make a meal of those if you want."

Maddie tried, but her eyes were bigger than her still tipsy stomach. She managed to eat half of what was on her plate while around the counter an animated discussion about the field hockey team's chance for

178

a state championship kept them busy through most of the meal. Afterwards the kids cleared the dishes and went upstairs to start their homework.

Scott watched them go as he stood by the sink next to Maddie. "So want to tell me what had you looking like a scared rabbit when we came in here tonight?"

Maddie met his gaze, surprised he'd noticed.

"Are you feeling all right?" Scott persisted.

Maddie shook her head. Her eyes stung again as she reached into her pocket and withdrew the wad of blonde curls.

"Oh, Maddie, I'm sorry." His hands gently squeezed her shoulders.

She couldn't take her gaze from the clump of hair. "I knew it was going to happen, but I'm afraid to even touch my head now for fear I'm going to lose the rest of it."

"Maybe you and Kylie should take that trip into Boston and buy a hat or a wig," Scott suggested.

Maddie looked at him and laughed. "Subtle, very subtle. Are you afraid to have a bald wife?"

"Not at all," Scott said, closing her fingers around the hair so she could no longer see it.

Maddie couldn't decide whether he was telling the truth or not.

"I just thought you might want an excuse to go shopping," Scott said just as the phone rang. He grabbed it, listened for a bit and then said, "Sure, why not. See you then."

"Where are you going?" Maddie asked, starting to load the dishwasher.

"To a Bible study on Thursday night with Phil."

Maddie almost dropped the glass in her hand. "A Bible study?"

"Yeah, I figured if I'm going to be taking the kids to church for the next few months then I better know enough to answer their questions."

"Is that the only reason you're going?" Maddie asked, impressed by Scott's newfound commitment to parenting.

"Do I need another reason?"

"No, of course not; I was just surprised is all."

"You don't know me as well as you think," Scott said.

At another time and in another place Maddie would have fired off an angry retort about his never being home to let her know him. But tonight Maddie took one look at the kitchen around her and said, "I think you might be right about that."

Thirty

The mind's ability to forget was a blessing, Maddie decided, holding on to the porcelain bowl. Because if she'd remembered how truly terrible this was, she didn't know how she'd get through the month in between chemo sessions. With Halloween fast approaching she wouldn't even need a costume this year to look like an ethereal waif.

Maddie pressed her hands to the toilet rim and pushed herself to stand. She threw open the bathroom window and stepped to the sink to wash her face. Blotting her face with a towel, she stared into the mirror. Her skin, normally pink and healthy, was a pasty white with undertones of yellow. Her face looked puffy, and though she knew she had lost weight from last month's treatment, her body appeared bloated as well.

But the sight of her hair made Maddie want to cry. Once blonde and shiny, her hair was dull and dry and patchy in spots where clever arranging couldn't hide the thin coverage. Another month and she'd be bald completely. And maybe that wouldn't be so bad, Maddie mused, spying another large balding patch behind her ear.

She turned from the mirror and stumbled back to bed, wondering if she had the guts to go ahead with her plan. She'd need some help. She'd thought about asking Annie but then dismissed the idea. Annie was already doing so much for them.

Scott then. Two months ago Maddie would have rejected that idea out of hand, not willing to trust anything so embarrassing to her husband. But ever since the surgery, Scott had shouldered the load of home and parenting without complaint. Oh, he was still squeamish. Maddie could see it in his face, but his concern overrode his revulsion, and for that Maddie was grateful. She didn't know where he was getting the strength. It seemed he hardly slept anymore, but ever so slowly Maddie was starting to trust Scott to be here for her and the kids.

Falling on top of the comforter, Maddie reached for the patchwork afghan she'd made in college and pulled it up to her chin. With her eyes closed she still felt queasy, making sleep, at least for right now, not a viable option.

A knock sounded on the door. Scott came through the doorway struggling to balance a tray filled with tea and crackers while wedged under his arm he carried the newspaper, a magazine, and a book.

"I thought this might settle your stomach." Scott set the tray down on the bed. "It used to work when you were pregnant."

Maddie nodded, though her stomach recoiled at the sight of food. The crackers were out of the question, but she thought maybe she could manage something to drink. "I'll try the tea."

"Good." Scott grabbed a pillow from his side of the bed and propped it up behind Maddie before handing her the mug.

Maddie sipped. "What else did you bring?"

"The *Globe*. *Time* magazine. And an old classic, *To Kill a Mockingbird*. Which one would you like?"

Maddie shook her head. "Reading is kind of hard right now. It's hard to concentrate."

"That's why I thought we'd read it together. Or more accurately, I'd read and you'd listen. Like one of those books on tape, only live."

Maddie stared at Scott towering over her, remembering how they used to sit out on the college green while Maddie read aloud and Scott used her lap as a pillow. "Really? Don't you have work to do?"

"Nothing that can't wait an hour. So you choose which one."

"That's easy, *To Kill a Mockingbird*. It's one of the first books I ever actually enjoyed."

Scott nodded. "Me too."

He placed the tray in between them on the king-sized bed and propped himself up against the headboard, stretching out his legs and crossing them at the ankle.

Maddie wrapped her hands around the mug and sipped her tea as Scott's deep baritone began the story, so familiar and yet Maddie had forgotten so many of its nuances. After several minutes, Maddie relaxed against the pillow and closed her eyes, letting the words of the story weave images in her mind that carried her far away.

The story had lost none of its allure, and Maddie found herself trying to remember what came next. Scott's subtle change of tone for each character made listening a pleasure. A fleeting thought of Adam and the summer show came to mind, but Maddie pushed it aside, instead immersing herself in the story of Scout and her father, Atticus.

With her eyes closed she thought she might fall asleep, but the story held her in its grip right up until Scott closed the book with a soft thud.

"Maddie, are you awake?"

"I heard every word." She slowly opened her eyes and set aside the empty mug. "That was great. Thank you."

"We could read some more tomorrow if you'd like."

"You'll be here?"

"All week."

"Rob must be going crazy with you out again this month."

"He's getting used to it. I made all my deadlines last month so he can't really complain."

"That never stopped him before."

Scott nodded with a wry smile. "True."

"You don't have to take this much time off every month. I can manage with the kid's help and Annie's, of course."

"I know I don't have to, Maddie. I want to." Scott rolled over onto his side to face her. "I like taking care of you and the kids. I like being home and going to soccer games and parent teacher conferences, all the stuff I've missed. If someone had told me that six months ago I'd have thought they were crazy, but I really do like it."

"The kids like it too." Maddie shifted against the pillow, angling her body toward him so she could see his face.

"They do?" Scott's face lit up, a smile crinkling the corners of his eyes.

Maddie nodded. He seemed so content, his tone warm and his face relaxed. "So tell me about this Bible study you're going to with Phil."

Scott plucked one cracker off the tray and popped it in his mouth. "We meet on Thursdays, but you know that . . ."

"What are you studying?" Maddie asked, reaching for a cracker and nibbling at the corner.

"This year it's the Gospel of John. The class is a mixed group, some guys who've been coming for years and others who are new like me. I don't think I get into it as deep as the others, but everybody's just there to learn."

"So what have you learned so far?"

"Well, I didn't know that John the Baptist and Jesus were cousins, did you?"

Maddie shook her head, finishing the cracker and reaching for another.

Scott's expression grew more animated as he leaned in closer. "Their mothers were related so they were cousins. John was the older of the two. It was his job to prepare the way, to get people to change their lives because no one knows when they'll come face-to-face with the Messiah . . ." Scott looked up suddenly, chagrin clouding his face. "I'm sorry, Maddie; that wasn't a good example."

"No, you're right; we don't ever know. Not the people back then or any of the people today. Like me, for instance. I could be sicker a year from now, or I could be cured, or I could be . . ."

Scott reached across the tray and grabbed her hand. "Don't say it. We caught this early, and now you and I are going to beat this. And a year from now we're going to take a trip to the islands, just the two of us, and celebrate your health and your new hair and all that we have to be grateful for."

Maddie's hand drifted to her hairline and tucked a few thin strands behind her ear. She paused then looked up at Scott, meeting his gaze. "I need to ask you a favor."

"Name it."

"I want you to help me shave my head."

Scott's eyes grew wide, but his gaze never wavered. "When?"

"Now, before I lose my nerve."

Scott stood up and came around the bed. "Are you sure about this?"

Maddie nodded. "I just can't watch it fall out. I'd rather be done with it."

Scott held out his hands and Maddie placed hers in his. "You're sure you can do this?" she asked. "I thought about asking Annie but . . ."

"Hey, when it comes to shaving, who knows more about it than a guy who has to do it every day?" Scott led her into the bathroom. "Can I make a suggestion?"

Maddie nodded.

Scott steered her to the edge of the tub. "Just let me do it and then take a look. You'll just have to trust me."

"I do," Maddie said, and for the first time in a long time she meant those words.

Scott draped a towel around her shoulders and found a pair of scissors in the vanity drawer. "This may take a while, so just close your eyes."

Maddie knew she didn't want to see him cut away what remained of her hair. She squeezed her eyes closed.

"So did Annie tell you that the paperwork on their foster-parent status just went through?" Scott asked, the snip of scissors punctuating his words. "Phil told me about it last night."

"What about the home study?"

"They've got an appointment for next week."

"I feel so out of it. You know more about our friends than I do."

"For a change."

Maddie was tempted to reach up and run a hand over her head but controlled the impulse.

"You know Phil gives you the credit for convincing Annie to go ahead with the foster-care application," Scott said.

"I didn't do anything."

The faucet in the sink ran in a steady stream, a wisp of heat touching Maddie's cheek.

"Do you remember what you said to her last month?"

Maddie paused, feeling a warm soapy mixture coat her scalp as Scott rubbed it in and then used the razor in long strokes to take it off. "I told her that being sick makes you scared, and that everybody deserves to have someone taking care of them when they're scared."

"And that's what put Annie over the top. She hated the idea that some little girl with HIV would be living in a group home with no one to care when she was scared."

A cool breeze from the open window chilled her scalp before Scott rubbed her head with a dry towel. "You ready?"

"Sure. I mean, it's just hair, right? How bad could it be?"

Maddie stood in front of the sink.

Scott stepped behind her, his hands gently resting on her shoulders.

Maddie stared in the mirror at her pale, shiny, utterly bald head. Her eyes widened and filled with tears as she bit her lower lip.

Scott gently pulled her into his arms. She let him take her weight, afraid that her legs wouldn't hold her up much longer. Maddie turned her head to the side, unable to look any longer. The coarse weave of Scott's sweater abraded her cheek as she turned in his arms and buried her face in his chest. Great sobs racked her body.

Ugly. So ugly. Bloated and pale and ugly. Maddie's mind whirled. This was no time to be vain, she told herself. She was fighting for her life, and she had more important things to worry about than a few missing curls. But none of that mattered, not when the voices in her head screamed how terrible she looked.

Maddie clenched her fists and cried.

And she couldn't seem to stop until Scott silenced her choking gasps with a single kiss to her freshly shaved head.

Scott couldn't let her go. He kissed the top of her head and held on tight as Maddie grew still in his arms. Her heart-wrenching cries subsided and still she didn't move. Scott pressed his cheek to her head. It felt strange, but nothing he couldn't get used to if she would promise never to move again. He'd waited a long time for this, for her to turn to him, to trust him enough to ask for his help. He'd never thought their reunion would take place in a bathroom with a floor full of hair at their feet, but he didn't care. Perhaps she was desperate, or just in need of reassurance. He didn't care about that either. She stood here in his arms and that was all he wanted.

Maddie sniffled and wiped her eyes with the heel of one hand. "I suppose I should say thank you for doing what I asked, but you won't mind if I wait a few days until I really mean it?"

Scott tipped her chin up with his knuckles. "I can wait." He stared at her, examining the contours of her face, the strong lines of nose and chin he'd never noticed before.

Maddie met his gaze. "Don't you dare tell me I'm beautiful because I'll never believe you, and you'll lose all the credibility you've been building up for the last few months."

Scott chuckled. "Well, I wouldn't want to do that." His knuckles traced the outline of her jaw and moved up around her ear before he opened his hand and slowly ran it over her head. "But it is kind of sexy." His hand caressed the back of her neck.

Maddie opened her mouth to protest but then snapped it shut, evidently convinced of the truth by the look in his eyes.

And in that moment Scott came as close to kissing his wife as he had in months. It would have been easy enough to do, but something held him back. Not desire. No, he'd underestimated the sheer force of that emotion now that he and Maddie spent so much time together. What held him back was all that still lay undiscussed between them. He didn't want to build a new relationship with Maddie without putting to rest what had happened in the past, particularly this summer. And he wanted to know in every fiber of his being that his wife wanted him, not just to take care of her and their kids but wanted him as a man. He wanted to know he was her choice to spend the rest of her life with, and until she said as much, he wasn't about to blur the lines of their relationship with physical intimacy.

For too many years they'd taken that part of their relationship for granted, entered into the act without truly experiencing the joining, the love that should have accompanied the pleasure. No, when they were ready to take that step, it would be because he and Maddie had fallen in love again.

"Hey, Dad, you up there?" Shaun called.

Maddie stiffened in his arms, her eyes wide with panic. She ran a hand over her head. "This is going to scare him."

Scott could hear feet pounding on the stairs. Glancing back at the open doorway, he grabbed a towel from the rack behind the door and tossed it at Maddie. "Do that turban thing you do when you wash your hair."

Maddie bent forward at the waist and wrapped the towel around her head, twisting it into a high knot as Scott tossed another towel over the hair on the floor.

Shaun burst into the bedroom at a run. "Dad, I'm going to start in the county game. Drew Martel broke his collarbone and coach is putting me in the starting lineup." He pulled up short at the bathroom door, breathing fast, his face beaming.

"That's great, Bud." Scott said.

Maddie stepped up next to him. "When's the big game?"

"Sunday. Can you come?" he asked hopefully.

"I think I can make it. I might have to watch from the car, though."

"I don't care, just so long as you're there." Shaun hugged her and then dropped a kiss on her chin. "I'm starved. What's for snack?"

He didn't wait for an answer but vaulted from the room and down the stairs.

"Sunday?" Maddie squeaked. "I'd better call Annie and see if she'll go shopping with me."

"Are you feeling up to that?"

"By the end of the week I think I could manage."

"Why don't you take Kylie with you? Make it a girls' day out."

"Good idea, but how about, for now, we find me a hat."

Thirty-one

"I can't believe you're letting me skip school to go shopping." Kylie grinned, sticking her head between the front seats as Annie parked the car in front of a store advertising natural wigs.

Maddie smiled, adjusting the floppy hat that covered her head as they stepped out of the car and made their way into the surprisingly large shop. "Hey, unless I plan on wearing this hat for the rest of the year, I need your help."

The wig boutique served a wide clientele indicated by the merchandise on display. Men's toupees, children's wigs as well as synthetic and natural wigs in every shade were displayed on plastic heads arranged on glass shelving around the room. Maddie marveled at the selection. As they wandered around the oblong room, Maddie noted the private fitting rooms in the back and the mirrors placed at strategic intervals throughout the shop.

An older woman stood behind the counter but merely nodded as if used to giving her customers a little space before offering her assistance.

"Can we make you a red head?" Kylie asked, her eyes gleaming as she tapped Maddie on the shoulder. "Something short and sexy and auburn." She pointed at a beautiful natural wig that fit the description.

"Or something dark and long and sleek," Annie suggested with a smile and winked at Kylie.

Maddie glanced from her friend to her daughter and back. "I don't want to stand out in a crowd; I just want to look normal again. So I won't scare little children and make grown men stare."

"I noticed Dad doesn't seem to have a problem with it," Kylie said. "I think he kind of likes it. Now that's a little creepy."

"Maybe he's looking at the woman and not just at her head," Annie suggested, stopping in front of a platinum blond pageboy.

A warm flush crept up Maddie's neck and settled in her cheeks. "That doesn't seem possible. Have you looked at me lately?"

"You don't look bad. And Annie's right. Dad really has been paying more attention to you lately, to all of us. It's like he's a different guy since you got sick," Kylie said softly.

"He's a different guy, all right. In fact, I'd say he's a whole new creation," Annie offered.

"What do you mean?" Maddie asked.

"You should ask him about it," Annie suggested.

"She'll never do that," Kylie chimed in. "She's too afraid if she points it out that he'd go back to the way he was before."

Maddie stared at her daughter, but Kylie had already wandered off. How did she know? How did she know that Maddie's biggest fear now was that Scott would stop taking care of her? Her illness had changed him. At least she thought that's what had done it, but she wasn't sure.

"Would you like to try anything on?" the woman behind the counter asked. An ample-breasted lady in her midfifties, her smile was open and welcoming. "My name is Anita, and I can bring anything you like into one of our private fitting rooms."

Maddie smiled. "I'm not sure what I want."

"Well, we could try a variety of things then. Why don't you get settled and I'll bring a few things in?"

"Can I help pick them out?" Kylie chimed in.

"Certainly."

Anita escorted them to a curtained area where she settled Maddie and Annie in two comfortable chairs. On the table between them a large hand mirror rested at the ready.

"Do you know who Scott reminds me of lately?" Maddie asked, eyeing the mirror.

A knowing smile creased Annie's face.

"He reminds me of Phil." Maddie sat in silence for a minute. "You'll never know how much I envied you your relationship with your husband. You two are so in tune with each other."

"That's not exclusive to us, you know."

"I'm beginning to figure that out, but sometimes I wonder why Scott's so different. Maybe he's afraid I'll die and he's decided to pay attention to me while I'm still here."

Annie shook her head. "The change in Scott isn't external, though you two have had a lot to deal with lately. It's in his heart."

Maddie ran a hand over the mirror's handle, unable to meet Annie's gaze. "Well, no matter where it came from, I don't deserve it. Not after last summer."

"After what happened with Adam, you mean?"

Maddie nodded, glancing over at the closed curtain and lowering her voice. "I was ready to throw my marriage away, and I might have done it too, if circumstances had worked out differently." Maddie paused. "And now the guilt is driving me crazy, especially with Scott working so hard to take care of us."

"Have you talked to him about it?"

"No." Maddie recoiled at the thought. "It would just be dredging up old hurts. What good could come of that?"

"You can't ignore what's happened, and yes, it may be painful, but before you two can move forward together you have to take a hard look at where you've been. You need to talk about Adam."

"I don't know if I can do that."

"Scott doesn't need details. What he needs is your renewed commitment to your marriage."

"In other words an apology."

"That's part of it. You made a mistake, Maddie. You actively went into that relationship with Adam and let those feelings grow. You aren't innocent. But more than that, Scott needs to know that you're with him, not because you're sick but because you love him."

"I don't know if I do," Maddie said quietly. "I did once, and I appreciate all he's done for me, but being in love with him again . . . I don't know. I'm not ready to commit to that until I know he's not going to turn around and go right back to the way he was before."

"You have to trust that he's a new man, Maddie." Annie leaned forward. "The evidence is right there in front of you, but you're going to have to take that leap of faith. You need to trust God to change your heart just like He's changed Scott's."

"I don't know if I could ever trust anyone that much, not even God."

"Sometimes it's funny how we can put our trust in doctors to heal our bodies, but not in God. We all have reasons, things in our past that make it hard to trust. But God loves you, Maddie. He wants to be in your life."

"He's already in my life. I go to church every Sunday."

"And your head is filled with lots of facts about him, but God wants to move from your head to your heart." Annie's hand splayed across her chest in an unconscious gesture that was as simple as it was beautiful.

"And how does he do that?"

"It takes an act of faith where you ask him into your heart."

"The thing is, if I did that now, I'd only be doing it out of desperation," Maddie said, voicing aloud her doubt. "I'd do it now because I'm afraid to die and not because I feel any deep and abiding love for God. I respect Him and I'm a little afraid of Him, but I don't know as I trust Him or love Him, not the way you talk about."

The curtain swung open. Kylie swooped in carrying several wigs, followed by Anita with several more. "Wait 'til you see these. This one is my favorite." Kylie had chosen a short blond number with a punk feel, spiked on top and feathered around the face.

Anita looked at Maddie a bit skeptically. "Would you like to try this one on first or one of the others?"

Maddie grinned at her daughter and tossed her hat at Annie, who caught it with a chuckle. "Definitely that one. It'll make me look ten years younger."

Anita stepped in front of Maddie and began to fit the wig to her head, her ample body blocking Maddie's view of the rest of the room. She closed her eyes, listening to her best friend and her daughter chat amiably as they awaited Anita's handiwork.

"So whatever happened with Kevin this year?" Annie asked Kylie. "I haven't heard you talk about him much lately."

"I dumped him."

"You did?" Maddie eyes flew open. She tried to lean around Anita, wondering how many other major events in her family she'd missed.

"Yeah. Dad said something last month that made a lot of sense."

"What was that?"

"He told me I deserved better, and when he said it, I knew he was right. Kevin just wanted sex."

Anita paused before resuming her professional duties.

"And I will too someday," Kylie continued, "when I find the right guy to share it with, but Kevin wasn't it."

Thank God, Maddie thought as Anita stepped out from in front of her.

Annie and Kylie smiled.

"Cool, Mom."

"I love it, Maddie."

Maddie lifted the hand mirror on the table to take a look. Anita had calmed the spikes with a skilled hand but left the gentle curving hair around the face. Maddie winked at her daughter. "Not bad, but let's try on one of those red ones."

Thirty-two

S cott tossed his portfolio case on his desk, resigned to being back in Boston though he'd just had a week off. Not that Maddie's third round of chemo could be considered a vacation, but Scott found that each month he was more and more reluctant to return to Boston. And next week with the Thanksgiving holiday would be a scramble. He only had the one day off. He couldn't afford to take any extra days, not with all the time he'd already taken this year, and more to come in the next several months. Scott mentally checked off all the things he had to do before the Baldwins and the Alexanders would sit down to celebrate Thanksgiving together.

"Scott? Got a minute?" Rob Sanders knocked on the open door and walked in.

Scott tensed. Rob never visited anyone in their office. Usually, he had his secretary call and summon them upstairs. "What can I do for you?" Scott asked.

"I'll get right to the point," Rob began.

Scott's pulse raced, a cold sweat breaking out on his back. He tried to focus. He'd been expecting this conversation but still felt like he'd been sideswiped by a bus.

"Sarah Hingemen is a great admirer of your work, but given the time constraints and need for day-to-day supervision on the project—"

Scott interrupted him. "You're taking me off the Hingemen project?"

Rob paused and then looked up, his gaze direct. "No, Scott, we're letting you go. We need employees at the senior level who are committed to the firm."

Scott held his anger firmly in check, knowing nothing good could come of a shouting match. "Just so we understand each other . . . you're firing me because I lack commitment to the firm or because I've taken too much time off?"

"Your working at home isn't right for the firm." Rob held up two hands, palms open, as if to forestall Scott's objections. "You've made all your deadlines, but the bottom line is we need a senior man here in the office available for the jobs that can't be done by fax, like the relationship building over dinner."

In other words, the schmoozing. A pervasive calm settled over Scott. Only one thing mattered now and he had to walk out of here with it.

"And the Hingemen project?"

"Remains the property of the firm since all your designs were submitted when you were on staff here."

"So, you're firing me because my wife has cancer."

Rob flinched. "We realize your family has needs at this time, but the firm also needs employees who can work within our corporate structure and not make their own rules. Since you've been with the firm for so long I'm willing to offer you a six-month severance package and full vesting in the retirement plan."

"I'll need a one-year continuation of my medical insurance," Scott insisted. "You pay the premiums and after that I can COBRA the plan and get the group rate for another eighteen months."

"Done."

Rob looked relieved to be getting off without a fight. Scott suspected he was worried about a lawsuit, which if it went to court would certainly cast the firm in an ill light.

Rob stuck out his hand. "It's been good working with you. I wish you all the best. If you need a reference, feel free to use my name."

Scott bit his tongue so hard he could taste the blood in his mouth. "So you'll tell human resources about the severance, the retirement plan, and the insurance, right?"

"Yes, they'll be expecting you for an exit interview in an hour."

Scott nodded and turned his back on Rob Sanders. He had an hour to pack up his office, but he'd gotten what he needed most. His medical insurance would remain in force and Maddie's treatments would be covered, and that was all he wanted from this firm.

"They fired you?" Maddie's lower lip trembled. "Because of me?"

Scott sat on the edge of their bed and tipped her chin up. "Admit it;

you never liked me working there anyway."

"You're right, but . . ." Maddie's hand massaged her forehead, brushing back the bangs of her short-haired wig. "Maybe you could sue them. It doesn't seem like it could be legal for them to just let you go because of a family illness. I'm sure we can find a lawyer . . ."

"Hold on, Maddie. I don't want to sue. In fact, I'm glad they did it." Scott smiled.

"You're glad?"

"They packaged me out with enough money to keep us going for a while. I never would have left, not with seventeen years of my time in there, but now they've forced my hand. I can finally do what I've always wanted."

"Start your own firm."

"You knew that?" Scott looked stunned but also pleased as he grabbed her hand.

"I knew you weren't happy, and I always thought what we talked about when we first got married sounded like a nice way to live."

"The office in the boathouse." Scott grinned. "I was thinking of doing most of the work myself; maybe bring Phil in for the heavy stuff. You do know this means I'll be home full-time."

"I think I can handle that." Maddie smiled.

"We're going to be tight for money for a while until I can get my name out there and get a few recommendations."

"We'll make it work."

"We . . . I like the sound of that." Scott reached up and cupped her cheek in his hand. "I think this is going to turn out to be one of God's greatest blessings, Maddie."

Heat wafted from the kitchen. Thanksgiving dinner was well underway, and Maddie hadn't done a thing. She hadn't shopped or cleaned or cooked. She felt a little guilty about it, but a part of her enjoyed sitting back and watching Scott order everyone around the kitchen. He put Kylie to work mashing potatoes while Shaun was dispatched outside to bring in logs for the fire. Phil sharpened the knives for the great turkey carving while Scott basted the turkey with a baster the size of a small accordion. Striding across the kitchen with a dish towel thrown over his shoulder and a glass of tomato juice sprouting celery stalks in one hand, Maddie thought she had never seen her husband look happier.

"How are you feeling?" Annie settled in on the sofa, having finished her assigned tasks of whipping cream for the pies and making gravy.

"I just hope I can do justice to all this effort," Maddie said. "I'm still a little queasy from last week's treatment."

"Just take it slow. No need to eat the whole meal in ten minutes when it took seven hours to prepare. Scott seems to be enjoying himself," Annie added with a wink.

"And to think that's the same guy who spent the last seventeen Thanksgivings sprawled on the couch watching football while I cooked the whole meal," Maddie said, scratching her head. "He's really in his element."

"He likes being needed," Annie said.

Maddie watched Kylie hip-check Scott into the counter, a bowl of hot rolls almost falling out of his hands. A year ago if he'd carried anything to the table at all, he'd have admonished her for being clumsy. Now he smiled and pretended to drop them on the floor, catching them at the last minute to everyone's amazed smiles.

In the last few months he had become her best friend, the man she counted on to care for her and the kids. She didn't know if love would grow from the trust and companionship she felt but if it never did, what they had now was so much more than they'd shared in the last decade. Maddie tucked a finger under the bangs of her wig and scratched her head, the heat from the kitchen spilling over into the family room and making Maddie's head sweat.

"Ladies, I think we're ready," Scott said, striding to the couch and offering his hand to Maddie. "Dinner's on."

She slipped her hand into his as Annie headed into the kitchen to join in the parade of dishes being carried to the table.

"You okay?" Scott asked.

"Just a little hot. Who knew wigs were so much warmer than regular hair?"

"So take it off."

"You're kidding, right? I'll scare everyone, especially the kids."

"It's nothing they haven't seen before." Scott took a step toward her. "Besides, I think it's sexy."

Maddie stared up at him. He met her gaze squarely, his eyes earnest as just a hint of a smile deepened the lines around his mouth.

Maddie reached a hand up and pulled the wig from her head, closing her eyes at the blissful feel of cool air across her scalp. These days her life was filled with so many unpleasant sensations. She took her pleasure where she could get it.

Scott slipped an arm around her shoulders and kissed the top of her head before leading her to the table.

The feel of his lips on her bare skin lingered long after she sat down opposite her husband at the long table. Covered dishes ranged along the lace table runner, while candles flickered in their silver holders.

"Before I say grace I thought we might each want to thank God for one of his blessings this past year," Scott began.

"Well, I'll start," Phil said. "And I promise to keep it short because you all know how I love to eat." He patted his belly as the others laughed. "I want to thank God for good work, good friends, and a lovely wife who fills my days with love and laughter."

"My turn," Shaun piped up and winked at his sister. "I thank God for helping Mom to get well again."

Kylie stood. "And I want to thank God for my dad, and all he's done to help us these last few months."

Maddie looked at Scott and thought his eyes looked a bit shiny in the candlelight.

"I guess I'm next," Annie said. "Phil and I have a surprise to tell you about but mostly it's a big thank you to God for answered prayer. On Monday Phil and I are going to Manchester to pick up our new foster child. She is three years old and HIV positive. Her name is Grace, and I can't help but think how appropriate that is because she is a blessing in our lives."

Maddie reached across and squeezed Annie's hands, her eyes damp with tears. "I'm so glad for you." She paused, knowing it was her turn and not sure where to start or what to say. "You might think in this year with all my health problems that I would find it hard to be thankful. But instead I find I have more to thank God for than ever before. I want to thank him for my friends and how they care for me, for my kids and how they make me laugh, and for my husband, who has taken on the care of our family and does it with such joy. I am truly blessed."

Scott met Maddie's gaze, his lips curved in a slow smile before he bowed his head.

"Heavenly Father, we come before You this evening to thank You for Your abundant blessings, for Your ample provision to us when others have so little, for the power of Your mighty hand providing us with good friends to share our days with and lead us closer to You. And Father, I especially want to thank You for the blessing of family. Everything I have comes from You, Father—my radiant daughter, my compassionate son, and my beautiful wife. I love them without measure, and I thank You every day for allowing me to share my life with them. Bless this food and our time together that we may go from here today and be as thankful tomorrow as we are today. For we pray to a great God with great expectations and thanksgiving in our hearts in Jesus' name. Amen."

Maddie blinked back tears. Where had Scott learned to pray that way? His words were so sincere, and though he had known she was listening, he had not said them to impress her but to thank God. A warm sensation spread through her chest and into her face as she met her husband's gaze. He lifted his glass. "To good health and long days to enjoy it."

Maddie smiled, the warmth in her heart invading each fiber of her being as she recognized the sensation for what it was.

Love.

Thirty-three

The tree's lights glimmered in the dark room. Maddie curled up on the couch beneath the fleece blanket Kylie had given her. She couldn't remember a better Christmas, not ever. There hadn't been a lot of presents. With Scott out of work they'd decided to be more cautious with their money, but the kids had each gotten the one thing they wanted and a few small goodies in their stocking. She and Scott had agreed not to buy each other gifts.

The whole holiday had been remarkably worry-free. She hadn't mailed a card or baked a cookie and what little shopping she'd done had been on-line. Stripping the holiday of all its trappings had helped them remember what Christmas was really all about—the birth of Christ. Instead of spending all their time and money in the commercial commotion of the season, they'd adopted a family through their church, and along with Annie, Phil, and Grace, they'd put together an entire Christmas celebration. Decorations, presents, and food had made their way into several large boxes, which Scott and Shaun had dropped off at the church ten days ago. They would never know where the boxes went, but Maddie hoped whoever received them had enjoyed their Christmas as much as she had hers.

A light touch on her shoulder made Maddie look up.

"Good, you're awake," Scott said.

Maddie shifted her legs, making room for him on the couch. "I was just enjoying the tree."

"I have something for you." Scott handed her a velvet box.

Maddie inhaled sharply. "But we said we weren't going to—"

Scott laid a finger against her lips. "It's not a Christmas present. I bought it a long time ago." His finger traced the line of her jaw. "I want you to have it."

With the heat of his touch still on her skin, Maddie examined the square box in her hand. "When did you buy this?"

"Last summer. I meant to give it to you the night I made

reservations at the Riverboat."

Maddie's eyes widened, a hot flush creeping up her neck. "The night I went to the drive-in instead."

Scott's gaze met hers. "We never were very good at surprises. Open it."

Maddie stared down at the box. "I can't." She held the box out to him.

Scott didn't take it but instead tipped her chin up with his hand. "Why not?"

"Because I can't even think about last summer without feeling guilty."

Scott grew still, though his hand did not leave her face. "About Adam."

Maddie nodded. "I think we need to talk about what happened."

"I agree," Scott answered, and though he had not moved, Maddie could hear the pain in his voice.

She cringed, knowing that her actions had caused him such pain and worry. Ever since her diagnosis they had grown closer as a family and as a couple, but in this last month Maddie had been stunned by her reaction to this man who had been her husband for seventeen years. Her heart raced when he touched her, which he seemed to do frequently. Her breathing grew quick and shallow when he walked into a room and slipped an arm around her. And when Maddie turned toward him, Scott would wrap her in his arms.

Maddie had come to love these simple gestures of affection, and she feared their passing after this conversation. She knew they needed to clear the air about Adam before they could truly resume their life as a married couple and share completely their growing love. But Maddie flinched, thinking of the minutes ahead, knowing the pain they would cause this man she had come to love again, though she had yet to tell him.

Scott picked up the box in Maddie's lap and set it on the coffee table. "I need to ask you one thing before we talk this through and I need you to tell me the truth . . ."

"I never slept with Adam," Maddie said softly.

Scott met her gaze. "But you wanted to."

Maddie didn't know how to answer. Tears stung her eyes and, looking at her husband's handsome face, she knew she owed him no less than the truth. "Yes," she whispered.

Scott's eyes closed and his shoulders sagged, and all Maddie wanted to do was reach out a hand to comfort him. But she held back, fearing his reaction. She didn't need to recall Annie's words to know what she had to do next.

"I'm sorry, Scott. I was wrong to walk away from our marriage and look elsewhere for what I thought I needed. I should have tried talking to you first."

"I wouldn't have listened, not then," Scott said, his tone terse.

Maddie sensed his anger was not with her but with himself.

"I was so caught up in my own pride, in making myself a success, that I couldn't see anything else." Scott turned to face her. "I don't need or want all the details, Maddie, but I need to know if you loved him."

"No, I never loved him."

"But you were going to see him the night of the accident?"

"Yes." Maddie leaned forward, her voice urgent. "There are no excuses for what I did. I'm sorry for the pain I caused you, for running out of here that night and getting in that accident . . ."

"I'm not sorry about the accident," Scott said softly and reached for her hand. "Because without it we wouldn't be here today. You'd still have that tumor growing inside you and we'd never have had the last few months together. You might have died if not for that accident, Maddie. I think about that every night and it scares me to death." Scott's gaze held hers. "So, although I want to hate Adam Slater, I can't, because he gave you back to me."

"I think God gave us a second chance to get it right, to make the kind of choices we should have been making all along." Maddie ran the tips of her fingers along the side of his face. "And now I choose to love you, not because you're the father of our children and not just because you're my husband, but because I love the man you are."

Scott's eyes grew wide as his grip on her hand tightened. "I didn't know if I would ever hear you say that again."

"Do you know what won me over?"

"My cooking?" Scott joked, drawing her into his arms.

Maddie rested her head on his shoulder. "It's the joy I see in you every day, the patience you have with the kids, the gentleness you've shown in caring for me."

"The fruits of the Spirit," Scott said, his lips close to her ear. "I didn't find those on my own. They were a gift."

"So, can you give them to me?" Maddie snuggled in closer.

"I can't, but God can if you want Him to."

Maddie grew still. "I've been thinking a lot about that lately. I didn't want to come to God out of desperation when I was sick and just use Him like some spiritual emergency room. I knew I had to want God in my life, not because I was scared to live without Him but because I recognized how much He loved me, how much He sacrificed for me."

Scott nodded, a day's growth of beard tickling Maddie's head. "It says in the Bible, "'For God so loved the world that he gave his one and only Son that whoever believes in him will not perish but have eternal life.'"

Maddie looked into his face. "I've heard that verse all my life and never really understood what it meant until I watched you these past few months; all the sacrifices you made for us, and you did it with such joy. How could I not want what I see in your eyes every day? I'm not quite sure how to get it, though."

Scott grinned. "It may not be pretty, but I think we can muddle through together." Scott faced Maddie and took her hands in his. He rested his forehead against hers, their breathing mingled in a united prayer.

"Father, thank You for showing Maddie how much You love her. Thank You for allowing me to be here at this moment when she is ready to open her heart and ask You into her life. I love her, Lord—totally, completely, and I know that You love her more than I do. Hear her prayer, Lord."

Scott squeezed her hands. "Your turn."

"I don't know what to say," Maddie whispered.

Scott kissed her forehead. "It doesn't matter as long as it's from your heart."

Maddie collected her thoughts, setting aside the wonder of being here praying with her husband, in order to fix her mind on the One who had saved them. "Heavenly Father," Maddie began, "I know it was my pride that kept me from coming to You months ago. I thought I needed to clean up my act first, to leave my sins behind before I came to You. Annie told me not too long ago that 'a contrite heart You will not spurn.' So, Father, I'm sorry. I'm sorry for my pride. I'm sorry for my behavior last summer, and I'm sorry for hurting this wonderful man who loves me more than I deserve. You sent Your Son to die for my sins—all of them. I thank You for that and I ask You now to come into my heart and make me the woman You want me to be."

Maddie peeked one eye open. "Is that it?"

Scott smiled, holding her face in his hands. "Welcome to the kingdom." His voice rang out with joy as he leaned toward her.

Maddie smiled and closed her eyes. She'd been waiting for this a long time. She still might be pasty and her head bald, but Scott's kiss made her feel beautiful as his lips lingered on hers and he drew her into his arms.

Maddie couldn't reach the door handle. Her hands were so filled with packages.

Annie stepped around her and pulled it open. "Scott's going to think this is an April Fool's joke."

Maddie side-stepped through the door. "I needed a few new things for our trip."

"A few?" Annie chuckled, holding aloft her single bag and pointing at the multitude of bags Maddie carried to the car.

A brisk wind buffeted the bags and sent a chill down Maddie's back. She almost wished she'd opted for the wig or at least a hat to keep her head warm, though these days she hated covering up what little hair she had. Shaun called it her #4 crew cut, but Maddie didn't care how short it was. Finally after months of waiting, her hair was starting to grow back, maybe with a few more grays mixed in with the blonde, but it was all hers. By the time she and Scott left for the Cayman Islands at the end of the month, Maddie hoped her hair might qualify as short and sexy instead of boyish.

Annie unlocked the car door. "You up for lunch?"

"Don't you have to get back to Gracie?" Maddie asked, pulling open the back door and loading the bags inside.

"Phil's taking her to play group this afternoon. And the new girl we hired is minding the store."

Maddie closed the back door as Annie got into the car.

"Maddie?" A familiar voice made her turn.

Adam stood on the sidewalk, his hands jammed into the pockets of his leather jacket.

A fleeting thought crossed Maddie's mind about her nearly naked head, but she pushed it aside. She had wondered what she would feel if she ever saw Adam again. And here he stood just a few feet away, looking as handsome as ever in jeans and black leather. "How are you, Adam?"

"Better now that I've seen for myself you're all right." He stepped toward her. "Emily Tuttle told me you finished your chemo."

"Two months ago."

"Was it as bad as I hear?"

Maddie nodded. "Pretty rough, yes, but I'm feeling better now. Still a little tired and I nap more than my kids do, but I'm coming back." The words came easily, and Maddie was surprised to find she felt no attraction to this man who had held sway over her thoughts for so many months. In fact, looking back on it now, she wondered how she had ever let things between them go so far. It seemed unreal. Time and distance had given her a different perspective.

"Are you going to try out for this year's show?" Adam asked.

Maddie shook her head. "No. Scott's starting up a new design firm and I'm going to be helping him with the administrative side of things."

She didn't want to hurt Adam, didn't know if she was still capable of hurting him, but she wanted him to know how her life had changed and where her priorities now lay.

"You sound happy, Maddie."

"I am. Eight months ago I couldn't have said this, but having cancer has changed my life." She smiled at the irony of cancer giving her not death but life. "How have you been?"

"Busy at the paper and with my dad. He took a fall this winter and broke his leg. It's been a slow road back."

"But you've been there to help him."

Adam nodded.

An awkward pause followed. Maddie turned toward the car and reached for the door. "I'd better go."

"Maddie?"

She turned back to him.

"Where were you going the night you got into the accident?"

Maddie drew in a deep breath. "I was going to Annie's."

Adam's shoulders sagged almost imperceptibly.

Lord, forgive me for lying. I can't hurt this man anymore, Maddie silently prayed.

A clear impression in her mind made Maddie's eyes widen.

Then tell him the truth about your marriage and let him go.

She blinked and obeyed. "The truth is, Adam, that Scott and I had a terrible fight that night. I was distracted and I drove my car into a tree, but that accident and my illness helped us find our way back to each other. We'll be married eighteen years at the end of this month."

"So you love him?"

"With all my heart."

Adam's jaw tightened, though a sad smile touched his lips. "That's all I wanted for you. I just thought I was the guy who could give it to you." He stepped backward and turned away from her. "Be well, Maddie."

Maddie didn't watch him walk away. She climbed into Annie's car and buckled her seat belt. "Sorry to make you wait."

Annie started the engine. "No problem."

"I hope he finds someone wonderful to share his life with."

"Maybe he can now."

Maddie sat in silence for a moment before admitting, "I wondered what I would feel if I ever saw him again."

Annie nodded. "And God knew you needed to see him, not for now but for later. You and Scott are back in the honeymoon phase of your marriage, but no marriage is perfect. And I think God wanted to confirm in your mind that you made the right choice, so you wouldn't revisit that choice later."

"All part of the plan?" Maddie said with a smile.

"Don't you just love the way God works? Although I don't know as it was part of the plan for you to buy out the lingerie department." Annie inclined her head toward the backseat.

Maddie laughed. "Hey, a girl needs a few new things for her second honeymoon."

Standing on the steps of their home, Scott hugged Kylie and then Shaun, and waited for Maddie to do the same. Phil and Annie looked on as little Grace fought to get down and run to her new playmates.

Shaun squirmed under Maddie's lengthy good-bye. "Gee, Mom, you'll only be gone a week."

Kylie took Grace from Annie. "It'll be fun having a little sister for a week." Kylie narrowed her glance and shot her parents a look tinged with horror. "Though I wouldn't want that to become a permanent arrangement."

Shaun grimaced. "Yuck. Don't even talk about it."

Maddie snatched his hat from his head and tossed it back to him. "Don't worry; you'll always be my baby."

"I don't know if that's a good thing or not," Shaun said, catching the hat.

Annie stepped up to Maddie. "We'll take good care of them, I promise."

"I know you will." Maddie hugged her hard. "Thanks."

Phil held out a hand to Scott. "Have a great trip and don't worry about the kids or the house."

Scott shook Phil's hand and then on impulse clasped his friend in a hug. "Thanks for everything."

Moments later they were in the car waving a final good-bye before they turned onto Lake Shore Drive. They drove in silence through the little town of Stoddard and past the general store.

"You okay?" Scott asked, knowing that saying good-bye to the kids was never an easy thing for Maddie. She cried leaving the kids at summer camp.

"I'm fine. Better than fine actually." Maddie grinned, tossing her head in a carefree gesture that might have made her hair bounce if it was just a little longer. "I'm a little nervous about the flight, but do you realize we haven't been away together since before Kylie was born?"

"I'm looking forward to it," Scott said reaching over and taking her hand. "It's been a long year and we deserve a break."

Maddie turned toward him in her seat. "Scott, I need to tell you something. I don't ever want us to go back to the way we were before."

Scott squeezed her hand. "Neither do I."

"Right, so that means we talk, about everything good and bad."

"Why do I get the feeling this is going to be bad?" Scott groaned. "Okay, let's get it over with so we can enjoy our vacation."

"I saw Adam earlier this month."

Last year Scott would have bristled with anger before he heard the explanation but now he waited, knowing Maddie wouldn't have brought it up if it weren't important. "Where?"

"On the street in Kerry when I was shopping with Annie. We only talked for a few minutes, and I've debated telling you about it ever since because it was so unimportant it didn't seem necessary."

Scott nodded, liking the unimportant part.

Maddie's tone was thoughtful, her eyes intent on his face. "But then I realized I was doing what I'd done a thousand times before in our marriage—keeping something from you because it would hurt you or make you mad. That's how we got to where we were last year, so now you're going to hear it all."

"Sounds like a good plan. So can I ask a question?"

"Sure."

"What did you feel when you saw him?"

"I guess what I felt mostly was sad. I hope he finds someone to love him as much as I love you." Maddie laid her head on his shoulder.

Scott loved the feel of her beside him, of the way she reached out to him and touched him as naturally as if she'd done it every day for the last eighteen years. He kissed her forehead. "I love you too, Maddie, and I thank God every day that he helped us find our way back to each other."

"Me too."

"Now, want to hear some good news?"

Maddie sat up straight. "About the phone call this morning?"

Scott grinned. "Exactly. Sarah Hingemen wants me to design her new summer house."

Maddie beamed. "That's wonderful. What is it, a little beach house on the Cape?"

"Well, it's hardly little, more like a small museum actually, and it's a lot closer to home than the Cape."

"Where is it?"

"Across the lake. She's going to be our neighbor." Scott chuckled, pulling the car onto the highway as he glanced at his beautiful wife. "Lately I'm convinced that God is not only a great provider, but He's got quite a sense of humor."

About the Author

CHRISTINE ANDERSON's life has taken many remarkable turns in the last year. In addition to publishing this first novel, after many years as a stay-at-home mom, she has returned to work as a nurse in Labor and Delivery. She continues to teach and speak at Creative Living Bible Study in New Jersey. She and her husband, Rodd, will soon be sending their youngest child off to college. God has filled her life with many new challenges even as her house grows a bit quieter.

In choosing a setting for this novel, she picked a familiar one. Her first vacation as a child and for the next twenty years was in New Hampshire on an idyllic lake much like the one in this story. Those fond memories made it a perfect setting for this story of redemption.

For more information on Christine, go to www.capstonefiction.com. You can contact her by: e-mail at Chrissi722@aol.com or visit her Web site at www.christineanderson.org.

Printed in the United States
91560LV00003BA/29/A